Seducing Sigefroi

Curse of the Lost Isle Book 3

By Vijaya Schartz

Print 978-1-77362-859-2

Chapter One

Lucilinburhuc, Northern Europe - Spring of 963

Icy water from melted snow chilled Melusine's naked body in a delicious embrace as she stretched into the Alzette River and let the current untangle her flowing hair. She glanced up at the jutting cliff crowned by the old Roman fort. No one had walked the ramparts in centuries, but she could not afford any witnesses. Extending her mind eye, she searched for signs of human presence.

Satisfied that no mortal lurked, Melusine flicked her serpent tail and dove into the green depths, then surfaced in a pool of pale sunshine. From a floating branch she plucked a twig. Then she heaved herself onto a rocky shelf and sat to comb and dry her hair.

Despite the timid midday sun, Melusine sighed. Hard as she tried, she couldn't accept her implacable fate. A hundred and forty years since her mother had cursed her, and still no sign of redemption. Soon, the Goddess had promised, her knight would appear and she would get her chance to serve and redeem herself. But soon could mean centuries in the eyes of the Great One.

A lark in the budding willow halted its tentative trill. In full alert, Melusine slid back into the river to seek cover under the stone arches of the old bridge. She held her breath, heart pounding. The road rumbled with the gallop of horses.

Melusine's wet skin quivered and her heart stumbled in her chest. Dear Goddess! If mortals saw her in serpent form, the priests and bishops would hunt her, and if they caught her they would torture her then sentence her to burn at the stake like a demonic creature.

The hoof beats slowed as the riders approached the bridge. Echoes of male voices reached Melusine's keen ears. She detected three sets of hooves, and enough jingle of chain mail and armor to frighten a hamlet. Closing her eyes, she focused her mind upon her inward gift of sight. Aye, two knights in full armor, and a young squire. The destriers halted.

"We'd better water the horses," a deep voice boomed from the bank near the end of the bridge.

Scabbards flapped on leather trappings, and metal clinked as the men dismounted. Boots rang on hard stone.

Flat against the first pile of the arched bridge, waist high in the river, Melusine held her breath. She dared not move or make a sound. On the changing patterns of the water surface, she spied the reflection of the approaching men. A huge black destrier snorted at Melusine's scent, but she calmed the warhorse with a soothing thought.

"What did I tell you?" The tall knight with the commanding voice removed his helmet and pushed back the mail hauberk to shake a full head of flaming red hair. A smile lit the strong planes of his clean shaven face as he stared at the little fort, atop the rocky cliff across the river. "This is the most magnificent promontory I've ever beheld!"

At the knight's side, a blond squire in brown wool led a broad-shouldered bay. The boy shaded his eyes to glance up.

"Impressive, my lord!" The lad turned to the other knight Melusine could not see. "Don't you agree, Gunter?" The boy took the fiery knight's helmet then led the two horses to drink.

The man named Gunter now appeared in Melusine's field of view, a stocky warrior with a dark beard, who led a big dappled steed. "Sigefroi my friend, you found an impenetrable place... even better than Stavelot."

Under the bridge in the shadows, Melusine felt her pulse quicken with hope. That name, Sigefroi! Could the red-haired knight be the same man the Goddess had named in her dreams? Could he deliver her from the curse?

4

Melusine closed her eyes and used her mind sight again. He looked quite rugged, slim and wiry from riding and swordplay, agile as a mountain cat as he walked on pebbles. He had a willful jaw and full, sensuous lips.

The young squire, after kneeling at the river's edge to fill up his master's helmet, offered Lord Sigefroi a drink.

"By the rood!" Gunter, the black-bearded warrior, chuckled. "I still can't believe that wretched abbot snatched Stavelot from under your nose. But this fort looks better yet." He slapped Sigefroi's back, then roared when the lord choked and spilled his drink.

Like quick silver, Sigefroi threw the rest of the ice-cold water into Gunter's face. Both knights, drenched, erupted in hearty laughter while the young squire joined the fun. None of the three seemed concerned about unsettling the horses, which wandered farther off alongshore toward a copse of chestnut trees.

Melusine heard the snap of branches and felt the horses' unrest before she caught a glimpse of a marauder in the bushes bordering the thicket, and he was running toward the horses. A thief? What dimwit would steal from fully armed knights?

The black destrier whinnied. Sigefroi swiftly unsheathed his broadsword and rushed to the horses, followed by Gunter and the squire.

The three companions ran. The trees and bushes came alive with running feet, tinkling mail, and muffled sounds of struggle, punctuated by strings of curses. While they were occupied in the brush, Melusine thought of diving into the depths to flee, but curiosity held her in place.

What if this lord knight with the fiery mane were the man of her destiny? She must learn more about him.

Sigefroi emerged from the thicket, dragging a kicking, screaming lout by the hair. Even from a stonethrow away, Melusine could tell the churl hadn't bathed in several moons.

While the squire retrieved the horses, Sigefroi dragged the thief back toward the bridge. Melusine retreated behind the pile and peeked around to watch.

Gunter followed his friend, shaking his dark head. "What do you suggest we do with this horse thief?"

Sigefroi halted near a mossy stump, a few paces from where Melusine flattened herself against the foot of the stone arch, then he forced the culprit to his knees.

The knight pointed the sword at the lout's throat. "I should kill you right here and now as is my God-given right!"

The lout mumbled something Melusine could not understand.

"But in my clemency, I give you two choices." Sigefroi paused, staring cooly at the thief who groveled at his feet. "Either I deliver you to the bishop's justice, or I sever your right hand and let you go free."

Shocked by the cold-hearted threat, Melusine extended her gifts to read Sigefroi's thoughts, but to her surprise, his human mind remained closed to her probing. How could this be? She usually had no difficulty reading mortals. Had her abilities weakened?

Sigefroi shook the man's collar. "What will it be?"

At his feet, the horse thief paled. Small beady eyes darted right and left. "Have mercy, my lord," he whimpered pitifully. "Few ever return from the bishop's dungeon."

"You made your choice, ruffian." Sigefroi raised the heavy sword. "Gunter! Hold him."

Before Melusine's bemused eyes, Gunter jumped the thief, wrestled him, seized the man's right arm and extended it out on the tree stump.

"Nay," the thief cried, pinned under Gunter's weight. "I vow I'll never steal again. I beg of you. Please, my lords, have mercy!"

Sigefroi didn't even blink. A flash of metal, the hacking sound of severed bone, then the chopped hand, like a grey spider, bounced on the sand and pebbles. Bewilderment spread on the robber's face at the sight of gushing blood.

Melusine screamed, but her voice merged with that of the unfortunate thief who uttered a long scream, strident enough to chill the devil's spine.

6

Melusine seethed with outrage. A beating might have sufficed. She had seen barbarians show more compassion than these brutes.

Gunter moved away, wiping blood off his mail.

"Go now," Sigefroi ordered coldly, "afore I change my mind and decide to kill you after all."

Holding a bloody stump, the whimpering thief bolted for the thicket, leaving a trail of blood at the water's edge.

With a disgusted grunt, Gunter kicked the severed hand into the river.

"No one takes what's mine!" Sigefroi called after the fleeing churl, then he wiped the wide blade with his under tunic before returning the weapon to its scabbard.

Heart thumping, Melusine stared at Sigefroi over the shivering mirror of bloody water. The knight glared back at her with wide amber eyes, like a great lion bloody from a kill. Then Melusine realized with terror that she had moved from behind the pile and he could see her.

"Gunter," Sigefroi called calmly, his wide amber eyes riveted on hers. "We found ourselves a maiden... and she's naked!" He pointed at Melusine waist high in the river. "Over there!" He motioned for her to come out of the water. "Come forth, lass!"

Gripped by the sudden urge to run out of the water and lose herself among the trees, Melusine realized she had no legs to run. And diving like a fish might raise suspicion. Why did it have to be the first Wednesday of the month?

"Where? Is she pretty?" Gunter winked at his friends and waded into shallow water, hooting from the sudden chill.

Despite the risks, Melusine slipped into the frigid depths with a swish of her serpent tail.

* * *

Sigefroi blinked and the girl was gone, but where? He felt a disturbing void at her disappearance.

Thierry, his young squire who just returned with the horses, guffawed. "All I saw was a big thrashing fish."

"A naked wench? A big fish? Sounds like an ondine to me." Gunter laughed, dunking his gauntlet in the river to wash away the blood. "Congratulations, my friends!" he railed. "Now, you'll have to confess afore attending mass. I wonder what's the penance for consorting with such evil creatures. Excommunication?"

Thierry signed himself.

Gunter ruffled the lad's blond hair. "That was in jest. Still, some villagers claim to have seen them ondines. I wouldn't mind meeting a pretty one myself."

Thierry ducked away from the bigger man. "I'm not a child anymore!" His changing voice cracked, belying his words. "I'm sixteen, I'm a man!"

"Stop it, you oafs!" Sigefroi shook inside, partly from the swift justice he had meted out, but mostly from the heavenly lass. "By the sacred foot of St Andreas, I know what I saw. It was a naked lass."

His companions fell silent. So did Sigefroi as his gaze swept the calm waters of the Alzette River. He took the reins from Thierry and mounted his destrier.

"Let's go find her. She must have run up the other side of the bridge. She can't have gone very far." He spurred his mount and rode ahead along the river.

Gunter and Thierry mounted and followed him in silence as Sigefroi galloped his horse back and forth along the river bank, scanning the woods and mossy boulders. Nothing moved across the river toward the cliff either. Where had the lass gone?

Sigefroi spurred his horse toward the bridge. Without waiting for his companions, he rode across the stone bridge ahead of them.

How did he manage to lose the most enchanting woman he'd ever laid eyes upon? Graceful as a nymph, with delicate curves and tan skin, flowing hair dark from the water, and astonishing eyes. Although he couldn't be sure, he'd wager the eyes were a deep gray, the color of a stormy sky. The shocked expression on the girl's lovely face, as if she'd seen the devil incarnate, kept flashing in his mind.

No wench had ever touched Sigefroi's soul before, but this lass intrigued him. She looked young and helpless. He wanted to protect her, kiss her, bed her, betroth her... Had he lost his mind?

He'd remained unwed all these years, waiting for an alliance that would increase his holdings. Only a princely heiress would satisfy the ambitious Sigefroi of Ardennes, and no one in the surrounding hamlets could possibly meet his requirements.

When he reached the opposite bank, Sigefroi slowed his horse and waited for his companions. He had come to assess the fortress, and the three of them needed their midday meal. Without a word, Gunter and Thierry caught up with their lord.

Sigefroi led them past an unattended watermill, its creaking cogwheels left to turn by themselves. The fishermen's huts on stilts looked abandoned as well, and no one manned the few barques attached to the stilts. They rode by a tanning shed, judging by the stink of urine... empty as well. The knights' arrival had scared the villagers into hiding.

The rutted dirt road ended at the foot of a narrow trail winding up the cliff side, a treacherous climb that led to the main plateau.

Gunter frowned up at the cliff. "Does this place have a name?"

Sigefroi pointed to the right. "Hither, the Petrusse flows into the Alzette River." He motioned upward with his chin. "That's the Rham plateau up there, and the rocky tooth next to it is called the Bock. The Romans built the fort on top and called it Lucilinburhuc, but the locals call it Lutzelburg."

Thierry nodded. "What does it mean?"

Sigefroi smiled. "It means little fort."

"Aye?" Gunter sounded unconvinced. "Lucilinburhuc could just as well mean the fort of Lucine, Mal-Lucine, the evil one. I hear tell the infamous ondine dwelled near Aachen when the bishops excommunicated her. But that was over a century ago."

9

"Truly?" Thierry sounded fascinated.

"Perhaps that was her in the river yonder." Gunter chuckled. "They never caught the vixen."

"Of course they didn't!" Sigefroi scoffed. "Ondines are pure legend. Even the devil wouldn't dare spawn such an abomination."

He shook his head at such absurdity and let his big warhorse pick its way along the narrow climbing trail. His companions followed in a single file on the steep incline.

"The fort certainly looks wicked," Thierry ventured. His young mind obviously favored the legend. "Like a gray predator watching us climb."

Sigefroi smiled at the boy's naivety. "That's why I like it!" Loosening his grip on the reins to give his mount more freedom to pick its steps, Sigefroi controlled his exhilaration and kept an even tone. "Can you feel the power emanating from the rock?"

He wondered whether his companions even understood what he meant. When he glanced back, he only met puzzled looks.

"That's what my father said the first time we saw it. I was only a child," he added in lieu of explanation. "This place must be mine."

Gunter cleared his throat. "Only if the abbot of St Maximin and the Archbishop of Trier let you have it."

Sigefroi smiled to himself. He understood Gunter's skepticism. "Don't worry. I will make my offer palatable enough."

"After the Barbarian and Norman invasions, now is the perfect time to rebuild," Gunter suggested behind him.

Sigefroi smiled. "And expand my holdings through alliances." He turned in the saddle and winked at Gunter. "Or appropriate by force what cannot be gained through peaceful trade or intrigue."

"Amen to that." His friend chuckled.

Sigefroi excelled at all these skills. In this opportune time of reorganization, he intended to carve himself a kingdom.

Conversations died as the trail grew steeper.

Sigefroi remembered the same climb as a boy, with his father, Wigeric of Lorraine. At the old man's death, the estate had been divided among his five sons, destroying the family's might. But Sigefroi refused to be less than his father. He'd vowed long ago to own more lands, and become richer and more powerful than old Wigeric of Lorraine ever was.

After an arduous climb, the riders finally crested the cliff. The vast triangular plateau sported thick woods, fields in fallow and newly sowed patches. Sigefroi noted with satisfaction the good, dark, arable soil. They rode past huge tree trunks... probably felled to build barricades against the most recent invaders.

Sigefroi directed his mount toward the fortified village at the narrow tip of the plateau. The small community faced the free standing needle where the fort proudly stood. Even from a distance, the village walls looked in disrepair. Atop the crumbling stone fortifications, wooden watchtowers in ruin, like gutted scarecrows, attested to decades of barbarian assaults. Such a shame to neglect the defenses. Sigefroi would rebuild them stronger than ever.

They rode into the village through the broken gate. Chickens and geese flew before the horses. A skinny hound barked at the three horsemen as Sigefroi led his party between wattle-and-daub huts... enough to house several large families of serfs. The chilly breeze carried away the smoke that wafted from holes in the thatched roofs.

Goats and sheep bleated in the distance, but the population remained hidden. Villagers didn't trust strange warriors in bloody battle gear, and for good reason. Over the past decades, they had seen what prowling knights could do on a whim.

The eastern corner of the Rham plateau, where the village stood, ended abruptly in a point at the edge of a deep gorge. An old wooden bridge spanned the void between the plateau and the fort crowning the rocky promontory on the other side.

Sigefroi halted his destrier for a closer look. The fort proper seemed in much better repair than the village walls.

"When I own the place," Sigefroi declared proudly, "the first thing will be to replace this rickety contraption with a mechanical drawbridge."

"A clever plan, my lord," Thierry concurred with enthusiasm. "The perch is surrounded by a precipice, with water on three sides. The enemy can only attack from the plateau, and no one can reach the castle if the bridge is drawn."

"You learn fast, lad. Even in Roman times, this fort has never been taken." Sigefroi grinned, proud of his squire. "You will make a fine knight someday."

Gunter shaded his eyes with a gloved hand, appraising the scenery. "You can see for leagues around and control the roads and the two rivers." He turned in the saddle to face Sigefroi. "You'd have to clear the woods to be able to see an army coming over the surrounding hills, though."

"That's my plan. It will make room for fields."

A roguish smile formed on the warrior's bearded lips. "I bet the southern slopes of these hills would be perfect for a vineyard."

Sigefroi laughed at Gunter's remark. "I wager you'll come taste my wine often."

"Aye!" Gunter offered a toothy grin and winked. "But only if it's any good!"

Sigefroi's stomach growled. "Let's pay a visit to the fort's bailiff, I'm starving!"

He kicked his horse and led his friends across the wooden bridge. As they traversed the gorge separating the plateau from the fort outcrop, Sigefroi could see the treacherous ravine below, with its sharp rocky spines. A fall would be fatal. He also observed that the timber under the old planks of the bridge could support heavy carts if needed.

When they reached the outcrop, Thierry pummeled the massive oak door with the hilt of his hunting knife. "Open the gate for Lord Sigefroi of Ardennes and his loyal companions," the lad shouted with practiced solemnity.

A small wooden shutter slid open in the upper part of the door, and a dirty boyish face appeared in the square hole. "What's your business in Lutzelburg, my lords?"

"Tell the bailiff to open the gate, or I'll have his head on a pike," Sigefroi snapped.

For a few seconds pandemonium erupted behind the gate, then a plump face with a drooping jowl appeared in the aperture. "Sigefroi of Ardennes, the mighty protector of our abbey in Trier, is of course welcome to this humble fort. But can you provide proof of who you say you are, my lord?"

Thierry turned crimson at the insult, and Gunter's hand closed on the sword hilt at his hip.

Controlling his temper, Sigefroi managed a cool smile. He removed his right gauntlet then thrust a closed fist toward the aperture, displaying the huge silver signet ring on his middle finger. "Will my personal seal suffice, bailiff?"

The plump face displayed an unctuous smile. "Of course, my lord. That, I do recognize. My apologies." The bailiff turned away. "Open the gate for Lord Sigefroi of Ardennes," he announced ceremoniously.

Sigefroi heard the locking bars lifted from their metal rests. The old door groaned and creaked as it opened on a vast courtyard. Ducks flew and hogs squealed in a desperate flight from the playful hounds. Apparently, the frightened villagers and part of their livestock had taken refuge in the fort as soon as they spotted the knights in battle gear.

The bailiff, in a silky brown tunic reaching well below the knees, met his uninvited guests at the gate, surrounded by a curious crowd of gawking serfs more than happy to abandon their chores. "You must understand, Lord Sigefroi, we've had a few bad encounters with marauding knights, and I had never met you in person."

"I appreciate your prudence, Bailiff, but I advise you to memorize my face, for I plan to come here often."

The plump man eyed him suspiciously but didn't comment. Sigefroi and his friends dismounted, then Thierry took the horses to the building that looked like the stables. The warm air carried the unmistakable aroma of yeast and baking bread.

Sigefroi patted his stomach. "We need nourishment, Bailiff. Show us your hospitality."

A cursory glance at the vast enclosure revealed only three stone buildings. A two-story villa dominated the space. The stables stood to the side, and a spacious, windowless larder looked large enough to store grain, nuts, dried fish, and meats for the long winters.

The bailiff led them to the luxurious villa probably built for the Roman general in charge of the ancient garrison. They entered through a wide double door flanked by two columns. Inside the main hall, a mosaic on the floor represented Pagan gods at play, but even Venus in the nude didn't compare to Sigefroi's earlier vision of the naked lass.

The baking aroma floated from a large oven built into the wall of the hall. Women stuffed a new batch of round loaves in the red brick mouth of the oven while children fed dry wood to the roaring fire underneath.

"Please, my lords, make yourselves comfortable." The bailiff indicated the massive table then walked away, giving orders to the servants in hushed tones.

Sigefroi and Gunter sat on benches. Sigefroi removed his helmet, set it on the table and stretched his legs, welcoming the warmth.

Soon, Thierry came in from the stable and, although the bailiff scowled, Sigefroi motioned for the lad to join them at the guest table. Servants usually ate in the kitchen but Thierry was a squire, a future knight. Sigefroi loved him like a younger brother.

Thierry smiled broadly and sat next to him.

Sigefroi ruffled the lad's blond hair. "You must be hungry."

The servants brought trays loaded with a healthy fare of goat cheese, oven-warm buckwheat bread, fresh butter, and boiled eggs, along with goblets and a pitcher of ale.

Gunter winked at Sigefroi then addressed the bailiff who fussed with the servants, "Don't you have wine to serve your important guests?"

The bailiff ambled toward the table, gazed down at his boots and pressed his thin lips together. "You see, we send the wine to the abbey in Trier... for celebrating mass."

Gunter frowned. "All the wine?"

The rotund man bowed. "I'm afraid so."

Sigefroi recognized the blatant lie. The man didn't get his rubicund face from drinking water or weak ale.

Grasping his sword hilt, Sigefroi half rose. "Do not tell me that the protector of St Maximin's Abbey can't have wine, Bailiff! Not if you want your head to remain on your shoulders."

The bailiff paled and bowed to Sigefroi, quickly, several times. "Of course, my lord. Anything for the protector of our abbey."

As the man retreated toward the stone stairs leading down to the cellar, Sigefroi wondered how many casks the weasel had managed to sneak away from the good monks. A pitcher of wine came, and they devoured the food.

Once his stomach full, Sigefroi inspected the ramparts and climbed the stairs to the square watchtower, made of the same stone as the fort itself and just as old. A choice bird's-eye view indeed. The tower overlooked the river, its stone bridge, and the wide Roman road from Rheims and Arlon to Trier.

Through the arched window, Sigefroi's gaze embraced a dark green valley, and at the bottom of the cliff, the Alzette flowed in a gracious loop encircling the Bock promontory.

This would be the perfect location for his purpose, only a short day's ride from Trier, the imperial city. Sigefroi could already envision his future might. From here, he would rule his lands, rally his vassals, and levy an army... the beginning of his dream.

Birds chirped in the vines, intruding on his thoughts. Sigefroi filled his lungs with crisp air, listening to the peaceful birdsongs. Among the twitter, he thought he heard singing. A pure angelic voice. He strained his eyes against the sun's reflection on the snaking river. There, something disturbed the even flow. It looked like the naked lass he'd seen earlier.

How could anyone enjoy such frigid waters for so long? Just then, a bright flash of sunlight on water blinded him. Sigefroi raised one hand against the glare. The furtive apparition was gone. He waited eagerly for her to resurface, but she did not.

Now Sigefroi remembered where he'd seen the girl before. In a dream. That must be the root of his obsession, a fantasy straight from his imagination. He shook his head to dislodge the spell. He had to focus on the real world. He'd neglected his body's needs. How long had it been since he'd ravished a woman? He needed to bed a wench... and soon.

* * *

Melusine had stopped singing to glance at the tower the moment she'd sensed Sigefroi spying on her from the high window. The barbaric knight had the piercing eyesight of a falcon. Good thing Melusine carried a small silver mirror in a pouch around her neck. Assessing the position of the sun, she'd angled the mirror to blind the importune knight.

That ought to teach him. As soon as Sigefroi shaded his eyes, Melusine dove, swimming upstream underwater. The man was becoming a nuisance. She needed to find out whether or not he was the one, and she knew exactly whom to ask. There were dangers involved, but she needed to know.

Past the safety of overhanging rocks, all the way to the Petrusse River, Melusine swam along the loops of the deep gorge until she recognized the grotto and the miraculous spring, where she worshiped the Mother Goddess. Despite the swollen river at this time of year, the grotto stood high up in the rock.

Melusine didn't dare venture so far on shore in serpent form. Without her legs to run, discovery would be deadly. And even if she managed to escape by sprouting wings, she would have to leave the Alzette, the home she'd learned to love.

So she followed the current on to the next place of worship along the gorge, where two lofty oaks framed a rock formation in the shape of a giant skull. A magic place to be sure, but as often evil as holy. Twisted mortals misconstrued its power and used it to summon dark demons. Melusine shuddered at the thought as she hefted herself upon a rock and sang.

Gradually, her pristine chant purified the place. When birds and insects resumed chirping, Melusine felt satisfied that no thread of evil lingered. Eyes closed, she summoned the Great Mother.

"O Magnificent Goddess, our guide and mother on this hostile planet since the birth of mankind, hear my plea and look upon me."

In the stillness that followed the invocation, the wind rustled, carrying a whiff of cherry blossom. When she opened her eyes, an eerie shimmer on the water told Melusine that her plea had been heard.

Upon Skull Rock, a giant face appeared, flawless and smooth. No emotions marred its serenity, but power stirred in the bottomless depths of the dark eyes.

"Unworthy daughter," the woman's voice whispered with surprising clarity. "How dare you summon me after your hideous crime."

Melusine shivered at the reminder. "That was so very long ago, Great One. I was but a child and knew not what I did. I have suffered the curse ever since. Shouldn't that be enough?"

"No curse can ever erase the torment you and your sisters caused to your loving father!" The strong whisper blew cold on her skin.

"I know that, Dear Goddess, and I will regret the deed all my life." Tears threatened to overcome Melusine at the memory of her father's fate. She also missed her two sisters, cursed and exiled to opposite ends of the civilized world with curses of their own. "But over fourteen decades of guilt ought to redeem my mistake."

"How dare you question your punishment!" The voice snapped and echoed off the cliffs.

Remembering the might of the Goddess, Melusine checked her temper. "I dare not, O Great One. Our birth mother punished us as she saw fit."

"That's better." The voice softened. "Now, state your request."

"I wish to know if my freedom from the curse is near." Melusine searched for a reaction on the giant stone face but saw none. "Is the knight I saw today the Sigefroi who can bring forth my release?"

The Goddess chuckled mirthlessly. "Aye, Sigefroi of Ardennes could release you from the curse, if you can get him to marry you."

Melusine swallowed painfully. Still a virgin despite her age, she couldn't fathom wedding this ruthless, unpredictable knight. The thought brought with it fear, but also a secret thrill at the challenge.

Her chest filled with bubbling hope. "All I have to do is marry him?"

The clear feminine laugh bounced against the tall cliffs of the gorge. "No, that's not all, child. There is much to do here. This countryside needs more peaceful fields, the rivers more traders, and the towns more markets. But above all, I want you to build formidable castles and stone fortresses to protect them all."

"Me? But I know nothing about building fortresses!"

The great face upon Skull Rock smiled mysteriously. "You used to know... Have you forgotten?"

"Oh!" Heat rose to Melusine's throat and cheeks. How humiliating to be reminded of such a simple principle as past lives. "I had visions, of course, but the knowledge is vague."

"Close your eyes, child. I will show you."

Melusine wanted to retort that she was no child, but thought better of it and obeyed.

18

Before her mind's eye stood a splendid fortress, built for giants in forgotten times of demigods, and half-mortals much like her. Troy! Magnificent and impregnable, and in front of its walls stood Achilles, her enemy... Melusine, who wore many names even then, was worshiped as Athena by swarms of loyal Greeks.

She did remember Troy clearly now. She had inspired Ulysses. Told him to build a horse. After the victory she had studied the pattern of the gigantic stones. She had pondered over the genius of skillful builders and military leaders. Aye. She knew all about building forts. "I do remember now, Great One. I shall design the best stronghold for Sigefroi."

"It may not be enough, though..." The whispering breeze stilled.

Melusine wondered whether the Goddess had departed. "Not enough?"

"Aye." The vibration resumed. The Goddess was still here. "You must not only win Sigefroi's love, but also love him back, become the source of his power, his pillar of strength, the root of his dynasty, the mother of his children. You shall protect and support him blindly, no matter what his actions bring. If you do, your heirs will rule from the North Sea to the lands of the Rus tribes in the east, and accomplish magnificent deeds."

"I see..." A secret thrill coursed through Melusine's body.

"But as Sigefroi becomes dearer than your own flesh and blood, you will suffer his disappointments, fear for his life, watch him grow old, and one day mourn his passing."

Melusine remembered what her aunt Morgane used to say. The hardest thing about living so long is to watch those you love grow old, wither, and die. So, that would be her true punishment, the only pain that could redeem her from the curse... loving a mortal. "I understand, O Great One."

"Yet, there is more, my child."

"More?" Suppressing a protest, Melusine braced herself as she felt the worst was yet to come.

19

The face of the Goddess on Skull Rock hardened slightly. "Your unholy secret and your Fae blood must remain undiscovered."

"Undiscovered?" Melusine stuttered with panic. "But if we live together, how can he not find out?"

"If by misfortune he chances upon your secret, he must take it to his grave."

Melusine swallowed hard. "And that will end the curse?"

"Only if he keeps your secret." The Goddess sighed, and Melusine felt her powerful breath on her cheeks.

Despite the harsh conditions of her release, Melusine allowed hope to warm her. "I thank you, for this rare opportunity to serve your higher purpose, O Great one."

The Lady's face on Skull Rock smiled sadly. "Beware, my child, of Sigefroi's entanglements with the Church."

The compassionate warning surprised Melusine. She shuddered at the words. "The Church?"

"Just as surely as he can save you from the curse, this ambitious knight can lead you to a horrible death." The words of doom echoed through the gorge.

Melusine bowed, her heart racing. "I accept the challenge."

"But in order to seduce a great knight, you will need a great sword."

Melusine felt the ripple of power as a glinting blade surged straight up out of the water surrounding her rock. She recognized the sword. She had seen it before. As she bent to take it from the shining water, she uttered with reverence, "Caliburn..."

A hissing sound, a rustle on the wind, and the eerie power vanished. The Great One had left. Between the two trees, Skull Rock looked like its old sneering self again.

Melusine caressed the sword of power with great respect. Caliburn had brought many victories throughout history, and protected its bearers without fail. It had been her father's sword for a time.

In a daze, Melusine realized that the sheen on the scales of her lower body had dulled. Her serpent tail had dried and itched. How long had she been out of the water? Holding the sword, she pushed herself off the flat rock and splashed into the welcoming flow.

The cold stream, however, did not ease her unrest. Like the splendid weapon, the offer from the Goddess carried a double edge. Would Melusine find with Sigefroi her redemption from the curse? Or would she end up burning at the stake?

Chapter Two

One week later, St Maximin Abbey in Trier, Ottonian Empire.

No music could charm Sigefroi's ears like the grating of quill on parchment, especially when the deed being drawn granted him a coveted property, like just now. Around him, the high arches of St Maximin buzzed with the voices of many nobles, guards, monks, and curious folk attracted by the public event.

Despite the giant log burning in the monumental fireplace, Sigefroi felt a chill as he sat at the massive oak table. He had traded his chain mail for a white silk tunic and red woolen chausses that molded the muscles of his legs. Armed only with a short blade, he felt vulnerable in court attire.

Paying no heed to the two archbishops in full regalia, or to his brother Frederick of High Lorraine sitting across the table, Sigefroi focused on the movement and sound of the abbot's quill. From somewhere in the monastery, the melodious voices of monks chanting the psalms marked the mid-morning prayers.

After returning the quill to the inkhorn, the abbot sprinkled thin sand to blot the rich brown ink then blew on it, sending the candle flames aflutter. Holding the open scroll, he cleared his throat and read.

"In exchange for the town of Feulen and its surrounding fields, St Maximin gives Sigefroi of Ardennes, son of the Duke of Lorraine, ownership of Lucilinburhuc, from the Alzette River to the old tree trunks lying about half a league outside the fortifications. The total property averages one manse, enough land to support a village of serfs and a noble family with the usual servants."

Sigefroi knew full well the abbey profited from the deal. "I gather the good lands of Feulen will compensate you handsomely."

The abbot offered a thin smile. "We appreciate your generosity, my lord."

When the abbot handed the document to Sigefroi, eight silk cords hanging from the deed brushed the table. The prelate then pushed toward him the wad of green wax and the lit candle. The wax stick crackled and spattered when Sigefroi melted its tip to the flame. Laying two of the hanging threads on the smooth table, he lavished on them a generous amount of wax. Then he made a fist and stamped down the flat of his oval signet ring.

Leaning back in the chair, the venerable abbot sighed. "This little fort is a piece of history... given to our abbey by Charles Martell of France, two and a half centuries past." He sustained Sigefroi's stare. "But of late, the crops do not yield enough to maintain it the way it deserves."

The face of the rotund bailiff with shifty eyes flashed in Sigefroi's mind. Remembering the overstuffed larder at the end of a long winter, he knew the man cheated the good monks. Sigefroi would see that the bailiff received just retribution.

The abbot looked upon Sigefroi with indulgence... his way of telling him he'd overpaid by exchanging fertile lands for a worthless pile of rocks.

Sigefroi didn't mind. He had what he wanted. Only a warrior could grasp the full value of an inviolable fort. "While you need churches and abbeys to spread the true faith, Lord Abbot, a Christian lord needs fortresses to gather his armies, ward off the heathens, and protect abbeys and churches from greedy neighbors."

Carefully separating the hardening wax from his signet ring, then the cooling wax from the tabletop, Sigefroi handed the document with its dangling seal to Archbishop Henri of Verdun, who had been talking in quiet tones with Archbishop Bruno, brother of Emperor Otto.

"And a Christian lord needs Holy Mother Church to validate his power," Archbishop Henri declared in a stentorian voice.

A hush settled upon the vast hall.

"For without God's rule and holy purpose, knights are naught but highway predators." For emphasis, the Archbishop shook his fist holding a heavy brass seal, symbol of his position and authority.

A murmur of assent rose from the standing crowd witnessing the event from behind the red ropes a few paces away.

Sigefroi repressed a smile as he finished cleaning bits of green wax from his signet ring with one nail. He'd heard the prelate's dramatic harangues before. "I couldn't agree more, Your Grace."

He knew better than to antagonize an archbishop. The Church crowned and excommunicated kings and emperors at will. Only with its support could any kind of power be achieved.

The prelate read the deed, mumbling to himself the Latin words, nodding at intervals. With a flourish that underlined the importance of the occasion, the archbishop delicately placed two silky cords across the base of his double seal. He filled the disk with melted wax before pressing the other half carefully upon it. Soft shiny waves oozed around the edges.

Sigefroi congratulated himself for his strong connections among the princes of the Church. Not all of them approved of a new power in their midst, however. Some corrupt prelates had requested outrageous donations to their cathedral funds while others demanded promises of military support. Once, Sigefroi even had to supply a comely wench to win a prelate's good graces.

But despite his personal fortune and his own titles as Protector of St Maximin and Lay Abbot of Echternach, Sigefroi did not hold enough clout to obtain this strategic piece of property. Two of his most influential brothers had intervened in his favor. And of course, as Sigefroi's friend, Emperor Otto himself had spoken to the archbishops.

Frederick of Lorraine, Sigefroi's oldest brother, ratified the document next, using the personal seal hanging from a silver chain on his chest. Equally tall, but thinner and older than Sigefroi, with the same reddish hair, Frederick wore a red silver-trimmed tunic. His aristocratic face, however, lacked the stern determination of a warrior.

"How does it feel, brother, to become my vassal?" Frederick raised one eyebrow. As Duke of High Lorraine where Lucilinburhuc was located, he had just become Sigefroi's new overlord.

Sigefroi smiled fondly. He rather liked the idea. "Better to keep it in the family. It will give us a chance to meet more often. Perhaps we could hunt a few boars together or meet in a friendly joust."

Frederick gave a nervous laugh, almost spilling wax on the parchment. "You still insist on violent sports, brother? I thought years of warring would have cured your battle frenzy by now."

"I hope I never change and always accept a worthy challenge." Sigefroi loved his brothers dearly but couldn't help noticing their shortcomings. Not one among the five had the shrewdness of a great ruler.

While awaiting his turn to seal the document, Archbishop Bruno of Cologne whispered in Sigefroi's ear. "My brother Otto wants to see you afterwards."

Sigefroi nodded. He hadn't seen the emperor in months and intended to pay his respects in any case. Despite the monarch's notorious cruelty on the battlefield, Sigefroi missed talking to the older man, or perhaps he missed slaughtering barbarians with him. The choices were simpler in his youth. Honor for the victor, shame, degradation, or death for the defeated, nothing in between.

Everyone at the table looked smug, but for different reasons. The Abbot of St Maximin had traded barren rock for a thriving town with farmlands. The princes of the Church gained a new military force to protect them, and Frederic of High Lorraine had now in his brother a most faithful and reliable vassal.

As for Sigefroi, he held the perfect perch upon which to build a fortress, right in the center of his scattered holdings, which he planned to consolidate into a powerful kingdom.

* * *

Safe inside her dwelling carved into the cliff, Melusine stared at the calm water of her divining basin. Tallow candles around the stone rim lit the mirrored surface. Not all her powers could be controlled at will, but visions on a water surface came easy to her.

Other gifts, like invisibility, required a glamour spell. Her powers of persuasion depended greatly upon the personal strength of the other person's mind. Dreams, on the other hand, came and went on the whims of the Goddess.

An unfamiliar scene appeared on the calm surface, unfolding miles away in Trier... the formal sealing of a land deal with Sigefroi.

Melusine tossed back her loose hair and shuddered at the sight of the archbishops. Her arms folded protectively around the sleeves of her blue shift. How could she, an accursed Fae, possibly live among such mortals and avoid discovery? Charlemagne had persecuted her mother. Bishops like those sitting at that table had also set a price on Melusine's head long ago. She feared the punishments the Church inflicted on Pagans, and the devastating effect of holy water on Fae folks.

"Dear Goddess," she whispered. "Give me the strength to walk into the lion's maw."

Her gaze returned to Sigefroi's reflection on the water surface, He smiled, self-assured, as daunting in fine silk as in bloody armor. Melusine wondered what feelings lurked behind his wide amber eyes. The permanent scowl creasing his fiery brow betrayed none of his inner thoughts.

During random spying, Melusine had discovered Sigefroi's reputation for ruthlessness and strong will, as

26

well as his political ties in the highest courts, but even for her, this fierce man's true nature constituted a mystery.

Hard as she tried, Melusine couldn't pry into the knight's mind. He seemed immune to her magic! If she could not bind him with a spell, Melusine would have to depend upon her personal charms. Somehow, the challenge of seducing this dangerous knight made her skin prickle all over as her insides flooded with warmth.

* * *

Later that day, in the imperial palace in Trier.

Sigefroi watched Emperor Otto toss a chunk of venison to the mosaic floor. Two hounds pounced upon it. Then Otto wiped his blond beard with the hem of the tablecloth. Blond ringlets fell on the green velvet of his broad shoulders, framing a smooth forehead, slim arched brows, and high cheek bones. Smiling, Otto pushed the silver platter toward Sigefroi then motioned to his man servant for more wine.

Since Otto didn't stand on ceremony with him, Sigefroi never felt intimidated in his presence, even in the austere grandeur of Trier's Roman palace. It took more than gem-encrusted furniture, marble paneling, domed ceilings, or golden mosaics to impress a knight of Lorraine.

Otto's enjoyment at reliving past carnage with deliberate accuracy, however, bothered even a rugged warrior like Sigefroi. Time to change the subject.

"By the by..." Sigefroi carved another piece of deer with his poniard and speared the hefty chunk. "I never had the opportunity to congratulate you on your recent crowning in Rome. Holy Roman Emperor has a much better ring to it than King."

Dipping his fingers in the bowl of salt, Sigefroi sprinkled the meat then bit into the savory morsel. The sweet roasted taste spread pleasantly across his palate.

Otto chuckled. "Not a small feat that crowning..." He lay back in his padded chair, blinking from the sun filtering through the high windows. "But it had naught to do with chance or mere luck, my young friend."

"How so?" Sigefroi admired the older man's ruthless tactics.

"You should have seen the pope's face when I declared my intentions." Otto's smile widened. "Of course, I made sure he had no choice in the matter. In order to succeed, you need a master plan."

"I agree." Sigefroi wiped his mouth with the hem of the table cloth. Even for a casual meal, Otto insisted on good manners.

Otto laced his hands on his stomach and stared at Sigefroi. "Do you know what you want to achieve?"

Sigefroi considered the question. Of course, he had a master plan. At an early age he had learned exactly how much force, courage, gold coins, tenacity, intrigue, and compromise it took to defeat an enemy or build an empire. "I've reached many goals over the years, but they were mere steps toward my main purpose."

"Which is?" Otto took the pitcher of wine from his body servant, waved the man away then refilled both silver goblets himself.

To hide his hesitation, Sigefroi took a sip. Sweet white Moselle wine, his favorite. "I shall surpass my sire in fortune, lands, and power."

Otto whistled, a soldier's habit. "Quite a brazen goal, but not impossible. I can see the fierce spirit of old Wigeric in you. That is why I value your friendship. The more powerful my loyal vassals are, the mightier I become."

Sigefroi breathed in relief. His father, Wigeric, had slain his own king to appropriate royal lands. "I'm glad you see it that way."

Otto raised his goblet. "Congratulations on today's acquisition. Soon, I understand, I may call upon your new army to defend my empire. I can always use reinforcements in Italy against the Byzantines."

"I see..." Sigefroi chuckled. "So, our friendship is naught but political interest, after all." He said it in jest but wondered how true the statement might be.

Otto grinned, reducing his slanted green eyes to mere slits and leaned forward. "An emperor must often combine rulership with pleasure." He took a long swig from his silver goblet then shook his head. "You, devil. Now that you have a fortress to call home, you need to find a wife and start making children for your future dynasty."

Sigefroi nodded. "The difficult task is to find the right woman."

Otto shrugged. "My daughters are still infants, much too young for you. If you had a legitimate son, though, I'd be glad to give him one of my little princesses in marriage."

Sigefroi winked. "I do have a few sons scattered about the empire."

"Nay!" Otto exclaimed, with exaggerated outrage. "I'll not waste my precious darlings on camp followers' bastards."

"I figured as much." Sigefroi chortled. "But I'm afraid I expect a lot from a prospective bride."

"You mean lands, breeding, fortune, influence?"

"All that, of course, but also intelligence, education, youth, and beauty." Sigefroi winked. "Don't forget beauty."

Waving away the comment, Otto shrugged. "Trust my experience. Beauty is not that important in marriage."

Sigefroi drained his goblet and brought it down hard on the table. "By St Peter's balls, I have to bed the wench to beget the sons I need."

"Aye, my young friend." Otto raised his goblet. "You're asking much, indeed."

Suddenly restless, Sigefroi rose and paced the mosaic floor, each booted step echoing in the vast room. "And beyond all that, I want her strong of body and character. I don't need a fragile flower who bends to my every whim or soon fades away and dies in childbed."

"You are dreaming, my friend." Otto's detached tone marked slight disapproval.

"And she must love me as I am." Sigefroi enjoyed the disappointing effect of his words on Otto. "For I refuse to change my ways."

The emperor rolled his eyes. "No wonder you never married. Most women are weak creatures of Satan, not angels from heaven."

"Still, there must be one waiting for me somewhere." Sigefroi sighed. "I have to find her, and soon."

Otto turned in his chair to face Sigefroi. "I had the entire civilized world to chose from, and even my sweet Edith is not perfect."

"Really?" Returning to his seat, Sigefroi smiled to encourage Otto's confidence. He found power in knowledge.

"She takes great care of our palace in Memleben, and I always find comfort in her arms after a victorious campaign... but she has no love for my bastard sons." Otto drank some wine and smacked finely chiseled lips. "May I suggest someone not quite flawless? I have a lady in mind for you."

"Don't go any further." Sigefroi silenced Otto with a simple glare. "If she doesn't have every quality I request, do not mention her name. I'd rather wait for the perfect maiden."

Otto raised both hands in surrender.

Sigefroi breathed easier. Briefly, the picture of a tanned naked girl under the Roman arch of a bridge crossed his mind. His heart beat a little faster. Was she the reason for his refusal to consider the nuptial offer?

* * *

Bent over the stone basin, Melusine let out a sigh of relief when she heard Sigefroi decline the offered bride. She had watched and listened in pure fascination, committing to memory every precious detail. Was she beautiful enough by Sigefroi's standards? If he preferred plump girls as the fashion went, he might not like her swarthy slender look.

The loving part could easily be feigned, though. Melusine had learned from spying on mortals that most men became dolts when it came to love, and flattery

30

usually worked miracles. Still. The Great One said Melusine must truly love the man in order to be redeemed.

From a faraway past, the image of her aging father, King Elinas, came unbidden through the water basin. Grief and disappointment distorted her father's kind face, making Melusine's heart ache at the remembrance. Why had he trusted her when she and her sisters only sought revenge?

She now understood that Elinas blindly believed in his daughters' love. How Melusine regretted sealing his unjust fate... much too late. The mortal king must have died over a century ago, miserable and alone in his cave. The curse forbade her to find out exactly when.

Turning away from the stone basin, Melusine struggled to bring her mind to present matters and consider her situation. She had a substantial dowry but no lands. Still, she fulfilled Sigefroi's breeding requirements.

Her mother, a royal princess of Bretagne, had become a queen in her own right. Her father had reigned over the kingdom of Strathclyde, now part of Scotland. Her family's tragic story, however, had since become local legend. She hoped Sigefroi wasn't familiar with the unfortunate dynasty of Strathclyde.

Melusine gazed upon her dwelling, carved into the cliff overlooking the Alzette River. For her safety, the secret entrance of her cave lay not only far from any trail, but she protected it with spells, and a veil of glamour that made it invisible to the human eye. Over the years she had faceted with care the many jutting pillars, shaped airy vaults, and smoothed the floor to a shine before covering it with thick rugs.

Opposite the divining basin still lit by its row of candles, stood a sleeping pallet. For comfort, Melusine had filled the huge leather mattress with wheat bran, then covered it with sheepskins. In the center of the room sat a stone table with two wooden benches. Along the walls, open chests and coffers revealed silks from the orient, rare spices, a hoard of coins, gold jewels, scrolls, and fine silver goblets.

On the cliff face, she had pierced openings in the thick sandstone, to let in light and fresh air. From outside, the windows looked like natural holes high in the rock wall, partially covered with hanging ivy. But from the inside, they had pleasant geometric shapes and harmonious balance.

Yes, Melusine could consider herself an architect of sorts. She'd used magic instead of a chisel, but she could visualize and supervise the execution of the most complicated project. Compared to her subterranean palace, fortresses couldn't be all that difficult to build.

Since spring had chased away the chill, Melusine removed and rolled away the oiled parchment covering the windows. A fire crackled in the hearth, but no smoke drifted into her lair. The draft followed a natural fissure that traveled far under the cliff before releasing the smoke uphill in the forest.

An underground stream provided pleasant sounds, as well as fresh water all year round. It also flushed all waste to the river, leaving her abode clean and sweet smelling.

And now the Goddess wanted her to leave this familiar place and marry a Christian knight? Melusine took pride in her Pagan ways. Could she play her part in the strange world of mortals? It might be her only chance at redemption. She would brave any danger to lift the curse that plagued her solitary life.

Melusine furrowed among the treasures heaped into her coffers, past a fine dagger and ornate metal boxes, to find a bejeweled scabbard. It sheathed Caliburn, the sword with a glorious past.

When she drew the heavy blade with a metallic rasp, the invincible sword gleamed blue in the candlelight. Now, thanks to the Goddess, the magic weapon was Melusine's to bestow anew. She hoped Sigefroi would prove worthy of it.

If this proud conqueror sought a strong woman, Melusine would give him a challenge. The wild knight would make a worthy opponent, even for a Fae, since he seemed impervious to her magic.

32

Melusine smiled in anticipation. But how would she fare in matters of love? Although she had never lain with a man in this incarnation, she remembered loving men in previous lives. Besides, she had eavesdropped on mortals long enough to understand how things worked, and what a man wanted.

In the faraway past, she had wooed kings and demigods, even gods, with the flutter of an eyelash. Could she do it again?

Chapter Three

Sigefroi relaxed, naked, in the decadent luxury of Trier's imperial baths, with successive pools of water at different temperatures to stimulate and relax the body and the mind. Despite having suffered from the invasions, the ancient city still offered many luxurious comforts preserved from Roman times.

With a busy day ahead, Sigefroi needed to sort out his thoughts. He'd dreamed of the naked girl in the Alzette River last night again. Why? It wasn't like him to obsess about a lass, no matter how beautiful or intriguing.

How different she was from the noble ladies he'd met at court, though. She had swarthy skin, a toned body, and long flowing hair with streaks of sunshine, as if she had spent her life outdoors... like a warrior. Although lithe, she was endowed with generous breasts. His manhood stiffened in the hot water at the recollection of her exquisite globes teasing the waterline.

Sigefroi glanced right and left. Fortunately the facility was almost empty at this early hour. Nobles and merchants rarely bathed before dawn. He waded waist high towards the cooler pools, hoping to chill his lust. Such natural reactions were difficult to hide while naked in a public bath.

What was happening to him? He always took or bought what he wanted. The girl was on his new lands, so she now belonged to him by right. He would have to search for her as soon as he took possession of his new domain. Since a serf could not be a nuptial candidate, he would ravage her, and cure himself of this ridiculous fixation.

His decision made, he stepped out of the cold water pool and dressed quickly. In city attire, but carrying his sword, he left the baths and walked to the river wharf to meet his companions. As he passed under the gigantic stone gates of the fortified city, he admired the statues and the engraved words of Trier's greatest emperors.

On the busy wharf along the wide river, sailors unloaded barges and soldiers loitered. As he approached the stone bridge spanning the river, Sigefroi couldn't resist peering under the nearest arch, half expecting to see a naked lass bathing in the current. But no such luck. This river was not the Alzette.

By the bridge, Thierry and Gunter waited with the horses. Sigefroi hurried toward them and waved. "Let's go see the vineyards. These horses need some exercise."

Sigefroi mounted then rode with Gunter and young Thierry along the Moselle River. On the hilly shores grew the grapes of his favorite wine. "These vineyards were planted by the order of Emperor Constantine himself, for the glory of Rome."

Thierry frowned. "How long ago was that?"

"Several centuries." Sigefroi smiled. "Vineyards last a long time."

They came into view of a monastery overlooking the vineyard on the slope. Sigefroi pointed to it. "Let's visit the monks and break our fast."

The monks received Sigefroi and his friends with the respect due his rank. They served a copious fare. The monks of Trier lived better than most.

After the meal, Sigefroi turned to the abbot. "Could I bother you with a taste of your sweetest white wine?"

The abbot nodded and disappeared through the refectory door.

Gunter chuckled. "Getting tired of red wine?"

Sigefroi smiled. "It will suffice for everyday fare, but for special occasions I need a sweet white wine, like the nectar I tasted at Emperor Otto's table."

When the abbot returned, Sigefroi found the wine to his liking and suspected that was where Otto's wine was made. Thierry and Gunter also approved with nods and smacking of lips.

Satisfied, Sigefroi purchased with gold coins four dozen vine stocks to start another vineyard on his new estate, as well as ten barrels of last year's wine. The order would be delivered shortly to his new domain.

By the time the companions returned to Trier, the sun already curved into afternoon. Back inside the city walls, they rode past a two-story villa, lit by many torches in sconces, and displaying a stone phallus higher than two men. A comely lass, tall and blonde with wide blue eyes, stood in the doorway.

She smiled invitingly while lifting her red robes to expose milky legs. "Half a silver coin can buy your fill of ecstasy, my lords."

Sigefroi chuckled. "Promises are cheap."

Gunter halted his horse and held his hand for his friends to stop. He turned in the saddle to face Sigefroi. "Can't remember my last wenching. Perhaps it is time to refresh my memory. Are you coming?"

Young Thierry blushed, looking expectantly at his lord, and Sigefroi surmised the lad had never known a woman. From an upper story window, muffled laughter drifted into the street.

Sigefroi smiled. "I reckon it looks better than a roll in the muddy grass with a camp follower after a battle." Surprisingly, he didn't feel aroused as he had so many times before. Although he usually enjoyed such pleasures and had the coin for it, lately he fancied a svelte, exotic woman with tan skin and sun-streaked hair.

On the breeze, Sigefroi detected the scent of perfumed oils such as burned in churches. It reminded him of a bishop who preached against sinful places but visited them often in secret.

Reaching for the leather purse hanging at his belt, Sigefroi extracted a silver coin and tossed it to Thierry. "Here, lad. Have some fun for me."

Thierry caught the coin in mid air, his blue eyes widening as he grinned with delight. "For me, my lord?"

"Aye. I still have much to do. Go with Gunter. I'll meet you two at the abbey for supper."

Gunter frowned in disbelief. "Are you unwell, my friend?"

Sigefroi waved away his comment. "Go. I will be fine."

With no more prompting, his two companions dismounted and tethered their horses to the metal rings in the wall. Sigefroi watched them hurry toward the inviting doorway, then he turned his destrier and rode away.

* * *

That night, at St Martin's Abbey, Gunter, in high spirits, told funny anecdotes. Thierry, despite the foolish grin on his face, behaved with more confidence and maturity than he ever had. The three men sampled the renowned wine of St Martin's own vineyards. Gunter approved when Sigefroi purchased several casks of the golden nectar for his new stronghold.

In the following days, Sigefroi hired stone cutters, carpenters, blacksmiths and stone masons. He also acquired three families of serfs and procured a body of servants for his new estate. At the free market in front of the cathedral, he bought horses, goats, sheep, and a sow with piglets.

While visiting noble friends and acquaintances from past battlefields, Sigefroi inquired about loyal soldiers for his personal guard.

No luck in finding an architect, however. The best ones were busy building new churches, expanding and beautifying the cathedral, repairing the city walls damaged by decades of warfare, or restoring the imperial palace. No matter. Sigefroi had seen the best fortresses of the civilized world and could probably direct the most urgent work without the help of a master builder.

Finally, one morning, the slow convoy of hand-pulled carts and horse-drawn chariots left Trier to cross the Moselle River. The thick wooden wheels groaned under the heavy loads. Toddlers sat on top of their families' meager possessions and other supplies for the fort. Going west, the train stretched for a quarter of a Roman mile along the Via Romana that cut straight through the green hills and valleys of High Lorraine. At the rear, the sow and squealing piglets traveled in the last cart, and behind it, goats and sheep followed on foot, bleating as young lads herded them with sticks.

Sigefroi rode at the head with Gunter and Thierry, while the new men at arms protected the column's flanks. Craftsmen, servants and serfs walked beside and between the carts. Among the serfs, a wife heavy with child struggled to keep pace. Sigefroi slowed his mount to let the train catch up.

Although he felt sorry for the woman, he couldn't show weakness in front of his new people. He needed to be feared as well as respected.

He composed a stern face to address her gruffly from the height of his black destrier. "Woman!"

"Aye, m'lord." When the wife glanced up, alarm widened her eyes.

"Get on a supply cart. You're slowing us down."

The woman mumbled her thanks with a furtive smile. In haste, she hitched up her skirts and hobbled toward the nearest slow-rolling horse cart, followed by her skinny husband. She caught up with the moving cart and grabbed hold of the back rail. With her man hefting her from behind, she stepped up the short ladder then settled between sacs of oats and wine casks. Once ensconced, the woman nodded to Sigefroi and smiled with relief. So did her husband as he walked alongside.

Their gratitude felt good, but Sigefroi revealed none of his pleasure. Was he getting soft? Nay, he reassured himself. The babe in the mother's womb was his property, and he must protect his investment. In order to prosper, an estate needed nurturing.

Despite their efforts, the score of mounted soldiers couldn't keep the long train tight and tidy. People, carts, and animals made for an unwieldy caravan.

Sigefroi sighed as he caught up with Gunter and Thierry. "At such speed, it will take three days to reach the fort, and I don't want to wait that long."

Gunter's brow shot up. "What do you propose?"

"Can you oversee the caravan all the way home?"

Gunter winked. "Easier than chasing stray enemy after a battle."

"I know I can count on you." Sigefroi smiled.

Leaving Gunter in charge of the convoy, Sigefroi motioned young Thierry to follow him. Thierry grinned and spurred his mount as Sigefroi forged ahead on the straight road. A cloud of dust billowed in their wake.

* * *

In a clearing on the knoll along the Via Romana, Melusine sat atop her white mare in full knight armor, watching the wide road. Two riders approached at a gallop. She recognized Sigefroi at his fiery mane. His young squire rode alongside.

Melusine bunched her hair under the mail hauberk, pulled down the helmet, and adjusted the nose guard. With a click of the tongue, she spurred the mare down the slope.

Her silver mail and long shield jostled awkwardly on her slender frame, but the bounce of Caliburn on her thigh reassured her as she rode. Besides, she had the advantage. This wouldn't be a fair fight.

Pushing the mare to a gallop, Melusine stormed through sparse woods and down the hill, then up the road toward the approaching riders, shortening the distance between them. Then she halted her mount short. Pulling on the reins, she made the white mare rear and paw the air in the middle of the road.

In challenge, she drew Caliburn in a wide arc. She knew she cut a striking figure, framed by two green hills with the stark fortress at her back.

The riders slowed. Sigefroi tugged on the reins and his body tensed. The squire followed suit. The two men came to a halt a dozen paces in front of her. Sigefroi grabbed the helmet hanging from his saddle and slipped it over his head. Then both riders drew swords.

His identity safe under the full helmet, Melusine smiled. Surprise, indeed!

"Return whence you came, Sigefroi of Ardennes!" she intoned in a strong clear voice, deep enough to be that of a lad. "You are trespassing upon nature's domain. You have no power over these woods, nor can you control the animals that populate them, the rivers, the wind, or the skies above. Your title means nothing to the forces that rule this land."

Sigefroi's grip tightened on the reins as he halted his destrier.

"Who dares challenge me on my own estate?" He sounded calm and in control, but the black destrier fidgeted, betraying his master's alertness.

Straight in the saddle, Melusine held her sword at the ready. "My name holds power and I do not give it lightly."

Sigefroi's gaze through the helmet slits darted to the tree line, as if he expected an army to rush out of the woods and fall upon him. After a short pause, he relaxed and erupted in laughter.

"Young man, you have balls of bronze to defy me alone!" He drew his mount closer, studying her. "I have every right to be here, and I will defend that right with my life if need be." There was no mistaking the threat in his even tone.

After so many years of isolation, Melusine felt rusty dealing with mortals. It set her nerves on edge. She managed to steady her breathing. "Is your heart so pure, Sigefroi, that you do not fear death or the forces of evil?"

"A righteous knight knows not fear, and I stand in my right." He led his war horse in a wide circle around her. "Two archbishops sealed the deed to this land."

Melusine tipped her visor and spat in the thick dust covering the stone road. "The princes of the Church are naught but the pope's minions... men of little faith and great ambition."

Sigefroi chuckled. "Some truths are better left unspoken, lad." He brought the big black horse about to face her. "Now, step aside and let us through. You are no match for my warring skills. I refuse to fight a youth with no whiskers yet." His gaze fell upon Caliburn. "Even one with a fine blade."

The remark took Melusine off-guard. "Why ever not? Since when does Sigefroi The Bloodthirsty hesitate to kill a boy?" As he didn't answer, she added, "I'm not as young as you think, and you'll have to fight me to get through. I leave you no other choice. "

"Pray, do not challenge my patience, lad!" The destrier sidestepped as Sigefroi raised his voice. "Faith! Be gone, or I might grant your death wish."

Melusine let out a derisive laugh. "I wager you wouldn't want your squire to think you a coward, and I say you are if you do not fight me here and now."

A few paces away, the squire watched and listened intently.

"If you get the better of me," Melusine said with emphasis, "you may do with me as you please, but if I defeat you, you'll do anything I say."

"I never concede." A dangerous glint in Sigefroi's eyes told Melusine he had taken the bait.

"Even in exchange for your very life?" She managed to sound vexing. "We'll see..."

"I always win," Sigefroi declared matter-of-factly. "Let's get it over with. On horseback, or on foot?"

"On foot, if you don't mind. My mount is no match for a warhorse."

Sigefroi dismounted with a grunt and slapped the destrier's rear. The warhorse trotted toward the squire who dismounted to retrieve the huge beast. While Sigefroi adjusted the shoulder belt of his shield and balanced his broadsword, Melusine slid off the white mare in a fluid motion. Her small size and lack of training might place her at a disadvantage, but she was quick and agile, with resources Sigefroi couldn't suspect.

Without warning, Sigefroi charged, uttering a blood-chilling battle roar. Melusine would have frozen in fright, were it not for Caliburn guiding and strengthening her arm in the appropriate countermove. Protecting its bearer was the magic sword's purpose.

Barely avoiding a lunge, Melusine side-stepped just in time, deflecting Sigefroi's sword in a clash of steel that sparked, releasing a flinty smell. The armor impeded her movements, and the shield strap bit into her shoulder.

Although her endurance would outlast his, exhausting Sigefroi by keeping to the defense would take too long. Attacking was also out of the question, for Melusine didn't want to kill or maim the man of her destiny. She only needed to humble him.

Sigefroi lashed out, battering her shield with a resounding blow. Under the sheer force of it, Melusine lost her footing. Dear Goddess! He proved stronger and faster than she'd anticipated. Focusing on balance, she called upon Fae power to spring back up. She needed more strength.

Without skipping a blow or missing a step, Melusine slowed her breathing and called upon the unseen forces that rule the universe. Mentally, she rooted herself in the earth like a tree, her head drawing strength from the sky. A shimmer of power flashed on Caliburn and glanced off her mail.

The next mighty thrust found Melusine prepared. Ducking sideways, she reacted with the right amount of speed and strength, forcing Sigefroi back as she feigned an attack. She now enjoyed the sport of avoiding the knight's blade as if she'd practiced the game all her life. Aye. Fae folks learned quickly.

When Sigefroi rushed again, Melusine countered with ease. She couldn't help but admire his physical strength, enjoying the full brunt of his wrath, a mighty wave of hot, unrefined energy. With every move, his battle-hardened muscles bulged under the mail tunic. She smelled the musky sweat pearling on his brow and his breath warmed her face. The formidable knight grunted and lunged with the powerful grace of a lion, but Melusine kept him at bay, enjoying the growing rage and frustration in his eyes.

Sigefroi's murderous glare drilled into her through the helmet slits. Would he recognize her? Nay. Melusine realized he didn't see her as a person anymore, but as an enemy, a vile thing to crush like a viper on the road. Such barbarism burned in his amber gaze, such determination. The close proximity of this ferocious man frightened and thrilled her at the same time.

Parrying high, Melusine caught a glance of the squire who held the horses at a safe distance. The lad watched with open curiosity, obviously enjoying his master's skillful demonstration. But Sigefroi's well-honed skills wouldn't bring him victory this day. To keep a semblance of fairness, Melusine kept fighting, making the combat look evenly matched.

When Sigefroi dealt a particularly fierce blow, Melusine sent through her parrying arm a wave of energy like a lightning bolt. Sigefroi was thrown back, flying through the air. His sword and shield clattered on the dusty stone of the road. His helmet flew off. He hit the ground in a pounding of metal. Flat on his back, the knight didn't move.

In two steps, Melusine had Caliburn's point at his throat. "Do you yield?"

Sigefroi blinked, and the slow realization of his desperate situation showed in the widening of his eyes, along with a spark of rage, and something else... Surprise!

When he did not respond, Melusine repeated louder, "Do you yield?"

The words came with difficulty. Sigefroi, no doubt, had to swallow a great deal of pride. "I... do... yield," he croaked.

"In exchange for your life, I shall exact an oath." Melusine made her voice carry so that the young squire could also hear and understand. "Within a week, a royal princess by the name of Melusine will ask for your hospitality. Not only will you treat her according to her noble rank, you will betroth her and take her for wife."

"What?" Sigefroi, in his surprise, had started to rise, but Melusine pressed Caliburn's point harder against the mail at his throat, forcing him to lie still.

"Swear on your knight's honor, or I kill you right now!"

In no position to bargain, Sigefroi finally said in a strangled voice, "I swear it."

"Louder!" Melusine insisted, applying more pressure.

The mail shifted as Sigefroi swallowed, and blood trickled at his throat under the sword's sharp tip. "I swear it on my knight's honor!"

Drawing back the weapon, Melusine returned the great sword to the scabbard. Sigefroi sat up slowly, coughing, shaking his red mane, and rubbing a grazed throat. Melusine didn't wait for him to get up or retrieve his broadsword.

When she whistled, the white mare came at a trot. She mounted swiftly and turned the horse around.

"Wait!" Sigefroi shouted in a broken voice.

Melusine halted the mare and turned in the saddle, a wide grin on her face. She'd been waiting for this moment to deliver the coup de grâce.

The knight rose on unsteady feet. "If you won't give me your name, at least let me behold the face of my victor!"

The humiliation in Sigefroi's eyes and voice delighted Melusine. Slowly, she lifted her silver helmet and pushed back the head mail, letting her long hair cascade over slender shoulders. Staring at him with glee, she however measured her deliberate reply.

"You were bested by a maiden, my lord."

Sigefroi's thunderstruck expression made her laugh.

"But have no fear, your honor is safe with me. I shall keep your defeat a secret." After a mock bow to Sigefroi and his dumfounded squire, she spurred the mare away and didn't look back.

* * *

44

Sigefroi couldn't believe what had just happened and stood openmouthed, staring after the lass riding off into the woods. By St Andreas' foot! He'd been undone by a maiden, the very same he'd seen bathing in the Alzette two weeks past.

He slapped his thigh in frustration, immediately regretting the shock that intensified the pain in his arm. Was this a bad dream? No. His sword lay on the road. So did the helmet and shield. He'd planned to find the maiden, but she'd found him first and humiliated him. How? Something didn't feel right.

Retrieving his gear, Sigefroi turned to Thierry menacingly. "Not a word of this to anyone, you hear? Don't ever mention it, not even to me!"

Thierry looked away in embarrassment. "'Course not, m'lord."

The blond lad avoided his master's gaze as he brought up the black steed and held it for Sigefroi to mount.

"I don't know what treachery this is, but I don't like it." Sigefroi hoped the steely tone would mask his growing embarrassment. "No maiden can defeat the best warrior in the realm in fair combat. Something is very wrong. I smell a rotten fish."

"Aye, m'lord." Thierry looked dejected, as if he'd just lost all respect for the knight he'd regarded as a hero all this time.

Sigefroi's joy at taking possession of his new domain suddenly turned sour. Neither of them spoke during the short ride to the fort. Sigefroi hated being played the fool. How could this frail maiden counter him blow for blow? Had he drunk tainted wine? Eaten poisoned food? If not, her strength and cunning surpassed his own. How could that be?

What bothered him most was his reaction to the elusive maiden herself. If he'd wanted to protect her the first time he glanced at her nude beauty, now he wished he could strangle the little hellcat. He'd show her he was the best warrior.

Jesu! Even now, he lusted for her. Why didn't he go wenching with Gunter when he had a chance? Shifting in the saddle to ease the discomfort in his groin, Sigefroi both envied and pitied the man who'd wed such a wild creature.

He didn't even know her name!

Judging by the expensive armor and fine weapon, she enjoyed great wealth. It shouldn't be too difficult to find out who she was. He would confront her and take back his oath, or strike a different bargain. He hadn't refused a bride from the emperor to accept one from a nameless wench. Unfortunately, he'd given his word as a knight... a promise he could never break.

And who was Melusine, the princess he'd agreed to take for wife? He'd never heard of such a lady in noble circles. The name almost sounded like Mal-Lucine, the evil goddess of antiquity who presided over childbirth and poisoned the mind of willful women with ideas of independence.

Gunter had mentioned Mal-Lucine as a possible translation for Lucilinburhuc. Sigefroi, however, didn't believe in the power of false gods, so he banished the thought from his mind until he could find answers.

* * *

Ten days later, the smell of fresh cut wood and the sounds of hammering filled the bailey. Sigefroi turned to meet Gunter coming at a run.

His friend's dark face shone with sweat but he grinned widely through his black beard. "Where do you want the guardhouse for the men-at-arms?"

Sigefroi motioned to a spot inside the wall near the gate. "This should be the best location, with quick access to the gate and the rampart."

Gunter nodded appreciatively. "I asked the women and children to collect the best fallen stones from the rubble of the village fortifications. They are cleaning and piling up the reusable ones."

Sigefroi smiled at his friend's efficiency. "And the stone masons are scanning the cliff for a possible quarry. The plentiful sandstone should be easy to work with, and suitable for strong walls."

Gunter guffawed. "Walls that bend rather than crack under the stone balls of the war machines?"

"Exactly." Sigefroi winked. "I want to be ready for anything."

The plump bailiff approached the two men with his family and servants in tow, all packed and ready to leave with carts and a few animals.

The fat man bowed to Sigefroi. "I guess it's farewell my lord."

Sigefroi refrained from showing his relief. The bailiff's departure afforded him the free run of the villa. For the first time since his arrival, he was truly lord of his new domain, and it felt wonderful. "Good luck managing your new appointed charge."

The bailiff nodded. "The abbey of St Maximin has been most generous, and the new appointment will prove easier to manage than this one." The plump man scanned the bailey with haughty detachment. "The lands are richer, too."

Sigefroi surmised that the bailiff would keep swindling from the monks wherever they sent him. After perusing the books, he had no doubt the man was cheating the abbey. As official protector of St Maximin, Sigefroi would send a missive to warn the abbot to keep a close eye on the man.

Gunter waved and left to follow a worker calling for advice.

Sigefroi watched the bailiff and his party make their way slowly through the wide open gate and onto the bridge. Then he climbed up the stone stairs carved along the wall and leading to the top of the rampart.

Looking up, he considered the gray clouds announcing more spring rain. He hoped the fair weather would hold for a few more days, enough time to finish the sowing. Already, the air had warmed and the fowl had returned to the woods. Soon, he'd go hunting again.

The top of the wall afforded a panoramic view of the activity. On the far plateau across the gorge, a group of serfs felled trees to clear the edge of the forest for new fields. The timber and larger branches would provide good lumber. Carpenters and masons erected huts in the village for the new families of serfs and free workers.

Over a week had passed since his arrival, and no royal princess had turned up at the fort. Sigefroi breathed easier. Perhaps he'd imagined the humiliating encounter with the wild maiden at the end of a tiring journey. After all, he'd seen her in dreams. She could have been an illusion.

His men had searched the countryside and found no trace of a warrior woman. Too bad. Sigefroi couldn't get the little hellcat out of his head. He would miss her.

Down in the bailey, Thierry glanced up at Sigefroi. When their eyes met, the boy turned away. Since the day of his stinging defeat at the hands of the brazen maiden, the lad avoided him. Sigefroi shook his head. He'd lost his invincible aura in the eyes of his squire. The boy would have to accept the fact that his hero was only human.

In truth, Sigefroi couldn't deny that the fateful fight had taken place. So why had the bold creature lied about a visiting princess? Why make him swear to marry the lady? To what purpose? It made no sense.

Still pondering the enigma, Sigefroi instinctively gazed east up the Roman road. In the distance, a small van made its way toward the Alzette. He counted five horse-drawn carts. Ahead of the train, a richly dressed lady rode side-saddle. Several loaded mules, a goat, and what looked like young servants followed.

A cold premonition gripped Sigefroi's gut. Hellfire and damnation!

"Gunter!" he shouted over the hammering of the carpenters below.

"Aye," the bearded man answered from the bailey, then ran up the stairs to join him at the top of the rampart.

Sigefroi pointed toward the approaching convoy. "What do you make of this?"

Shading his eyes to peer in the distance, Gunter whistled. "You have good eyesight, my friend. Quite a wealthy train, by the looks of it. Good beasts and fine carts, but I see no armed escort."

A guard appeared on the rampart, running toward them. "M'lord!"

"Aye, Medard. We've seen it."

"Should we inquire, m'lord?" The young soldier's eyes widened with eagerness.

"Aye. Take an escort and find out who it is." Sigefroi waved a dismissal then thought better of it. "Wait!" He hesitated, not sure how much to divulge. "If the lady is coming here, leave the escort with her and return to inform me immediately."

"Aye, m'lord." Medard bowed and turned back to climb down the stairs.

Sigefroi struggled to hide his apprehension. Why had he given his oath? Would the wild maiden have killed him if he hadn't promised to marry the princess? At the time, he believed it. Now, he wasn't so sure.

Gunter frowned. "You think she's coming here?"

Sigefroi cringed. "It's mid afternoon. I don't know of any other decent stop for this sort of convoy less than a day's ride away."

Gunter rubbed his black beard. "I see your logic. I'll go pick the best men to escort them here."

After Gunter left, Sigefroi remained atop the rampart, staring at the advancing van. Each passing moment seemed to confirm his fears. Despite the distance, the small woman sitting side-saddle on the white mare at the head of the van looked somewhat familiar. The girl sat very straight and had long hair streaked with sunshine.

His heart faltered. It looked like the maiden herself, the same he'd fought on the road, the same he'd seen bathing nude. The woman of his dream. Some gut feeling deep inside told him he was right.

By the foot of St Andreas! But he should've known. Indeed, she never intended to kill him, only to marry him! Rage invaded his mind.

But he could have his revenge no later than tonight. The little minx thought herself so smart, but she was only a maiden after all... and Sigefroi knew how to handle wenches.

In front of his entire household, the new Lord of Lucilinburhuc would retake control of his life. A good politician always turned a defeat to his advantage. Sigefroi would save face by taking credit for the marriage bargain and have some fun at it, too. If he scared her enough, she might even rescind the deal. Although he would enjoy bedding her.

In any case, the villa wasn't ready to entertain a princess. Fortunately, Sigefroi still had a few hours before the lady's arrival. His hospitality wouldn't be found wanting.

Bursting into the kitchen, Sigefroi startled scullions and cooks by ordering an impromptu feast, as well as the baking of fresh bread in the middle of the week. Then he gathered maids and servants and set them to scrubbing the recently vacated villa, the hall and especially his private rooms.

Used to giving orders to soldiers, he saw with satisfaction that the help scurried at his commanding tone. Sigefroi truly enjoyed playing castle lord.

An hour into the preparations, Medard entered the busy hall and bowed, then looked around, as if afraid to talk. The hall grew silent in expectation.

"Speak!" Sigefroi barked.

Medard blushed and swallowed hard. "It is Princess Melusine of Strathclyde, daughter of King Elinas. The lady sends her greetings, m'lord."

"A name and title? That's all she gave?" Sigefroi found the young guard's timidity irritating.

"Well," Medard took a deep breath. "She says she comes to wed you, m'lord."

Servants caught their breath in surprise.

"She brings a fine retinue, m'lord," Medard added with growing excitement. "Choice horses, and wooden chests full of dowry."

"How much dowry?"

Medard shrugged. "The lady didn't say. I'm not good at counting, m'lord, but the coffers filled with gold and silver are bigger than those in the imperial armory where we used to store the hauberks."

A murmur of approval washed over the servant folk. That much gold and silver amounted to an impressive fortune.

"Thank you, Medard. You can return to your post."

The guard saluted and left the hall.

"And she travels without an escort?" Gunter frowned. "That's suicide!"

"The lady is quite safe, I can assure you." Sigefroi allowed himself a private smile at the memory of his stinging defeat.

"Still, the roads are dangerous." Gunter looked shocked. "Did you know about this?"

"Aye, my friend, I knew of it." Sigefroi managed a conniving wink. "I can use a bride with enough gold and silver to buy me a small kingdom."

The fact that the little hellcat had emasculated him in front of young Thierry didn't seem important anymore. Even now, the squire who helped in the hall wouldn't meet his gaze. But marriage to the spirited princess might serve Sigefroi after all. In fact, he looked forward to a proper rematch... on his bed furs. The princess would find out then who wielded the mightiest sword.

"You arranged an alliance without telling anyone?" Gunter laughed and slapped his friend's back. "You devil of a man. Why all the secrecy? To avoid our jibes?"

"And right I was, I reckon." Sigefroi's chuckle lacked conviction.

If the royal maiden yielded such a fortune, she could wed any noble she fancied. So why did she corner a small lord over a well landed duke or a prince? The question chafed at the edges of his mind.

"Tell us more about the lady!" Gunter insisted, curious as a crone. "Is she pretty?"

51

"Aye." Sigefroi didn't have to feign the flush of embarrassment that crept up his face. "It is an arranged marriage." He cleared his throat. "She's wealthy, but as is oft the case, I know very little about her. I met Lady Melusine only twice, and we barely exchanged a few words, but she can tell us more at dinner."

Gunter roared, and the castle folk returned to their chores with renewed ardor in a buzz of animated conversations.

Only young Thierry, who'd been feeding the oven fire, didn't look happy with the news. He bent his head and quietly left the hall.

Sigefroi understood the lad's disappointment at his mentor's defeat, and even more at the coverup to hide his shame. Sigefroi knew they should talk soon but hadn't found the right words yet. As incredible as it sounded, he'd simply lost a fight to a lass. Sigefroi still couldn't face the facts. His honor, however, commanded that he keep his oath, and his body yearned for the enchanting beauty of Princess Melusine of Strathclyde.

Disrupting Sigefroi's thoughts, Medard came running and yelled from the wide open doors of the hall. "M'lord, the lady's gone!"

"What?" Answering to the urgency in the guard's voice, Sigefroi met him outside. "What do you mean, gone?"

"Come see for yourself, m'lord. Her caravan is gone. Vanished. She's not on the road anymore."

"Could she have turned onto a smaller road?"

"Possibly, m'lord. But she would have to know the land better than we do."

In a few long strides, Sigefroi reached the rampart wall and climbed the stairs to join the soldiers gathered to gaze at the road below.

"Return to your posts," he ordered grimly.

The guards scattered at his command.

"One moment she was on the road," Medard explained behind him, panting, "then when we looked again, she was

52

gone. No more convoy, no carts, no horses… even our men sent to escort her are gone, m'lord."

Sigefroi stared at the empty road. He could see several miles in each direction... nothing. By St Andreas' foot, what new game was the wild maiden playing now?

Chapter Four

When Melusine suggested to the astonished guards a little known roundabout way up a forested hillock, the men had readily agreed. This route avoided the steep cliff trail that might prove too difficult for her heavy carts.

Riding at a sedate pace between two rows of castle guards, Melusine welcomed the protection of the woods. Sigefroi's gaze from the rampart had made her nervous, so she'd sent a distracting thought to the men on the wall and veered off the straight Roman road. The gentle slope led to the far plateau. They would emerge from the forest into the fields surrounding the fortified village. It would take longer but made for an easier ride.

Lord Sigefroi probably wondered where she went. Melusine allowed herself a slow smile. Her disappearance would add to his frustration. She counted on his anger and wanted him off balance.

Melusine hated to arrive three days late, but it couldn't be helped. The fat bailiff had only vacated the premises this morning, and she'd wanted him out of the way. The rotund man, familiar with local legends and lore, might have suspected her as a Fae. Also, Melusine knew from spying through the divining basin that the villa was small, and she needed privacy to seduce her knight.

She could only imagine Sigefroi's shock at recognizing her and derived a certain pleasure from his quandary. Any Christian knight valued honor and immortal soul too much not to keep a solemn oath. The ruse had worked beyond all expectations. Now, she couldn't wait to see his face. He'd be livid, but she found it easier to sway a knight whose feelings raged out of control than to conquer a cool, calculating lord.

The young servants in the van talked animatedly about the prospect of castle life. Melusine had recently taken them into fosterage from humble families too happy to seize such an opportunity. At Lucilinburhuc, the lads and lasses would receive an education, learn valuable skills, and secure a better life than their parents could ever have hoped for them.

When her convoy emerged from the thick forest, Melusine noticed all the new activity. Groups of men and women worked in the fields. The large tree trunks lying at the edge of the forest had been sliced and cut for lumber, and the smaller branches neatly stacked into piles for firewood.

As they rode by, dirty children gawked, and workers stopped to stare at the unusual cortege. As she neared the village, she noticed that the battered wooden towers on the village fortifications had been dismantled.

The train entered the village at a slow pace. Melusine observed new huts mushrooming everywhere. The population seemed to have quadrupled. She had to admire Sigefroi's sense of organization. Dear Goddess, how she wanted to be part of such a grand project. Excitement flushed her cheeks, making her giddy.

Melusine never had a chance to build a new country before. But here, according to the Goddess, she could start a dynasty that might rule from the North Sea to Bohemia and the plains of central Europe.

As they approached the wooden bridge that spanned the gorge and led to the fort's wide open gate, the guards fell behind to allow for traffic. Laborers and servants came and went freely over the bridge from the caste yard to the village, lugging lumber, masonry blocks, baskets of victuals, livestock, lengths of hemp rope.

Once inside the fort, the flurry of activity seemed to increase. The smell of wood and the din of construction dominated. The breeze also carried the aroma of fresh bread and roasting venison.

In the middle of the bailey, wearing a white tunic and chausses that contrasted with his tan face, Sigefroi stood in front of his servants, arms crossed on his stolid chest. As she approached, Melusine saw a glint of amusement in his amber eyes.

Her heart stumbled. He had recognized her, and far from showing the rage she expected, he looked rather pleased.

Suddenly, Melusine didn't feel so sure of herself anymore. She'd just entered the lion's den. What if her carefully laid plan went awry? If he'd set a trap to kill her, the knave would be free of his oath. She straightened in the side saddle to hide her concern.

"Welcome home, my beautiful bride to be. Lady Melusine, is it?" Sigefroi smiled engagingly and took her gloved hand from the reins to kiss it.

Even through the riding gloves, Melusine shivered at the contact of his lips sending tingles up her arm. "My lord."

He then seized her waist and lifted her from the saddle like a feather pillow. "So, we were destined to meet again."

His warm breath fanned her face and hair as her body slid against his hard frame, ever so slowly. The heat of his hands branded her waist, and he kept holding her tight, long after her feet had touched the ground. As he towered over her, Melusine flushed hot with embarrassment. She hadn't expected Sigefroi to behave so gallantly.

After a hundred years of solitude, his attentions unsettled her. Never in this life had she been courted, and she suddenly wondered whether she'd made a grave mistake in accepting this undertaking.

Dear Goddess! Had he placed her under a spell? She didn't seem able to concentrate on anything but the magnificent and dangerous beast named Sigefroi of Ardennes, new lord of Lucilinburhuc.

* * *

56

Sigefroi deliberately let his hands linger at Melusine's slender waist after he helped her down from the mare. He smiled when he saw her blush.

"Melusine..." The name rolled pleasantly off his tongue. "An unusual name for a princess... or for a warrior."

She gazed up at him with wide eyes of a deep smoky gray. She trembled under his hold. The tiny spasm at the corner of her smile betrayed her jitters. Despite a rigid back and a noble bearing, she looked like a doe who'd sighted the hunters... just like that day under the bridge.

The sweet fragrance in her unbound hair, her closeness, and the memory of her naked body in the Alzette River stirred his loins. He also remembered her bold ardor in battle, which added to his lust and hardened his manhood.

Hellfire and damnation! His cool anger melted at the sight of her.

Her lips opened slightly as she moistened them with the tip of her tongue.

On impulse, Sigefroi tightened his grip around her waist and planted a rough kiss on her lips. In his strong embrace, her body tensed at first. Then her hands fumbled on his chest and she relaxed to meld against his frame, softening, offering herself to his plundering kiss.

He reveled in her willingness. Her sudden heat at his contact surprised and delighted him. The spunky little maiden would make a wondrous bed mate.

When he released her, Melusine stared at him with bewildered eyes. All arrogance was gone, and Sigefroi thought he saw a tinge of awe in the way she gazed up at him. He'd lost control for a moment and his body yearned for more than a kiss. But how he enjoyed befuddling her.

After a short silence, servants and guards in the bailey erupted in applauds, hoots, and jibes.

* * *

Once in her spacious chamber, Melusine smiled her thanks to the servants who had brought pails of hot water and filled the wooden tub. "I can manage on my own now. I'll call if I need help."

After the last servant left the room, Melusine slipped off her leather boots, shed her dusty traveling gown, and tossed it on a chair. She sprinkled dried lavender blossoms from a leather pouch into the steaming bath. Lifting her long tresses, she stepped into the tub and immersed herself, grateful for the fragrant, calming warmth.

Dear Goddess! The strange confusion that so scared Melusine threatened to upset her plans. She needed a clear mind to manipulate Sigefroi. How could she properly seduce him if his simple touch deprived her of her ability to think?

Was his shocking behavior acceptable among mortals? She felt violated but thrilled. Had her mother experienced the same agitation when she had lured King Elinas into marriage? If so, she never spoke of it.

Melusine must regain mastery of her senses. She couldn't show weakness in front of this brazen knight. Sigefroi played a wicked game, the rules of which she had yet to understand. He should be outraged. After all, she'd defeated him in battle then tricked him into marriage.

So why did he treat her like a beloved? Noble marriages rarely involved carnal passion, and mating with wives was limited to procreation by the Church. So, why would he bother to pretend liking her?

Melusine laid her head back on the wooden edge of the tub, letting her hair hang outside. The heat of the bath penetrated deep under her skin to soothe tight muscles.

The heavy drapes around the square canopied bed had been lifted and tied up to the four posts. Among fur pillows and bear pelts lay the dress she would wear at supper, midnight blue silk, embroidered with silver trim and silver stars that sparkled in the glow from the fireplace.

Along the far wall, her chests and coffers lay unopened, except for one containing her finest apparel. Outside, daylight faded to a gray blur, and the delicious aroma of roasting meats wafted through the open window. Melusine closed her eyes.

Behind her, a servant entered the room but she kept her eyes closed. She heard the crackle of a stick from the fire and recognized the fizzle and the smell of burning tallow as someone lit the candles around the room and closed the shutters. Unwilling to break her meditating state, Melusine ignored the interruption and kept her eyes closed, sinking into deep relaxation.

"Is everything to your liking so far?"

Jarred by the deep male voice, Melusine snapped awake. Sigefroi stood in front of her, one soft boot nonchalantly propped on the edge of the wooden tub. The white of his tunic matched his teeth as he stared at her with a wolfish grin.

Melusine glanced around in panic for something to cover her nudity but her clothes lay too far away. She pulled up her legs in the bath water and laced her arms around her knees. "How dare you intrude? Can't you see I'm taking a bath?"

Sigefroi's bold gaze swept over her exposed body. "It's not as if it were the first time. You seem to like bathing in hot tubs as well as in cold rivers."

Shocked at his effrontery, Melusine released one arm to point toward the door. "Get out of my chamber immediately!"

"Your chamber?" His grin widened. "This is the only private chamber in the villa, and it happens to be mine."

"Yours?" Melusine flushed in confusion. She knew the villa was small but hadn't really thought about all the details.

"I'll share it with you, unless you want to sleep on the hall floor with the servants." The scowl on his brow returned. "And as the lord of this place, I don't take orders from my guests... or my wenches."

Wench? Her solitary life hadn't prepared Melusine for such vulgarity. According to what she understood of men, however, she must not give herself too fast but rather let

Sigefroi grow hungry for her body as long as possible. "I am no wench and demand to be treated with respect!"

He chuckled and effected a mock bow. "You certainly have mine, my lady."

Melusine managed a forced smile. "If you give me your word to behave honorably, I could sleep on a pallet behind a screen at the far side of your bedchamber."

He rolled his eyes. "Truly?"

Melusine hoped her inaccessible proximity would work in her favor. "There is enough space for the two of us."

"Nay." The candles flickered in his amber eyes. "You don't understand, my lady." A slow smile spread on his sensual lips. "I intend to take you to my bed tonight. After all, we are to be wed."

"So soon?" Panic choked her voice. Impaired by Sigefroi's close proximity, Melusine couldn't think. He wanted to consummate their union tonight? She quickly regained her composure. "My lord, it's not proper. We hardly know each other and are not yet betrothed."

He pulled up the sleeves of his tunic. "A detail easily remedied, my lady. Do you mind if I wash my hands before dinner?"

Before she could react, he dipped his hands in her bath, caressed her knee, brushed the skin of her thigh. Delicious heat coursed through her entire body. He seemed to enjoy her confusion as he swept the length of her folded arms with the back of one finger.

Lifting her chin with the crook of one finger, he bent and softly kissed her lips.

Melusine melted into the bath water, waves of heat swelled and washed over her. His smooth, soft lips teased hers. Her mouth relaxed and opened under his. She let him gently probe her mouth then claim it as his own. Dear Goddess, she was lost.

How could she manipulate this man when she yielded under his touch? She had seen shameless wenches offer themselves to strangers when it served their purpose, or even withhold their favors at will, but Melusine could never do that. She could not refuse this man. She was exposed, vulnerable, and in great danger.

Sigefroi broke the kiss and pulled up a stool. He straddled it, disturbingly close, and stared straight into Melusine's eyes. "Why did you choose me, and how exactly did you trick me into this promise? I don't believe for one moment that you are my better with a sword!"

Despite her precarious position, Melusine felt a shred of her natural confidence return. Sigefroi's varnish had finally cracked to show where his insecurities lay.

She smiled mysteriously. "All in due time, my lord. All in due time."

As if regretting his show of weakness, Sigefroi scowled and rose. "I could force you to tell me, my lady, but I'll give you until after supper. Then, you will answer me."

Melusine raised one eyebrow in defiance. "Or else?"

He huffed a deep sigh. "I'll find ways to make you."

"Will you now?" Melusine rather enjoyed his frustration.

"Should I remind you that you are in my home, and Strathclyde lies far across the sea? I doubt that if you disappeared or suffered an unfortunate accident, anyone would know where to look for you."

The threat in his feral eyes sent shivers scurrying up Melusine's skin, but far from bringing fear, it raised sensual curiosity. Something told her he didn't mean her harm. Before she could think of a saucy retort, Sigefroi rose from his stool and marched out of the room.

Melusine allowed herself a sigh of frustration. How could she possibly tame such a wild knight, especially when she melted like wax at his touch? How could she manipulate the man if she fell in love with him? She must find a way to control him, or her life could be forfeited. And if he discovered her Fae origins, he could have her arrested for witchcraft.

* * *

After he left Melusine, Sigefroi berated himself for giving her an ultimatum. It gave away his concerns. Nevertheless, he had managed to scare and arouse the little minx without betraying his attraction to her. A small victory.

His incursion into the kitchen startled cooks and scullions. Various vegetable stews simmered in black cauldrons hanging above the hearth, while geese, lambs, and a whole pig finished roasting on slow-rotating spits turned by children over the embers of the main fireplace.

The chief cook wiped his sweaty brow with the hem of a stained tunic then glanced up at Sigefroi with a proud smile. "All is ready, m'lord. Just as you asked."

"Aye. Pray that it tastes as good as it smells." Sigefroi's mouth watered. "With all that hard work, everyone is hungry."

On his way to the hall, thoughts of Melusine returned. Sigefroi, who'd learned at court that things seldom were as they appeared, didn't trust the self-proclaimed royal maiden. Although he didn't personally know the present rulers of Strathclyde, he was fairly certain that no king Elinas had reigned there for over a century. The name evoked only the half forgotten legend of a would-be high king. Sigefroi would keep his eyes open, playing the game and enjoying all its fringe benefits.

Pulling aside the heavy curtain, Sigefroi glanced into the dining hall. In high spirits, servants, freemen and soldiers milled around the trestle tables lining the hall.

When the horn sounded the lord's entrance, Sigefroi stepped into the hall and took the central chair at the high table set for three on the dais at the narrow end of the dining hall, opposite the main door.

Upon a wave of his hand, everyone in the hall sat in front of a bread trencher on the benches lining the tables. Gunter took the chair at his left and smiled genially.

Rubbing his black beard, the knight indicated the empty chair on Sigefroi's right. "She's late. How can you tolerate such lack of respect from your future bride? You should send for her. Better to train them early."

"Aye." Sigefroi chuckled at the thought of taming the little hellcat. This one would require more tenderness than violence. "Perhaps it's my fault she's late, but next time remind me to give her a proper beating."

Gunter rolled his eyes. "I've never known you to beat wenches." He tapped Sigefroi's arm and pointed to young Thierry, who talked and shared his goblet with a lass his own age among Melusine's entourage. "Amazing how his first experience as a man has boosted the lad's confidence with the ladies."

Sigefroi smiled. "I wager his first encounter with the harlots went well?"

"Beyond his wildest expectations." Gunter frowned. "Didn't he tell you about it?"

"Nay." Just then, Thierry glanced toward the high table but turned away when he met Sigefroi's gaze.

Gunter squinted. "What's eating him?"

"Perhaps he's growing up and facing his first disillusions." Sigefroi shrugged. "He'll get over it soon enough."

He hated to disappoint the lad who had worshiped him like a saint, but he had no logical explanation for his stinging defeat under Melusine's sword... yet.

Gunter pulled out his knife. "Are we waiting for her?"

"No." Sigefroi gave the signal to start serving the good wine.

He glanced up when the tinkling of ewers and the conversations stopped. All eyes turned to the door as Melusine entered the hall.

Sigefroi held his breath. The light of the torches flirted with the silver specks in her dark blue gown tied by a silver sash to accentuate her tiny waist. A radiance illuminated her face and danced in her mysterious gray eyes. She walked head high, straight as a queen. Blue gems and silver sparkled at her throat and in the thick braid holding back her long tresses.

Even an emperor would envy Sigefroi his princess. A twinge of jealousy tugged at his gut at the thought of all these men staring at her. Then he reminded himself that she already belonged to him. But by what whimsical fate?

As she drew close, he detected a slight twitch of her lips. She flashed him a disarming smile, as if pleading for protection, eyes wide with fright. Small wonder. She'd never lain with any man, and tonight she would be his lover.

What did he do to deserve such a prize? What made this lamb come willingly to the slaughter in a fortress full of strangers?

"You look as dazzling as a Fae of legend, my lady. Did you cast a spell on me?" The gallant remark escaped his lips unbidden.

Melusine blinked. He heard her short intake of breath, but then she smiled. "I choose to take that remark as a compliment, my lord."

He drew the chair for her to sit, then handed her his wine goblet. Her hand trembled ever so slightly as she raised the cup to her parted lips. How he wanted to kiss the tiny drop suspended there. Instead, he took the goblet from her hand and gently knocked the blade of his poniard against it to call attention.

"I hope you all enjoy this special feast in honor of Lady Melusine," he announced, his deep voice filling the hall. "This is our official betrothal banquet. The wedding will be held in two days, on Wednesday."

Melusine laid a restraining hand on the silk of his sleeve. "Nay, not Wednesday, my lord."

He detected a trembling in her voice. Shock? Fear? She looked deathly pale.

* * *

Melusine swallowed hard.

The assembly gasped at the interruption, staring at their lord as if expecting his imminent wrath.

"Certainly you mean Sunday, my lord!" Dear Goddess! This Wednesday she would become a serpent

64

from the navel down! She'd hoped for more time. Why was he in such a hurry?

"Oh?" Sigefroi squinted at her sharply.

"Aye." She strained to smile under his scrutiny. "When the priest comes hither to celebrate mass, and the villagers can enjoy the festivities as well. Besides, it will give me more time to prepare and recover from the journey."

His face softened and he covered her hand with his over the white tablecloth. Although he was the cause of her trouble, it made her feel safer. She detected amusement in his eyes.

"Very well." Sigefroi turned to the assembly. "If Lady Melusine wishes to wed on Sunday, so it shall be."

She hoped her grateful smile rewarded him enough. Why was it so difficult? When it came to Sigefroi, none of the spells and glamours she used on common mortals worked. He often guessed too close to the truth and seemed to enjoy her dismay each time.

In a festive atmosphere, the kitchen lads and lasses served the first remove, ladling boiled chestnuts and turnips on the bread trenchers. Roasted geese were brought on silver platters, and the sound of laughter and easy conversations resumed in good cheer.

"So, m'lady," Gunter said casually waving a goose thigh. "Tell us of whence you came."

To cover her hesitation, Melusine pulled from her sash the chiseled dagger she used to eat and laid it on the tablecloth. "Strathclyde is a Briton enclave in the southwestern part of Scotia. Small and humble compared to the German empire, but I inherited my mother's fortune as well as my father's."

"Did your father arrange the marriage, then?" Gunter bit a chunk of roasted goose and chewed on it noisily.

"Nay." Sadness threatened to engulf Melusine at the thought of her father. Would his gentle soul ever forgive her and her sisters? "My father died long ago."

"So, who owns you?" Goose grease slicked Gunter's lips. "A brother? An uncle? Every woman belongs to a man."

Although she resented the concept of such ownership, Melusine didn't express her distaste. "After my half brother assumed the throne, my mother, my sisters and I led a spiritual life on an isolated island."

Sigefroi's eyes twinkled with sudden interest as he carved a breast and laid it on Melusine's trencher. "A monastery?"

"Of sorts, aye." Although a Pagan one dedicated to the Goddess, the Lost Isle could be called a monastery. Melusine cut a small chunk of goose with her dagger, then chewed slowly, enjoying its perfect taste and tender consistency.

"So, you only belong to God?" With the point of his poniard, Gunter attempted to dislodge a piece of meat stuck in his teeth.

"I belong to myself and make my own decisions," Melusine stated with emphasis.

Sigefroi gazed at her deeply, as if aroused by her unnatural desire to belong to no man. His lips curved into a half smile each time she evaded embarrassing questions.

Relentless, Gunter pursued, "How far have you traveled today, and why do you carry such riches without an armed escort?"

Melusine smiled. At least, Gunter was easy to manipulate. "I came from France, a day's ride west of here," she lied easily. "And as you just said, Sir Knight, no one would expect an unescorted train to carry anything of value. The lack of guards is my best protection against prowling war bands or greedy lordlings."

"But what about your virtue?" Gunter insisted. "You don't even have a chaperone. And your mounts and rich clothes could tempt petty thieves."

Tired of the subject, Melusine sent a dismissive thought to Gunter's mind. "I can handle molesters and petty thieves."

Sigefroi chuckled. "I can vouch for that."

Melusine observed Sigefroi as he ate and drank heartily. She suspected he committed to memory each and

66

every word. The next remove included mutton, lentils, and cheese. Melusine ate little, but everything tasted wonderful.

She smiled when he glanced at her. "I am impressed by your lavish hospitality, my lord."

Sigefroi smiled back. "You haven't tasted my bed yet, my lady. Its pleasures greatly surpass those of my table."

A hot flush flooded Melusine's face and Gunter roared with laughter.

Chapter Five

Acutely aware of Melusine's warmth, her thigh so close to his under the table, Sigefroi handed her the silver goblet they shared. When she declined the wine for the third time, he wondered whether she wanted to keep a clear mind for the rest of the night. Or perhaps she feared she might divulge some secrets if the wine went to her head.

If she were a maiden, as she claimed, she should be frightened, and drink would help. So why refuse? Sigefroi took a sip and set the goblet on the tablecloth while watching his feasting subjects.

At the moment, Gunter seemed captivated by the adoring eyes and generous bosom of the serving wench who sat on his lap and shared his cup. The brawny knight had gulped more than his share of wine. Around the trestle tables lining the hall, conversations and spirits soared while soldiers sang bawdy limericks that brought color to the women's cheeks.

Voices rose in anger at the far end of the guards' table. The soldiers stopped singing. A platter of food clattered to the center of the mosaic floor.

Gunter rose, unseating his wench who yelped and scuttled away, then the knight drew his sword and stepped in front of the high table, in a stance Sigefroi had often seen in battle. Except for two young men wrestling on the central floor usually reserved for entertainment, no one moved or talked.

Repressing the urge to vent his anger at the rudeness of his new guards, Sigefroi wiped his mouth with the hem of the tablecloth then stood up and cleared his throat.

"Separate them," he barked.

Soldiers grabbed hold of the struggling delinquents and shoved them before the high table. Sigefroi recognized the two bloody-faced recruits as Cedric and Conrad, both sons of old comrades in arms. But he could not let his friendship with their fathers soften the punishment.

"I keep discipline in my hall!" Sigefroi bellowed then paused to let his words sink in. Now more than ever, he needed to enforce the rules he had dictated only ten days ago. "Do you remember the penalty for fighting among yourselves?"

The two hotheads glanced at each other but remained silent.

Sigefroi nodded to Gunter.

The brawny knight pressed his lips into a line. "Twelve lashes, I believe."

Sigefroi surveyed the assembly for any rebellious reaction. "And how many for disturbing the peace of my hall?"

"Another twelve." All trace of drunkenness had gone from Gunter's demeanor.

Shock registered on Cedric and Conrad's faces. They stared at their boots, like children caught stealing.

Sigefroi considered waiting until the morrow to mete out the punishment but decided against it. For the first offense since he'd become lord, Sigefroi needed to make a swift example that soldiers and servants would not soon forget. His authority was in jeopardy.

"Do you feel up to it, Gunter?"

Gunter glanced toward his abandoned wench then grunted. "Aye, I'll do it."

Sheathing his sword the brawny knight deliberately walked to the back wall and fetched the three-pronged leather whip hanging from a bronze hook.

Sigefroi turned to Melusine whose face turned pale. "That's not the entertainment I would have wished for our betrothal, my lady, but it will have to do."

"I understand." Melusine sat very straight, yet he sensed in her tone more dread than true understanding of the value of discipline.

Sigefroi motioned to the soldiers still holding the culprits. "Strap them each in a chair!"

The soldiers pulled up the young men's tunics over their heads, while other recruits brought two heavy chairs and set them side by side. Bare-chested the contrite young men straddled the chairs backwards, then a guard tied their hands around the high backrest, stretching the smooth skin of their bare backs. Both Cedric and Conrad were strong and well built. Sigefroi noted the new bulge of muscles from intense training in the fencing yard.

In the palpable tension that hung around the hall, Sigefroi addressed his people. "No fighting will I tolerate among my men, nor disruptive behavior in my hall! Save your anger for the fencing yard." He motioned to Gunter. "Proceed!"

Sigefroi sat down to witness the execution of the sentence.

Both culprits accepted the rolled piece of leather to bite on, then laid their foreheads on the backrest. At Sigefroi's side, Melusine barely seemed to breathe as she stared at the two dissidents. Her nervous hand rubbed the hilt of her eating dagger. She hid her repugnance like a true princess, but Sigefroi wondered what she truly felt.

With all eyes fixed on him, Sigefroi couldn't reassure the maiden or even explain. Everyone present would think him harsh, but to avoid future incidents, a lord needed to establish a reputation for maintaining order. Feuds between soldiers led to their death in battle. Better a good flogging and a valuable lesson learned early.

During his many campaigns with Emperor Otto, Sigefroi had become a master at overcoming his revulsion for gruesome spectacles. He was glad for it now. How anyone could enjoy brutality was a mystery to him. A murmur of excitement circulated along the trestle tables while Gunter, whip in hand, made his way to the center of the hall. Fifty pairs of eyes stared with anticipation.

The first crack of the whip cut the air, leaving three lines of angry red welts on Cedric's back. The young man flinched but didn't cry out. Conrad tensed in expectation of the next lash. It snapped, eliciting only a wince and a muffled grunt.

A few men and women, enthralled by the spectacle, now released the breath they'd been holding, along with whispered comments. A soldier uttered words of encouragement to his unfortunate friend while others cheered for Gunter to hit harder.

Sigefroi glanced at Melusine. Tense and absolutely still, she kept her eyes on the scene, showing no emotion, but he could feel her disapproval. So, the lady had a heart. That was good news.

With measured strokes and none of the ferocity he displayed in battle, Gunter raised the whip and lashed each dissident in turn with consistent force. Half way through the chastisement, Cedric's skin broke and bloody welts trickled red. Still, he remained mute, barely twitching under the whip. Conrad followed his example.

While the small crowd gasped at the sight of blood, Sigefroi kept count. He appreciated the courage the two hotheads now displayed. Despite their disobedience, he would remember their valor when the time came to impart a dangerous mission.

The backs of both young men, now covered with a latticework of bloody crevices, would have made Sigefroi wince, were he not under scrutiny.

"That's enough!" he called out after counting the last stroke.

In a deliberate arc, Gunter lowered the whip and rolled the bloody leather braids then walked away toward the hook on the wall. Two soldiers untied Cedric and Conrad and supported them as they walked out of the hall.

Sigefroi wanted to forget the regrettable incident like he usually did after a bloody battle, in the warm embrace of a female body. After signaling for more wine to be served to the guests, he turned to Melusine.

"My lady, it's time to retire." He rose and extended his hand to help her stand up.

She remained seated, looking from his hand to his face. She hesitated. Confusion knitted her brow, then cold anger glinted in her wide gray eyes.

Finally she rose. "I was trained in the healing arts, my lord. I should tend to these young men's wounds."

"Nay. The louts don't deserve your care." Sigefroi lowered his voice in confidence. "Besides, I request your services in my bed."

"It's highly inappropriate, my lord." Melusine blushed but did not relent. "At least let me make a salve. It won't take long. I have all the ingredients in my coffers."

Although it infuriated him, Sigefroi had to admire the girl's tenacity. "I said nay, my lady. Others can care for the delinquents. Tonight you're mine alone."

Melusine's eyes narrowed. "I am no man's property."

Pushing down his displeasure, Sigefroi forced a cold smile. "As of tonight, this betrothal makes you mine by law. You will come to my bed, unless you would rather satisfy the sexual urges of a score of drunken soldiers?"

Under his stare, she glanced toward the soldiers' table then bit her lower lip. "I would rather not, my lord."

He offered his arm, and her small hand came to rest on the white silk of his sleeve, grasping his forearm as if she sought protection. He guided her out of the hall and toward the stairs leading to his bedchamber. As he covered Melusine's hand with his, the warm contact of her soft skin prompted heat to surge through him. All he wanted now was take the spirited maiden to his bed.

A maiden... Jesu! Sigefroi had never deflowered a lass. Other lords used their god-given right to sample any vassal's bride before her own husband, but Sigefroi had never taken advantage of that privilege. All his wenches had been willing and bold, eager to please him, and he'd always pleasured them without restraint. Would it be much different with a noble maiden? He burned to find out.

Nodding to the guard who opened the bedchamber door, Sigefroi lifted the heavy privacy curtain to let Melusine through, then he barred the door from inside. He wanted no interruption.

Melusine stood in the center of the room, holding her shoulders. Tall candlesticks burned around the vast room, giving off enough light for him to see her. How lovely she looked, like a doe facing the coup de grâce.

His smile came easily. "Cold, my lady?"

When she nodded, he threw a fresh log in the hearth. Bright flames leapt and the fire grew warmer. He wanted to enjoy his prize in total comfort.

Away from the bed, Melusine stood stiffly, as if she didn't know what to do next.

Sigefroi unbuckled his baldric and hung the sword and belt on a hook jutting out from the bedpost. He sat on the high bed and took the time to pull off his boots, then patted the furs next to him.

"Come sit by me," he said, as gently as he could.

Melusine still looked like a cornered doe ready to bolt at any sudden move. Her gaze steadied as she considered him for a moment, then she squared her jaw and faced him. "My lord, I'm afraid I'm still shaken by the incident in the hall tonight."

Remembering the whip, Sigefroi smiled, admiring her candor and her courage. Not many women would dare criticize him.

"It was necessary, my lady. What kind of lord would I be if I let my men disrespect my rule?" He patted the bed again. "Now, let's forget about it and delve into more pleasant matters."

"My present mood is hardly conducive to romance, my lord." Her voice trembled slightly. "Although I know very little of such matters, I understand that few women enjoy the deed when it's imposed upon them."

"Imposed?" Sigefroi rolled his eyes in disbelief. "It was your idea to become the lady of this castle. And as such, you belong in my bed."

"Aye." She flinched. "But so soon? I don't feel ready. I never imagined it would be so difficult."

"Difficult? Are you insulting me?" Sigefroi chuckled to soften the remark. "I could teach you to enjoy it... most women do."

"I know... I've often wanted to try." A timid smile flashed on her face.

Sigefroi rose from the bed and went to her. He enveloped her in his arms. Her head came to rest on his chest, and he caressed her long, silky hair. She relaxed in his embrace. Lifting her chin with the crook of one finger, he softly brushed her lips with his, willing her to warm up to him.

Her slender arms came around his waist. Short bursts of breath tickled his lips as she answered his feathery kisses with her own, timidly at first, then with more confidence.

Exhilaration filled him, like on the battlefield when victory was nigh. Strengthening his hold on her, he reined in his wild appetite to take the time to ravage her mouth. To his delight, she responded with unbridled ardor.

His mighty sword ached as his hands explored Melusine's firm curves through the silk gown and smothered her delicate body. She moaned under his kiss, the vibration heightening his desire in a flurry of new sensations.

Jesu! He must slow down, or he would spill his seed like an overwhelmed virgin before pleasuring her. Sigefroi wanted their first joining to be memorable. Breaking their embrace, he scooped her up and laid her among the fur pillows on the pelts covering the bed. With slow, deliberate caresses, he removed her shoes, then kissed her small feet. She didn't protest but only gazed up at him with liquid eyes that shone like polished river stones in the candlelight.

It seemed that she wanted him as much as he wanted her, but in her innocence, did Melusine realize it? Or was lust so new to her that she couldn't sort her feelings? He'd make sure she knew she wanted him. He'd make her beg for release.

"Sigefroi?" Hearing her say his name in that husky tone filled him with triumph.

"Aye, Melusine." His voice sounded rough, too.

She stared at the bulge in his chausses. He was a big man.

Sigefroi lay beside her and pushed back a strand of hair from her face. "Do you trust me to be gentle?"

Melusine closed her eyes as if wrestling with the idea. "I find trusting others most difficult. I've seen much betrayal."

"For one so young it can't be that much."

Tears welled at the edge of her closed eyelids.

He wondered what sad memory prompted them but didn't ask. Instead, he kissed her tears and landed a string of butterfly kisses on her cheeks, and down her throat. Even when her breath caught, he didn't stop.

"Let me see you," he whispered, tugging at her sash. He found the knot and loosened it. Then he lifted the hem of her skirt all the way above her head, so deftly that the sleeves slid off her arms in one motion. "Jesu, you are even more beautiful than I remember from the bridge."

She blushed, wearing nothing but blue sapphires at her neck! "I was afraid you wouldn't like my body."

"How could I possibly not like it?" He caressed her creamy skin slowly, from perfect toes to the inside of shapely thighs, then he brushed the tender side of her arms.

"I like this." A timid smile curled the corner of her lips and he saw her relax and tense to the rhythm of his methodical strokes.

Aye, she might be a maiden, but she wanted this as much as he did. Sigefroi traced concentric circles around her small breasts, teasing the tiny pink nubs. Then he let his fingers probe lower, toward the dark triangle of soft curls below.

Melusine moved away from his intrusive caress.

"Nay, my sweet." With one hand Sigefroi pinned both her wrists above her head, then laid a heavy foot to immobilize her leg. "You won't escape the blissful torment I have in mind for you."

She arched under his strokes and strained against his hold in vain. She looked so vulnerable. What had become of the fierce warrior who had defeated him in battle? "That's not fair, my lord!"

"Nothing is fair in love or war, my sweet." Sigefroi silenced her mild protests with a wanton kiss, ravaging her mouth while his free hand fondled her nether parts.

Melusine shuddered under him and her back arched under his probing fingers. She squirmed, warming to his touch with cries of delight muffled by their kiss. Letting go of her mouth, Sigefroi nipped her lips then kissed her throat and laved her breasts. When he seized one hard nub in his teeth, gently but firmly, harrying it with his tongue, her small cries intensified. Then he let go of her breast.

"Don't stop," she begged, "please, don't stop."

A devilish idea crossed Sigefroi's mind. Aye, she was begging.

"Why did you choose me?" he asked inexorably, still laving her breasts but not hard enough for fulfillment. His lower caresses elicited slow spasms of desire that remained unsatisfied. "Answer me and I will fill your need."

"Please..." She arched under his expert hand, in a futile attempt to find release.

"It will get worse until you tell me." He smiled, enjoying his power over her. The tip of his fingers circled the soft petals of her slick womanhood.

She gasped. "I had a dream that foretold we are destined to a great future together."

His tongue stopped exploring her perfect navel and he glanced up at her. "Indeed?" Sigefroi remembered dreaming of her, even before he saw her naked under the bridge. He studied her flushed face. "Who interpreted the dream?"

"My spiritual mother..." Melusine hesitated. "She said it was written in the heavens."

Suddenly Sigefroi needed to believe her. What was happening to him?

While he'd tried to convince himself that he only played a game, he truly wanted to seduce her, please her beyond his own satisfaction. He realized with a start that he sought her unconditional love, not for sport, but to feel complete. He wanted to share his life with her as an equal loving partner. So what, if they met under   strange circumstances? Beyond reason, he trusted her to be his perfect mate.

"How'd you know I was the man of your dream? Did you see my face?" he asked thickly.

"No. I heard your name." She arched against his still palm begging for his caress, breathing fast. "Sigefroi..."

"Aye?" He grinned and resumed the light stroking. "I like the way you say my name."

She stretched as if to expose more skin to his hand. "When I heard Gunter call you under the bridge, I knew you were the one."

The sweet fragrance of her hair enveloped him. Her arousal drove him wild with lust. "And what were you doing under that bridge, besides spying on me?"

"Bathing, my lord." Her head fell back, exposing a tender throat to his kiss.

"Aye. I noticed you like water... icy cold or steamy hot. Perhaps I'll take you to the Imperial baths in Trier, my little nymph." He suddenly remembered the angelic melody he'd heard from the rampart the day he first saw her. "I'd wager you sing like one, too."

"Aye." Her legs parted to better accommodate his hand. "I love to sing."

Releasing her, Sigefroi pulled off his tunic then tugged at the legs of his chausses. Stark naked, he knelt on the bed in fully erected glory and gazed down at her. "Then sing for me, my sweet."

* * *

Melusine never thought she could yearn for a mortal's touch, but this splendid naked man drove her to the edge of insanity. She never suspected her duty to give Sigefroi a Fae heir would prove so pleasurable. Dear Goddess! But he was huge.

She didn't resist when he took her hand and laid it on the silky head of his manhood. She felt him shudder under her touch. How strange that something so hard and big

77

could feel velvety and warm as it throbbed under her caressing fingers!

Heat suffused her nether parts and she felt her face flush with heat. Although she'd spied on mating couples through the divining basin, Melusine understood little of the strange ritual.

"Teach me," she whispered in a ragged breath.

"Aye, my sweet." Sigefroi slid a fur pillow under her head, then stretched beside her.

The shifting candlelight revealed ghastly scars on his chest and muscular thigh, but far from spoiling his looks, they contributed to make him formidable and dangerous, even in the nude. Melusine shuddered as his warm body brushed against her skin, hard all over, so strong.

She locked her gaze upon his feral eyes and for the first time found softness there. She saw tenderness in his smile. Dear Goddess! How easy it would be to love him. But although the Goddess wanted her to love him, such weakness would lower her defenses and place her in mortal danger. For now she would submit to him. Later, perhaps, she might love and trust him.

"Easy, now," Sigefroi whispered in her ear.

His tongue teased her earlobes, driving her wild with need.

"Trust me, my sweet." He lowered his weight upon her.

Far from crushing her, it heightened Melusine's desire. Trapped under him, entirely at his mercy, part of her wanted to trust while the other still feared him, but she couldn't ignore her need.

Responding to his lust, her body moved of its own volition, begging for a stronger contact. Deep in her womb, obscure forces stirred, conspiring to make her want this splendid animal, this fierce mortal who made her feel so vulnerable. His caresses unleashed a crescendo of sensations too much to bear.

"Take my maidenhood," she pleaded. "Even if it hurts, I want this."

"Are you certain?" His breath grew shorter.

78

She realized that he, too, wanted her very much. It pleased her that he didn't take her quickly but took his time.

Strong hands parted Melusine's thighs, then the pressure of his chest forced the air out of her lungs. Hungry lips locked on her mouth as his tongue dove deep into her throat, depriving her of breath and of all willpower.

The engorged head of his shaft now pushed at her virginal gate, seeking entry. Too big, she thought. But her wanton body kept moving in rhythm with his, in a desperate attempt to accommodate his manhood.

Hard fingers clenched her buttocks then his powerful thrust ripped her asunder. Deep inside, pain seared. Melusine cried out, but far from shying away, she met Sigefroi's thrust and dug her nails in his square shoulders. Why did he stop? Desperately, she moved her hips around his impaling sword, throwing herself against him.

As if spurred by her boldness, Sigefroi unleashed upon her a savage assault, tearing at her repeatedly, deep and forceful. Then he slowed his thrusts but went deeper. The powerful strokes made Melusine forget there ever was any pain.

She focused on the place in her womb battered with excruciating precision by his manhood. The growing sensation mounted to become almost intolerable. Sigefroi swelled inside her, filling her, pounding her slowly, with inexorable strength and endurance.

"This is too much," she pleaded between ragged breaths. Certainly this wild raking would damage her body, but she went on moving with him.

"No, my sweet," he panted. His grip tightened on her hips. "We can't stop now. I want to hear you sing."

Panic invaded Melusine's mind, but her body kept crashing and ebbing out of control. Surely, she was going to break if they didn't stop!

Instead, Sigefroi heightened his fierce tempo.

Heat engulfed Melusine, as if her entire body was melting. She wiggled in an attempt to evade his wild ramming, but he held her so tight that she couldn't move an inch.

Melusine heard a low moan that grew to a roar with each of his mighty thrusts. Then she realized the sound came from her throat. Wave after wave of exquisite pleasure washed over her, eliciting screams she never thought herself capable of. Her body undulated and shook in tremulous throes.

Over a century of pent up passion surfaced and swirled, drowning her in a sea of new sensations, all wonderfully pleasurable, all strong and magnificent, all thanks to the splendid Sigefroi of Ardennes.

Just when she thought she might faint, he sped up, heightening her ecstasy if it were possible. His face contorted as if with pain, and she felt him tighten and discard all control as he ploughed into her with unrestrained violence. He groaned and faltered. The erratic rhythm of his final thrusts brought forth a tremendous release that rippled through both of them. They shuddered together then lay very still.

"Jesu!" he exhaled, kissing her hair. "You are magnificent." He glanced down at her and frowned. "Are you well?"

Melusine chuckled, weightless, as if relieved of a burden. "You didn't lie, my lord, you made me enjoy it."

"I always keep my word." He eased himself to the side, but his arms still enveloped her possessively. "Are you comfortable?"

"Aye." She'd never felt this wonderful. "What now?"

Sigefroi smiled mysteriously. "Now is the time for truth."

"Truth?" Melusine should have been scared, but somehow, she felt safe in the knowledge that he truly cared about her. Why otherwise would he have bothered pleasuring her?

"Aye. It is said that during this special moment after lovers had their pleasure, they can't help but tell the truth. I want to know the truth, my sweet."

Relaxed and confident, Melusine placed both hands under her head. "Did you like it too?"

He exploded in a laugh that vibrated through the bed posts. "Like it? That's not a strong enough word, my sweet."

Melusine allowed herself a smug smile. She'd been right. He not only cared, but he'd known pleasure with her. "What would happen now if you had found me repulsive and wanted out of your oath?"

The amusement left his eyes. "I would kill you and keep the treasure."

The steely edge in his voice told her he would have done it without a second thought. The cold comment sobered Melusine who shuddered in retrospect. She'd taken a terrible risk.

"I appreciate your frank answer, my lord."

Rising on one elbow, Sigefroi scrutinized her face, his brow setting in a familiar scowl. "My turn to ask." He cleared his throat. "During that fight ten days past, how did you manage to defeat me?"

She traced the contour of his smooth jaw eliciting a smile. "It was the sword, my lord."

"The sword?" Sigefroi seized her caressing hand and kissed her fingers, but his amber gaze never left her face. "Pray tell."

"The fine blade you so admired is no ordinary weapon, my lord." Melusine traced a long scar across his chest. A battle wound, perhaps? "It's an ancient heirloom that has been in my family for centuries."

"In truth?" He frowned. "It's a fine weapon. I've never seen the likes of it. Not Saracen steel... yet it shines like no other. The point even damaged my chain mail. I had to have it mended. No ordinary sword can do that." His eyes shone in the candlelight.

"It is said to have been forged in the otherworld."

"You could have killed me with a feather push of that deadly blade." He twisted his neck as if remembering the sensation.

81

"Aye." Melusine smiled lazily. "But I never intended to kill you, my lord, or you would be dead. The blade makes the bearer invincible."

Sudden interest lit his amber eyes. "Do you have the sword here?"

"Of course, my lord." Languidly, Melusine rose and walked loosely toward the chest where she had stored the weapon. Surprisingly she didn't mind walking nude in front of Sigefroi who watched her every move.

She opened the chest, picked up the scabbard and drew the blade with a flourish. "Behold Caliburn..." A blue glimmer played on the steel. "A sword of great power."

* * *

Sigefroi stared at the blade in Melusine's hands. He could sense its power, like he felt the ancient power seeping from the cliffs of the Bock, and oozing from the surrounding forest. In retrospect, he had felt the mighty sword during their short battle. He could not deny what he felt. It had to be the truth. How could he explain his defeat otherwise?

Even the Church recognized miracles, and holy relics had been known to cure diseases and protect lives. So, why not a miraculous sword?

"Aren't you afraid I'll steal it while you sleep and kill you with it?"

A clear laugh answered him. "Caliburn would never hurt my lineage, my lord, I am its keeper. And only if given freely can Caliburn protect another."

"You plan to give me that sword?" The words had escaped him before he could think.

Frowning, Melusine dropped the bejeweled scabbard inside the open chest but still held the blade. "Your ability to guess is uncanny, my lord." Carrying the sword with great care, she walked up to the bed. "Aye. It is your destiny to wield the sword of power... in exchange for a solemn promise."

"Another promise?" He cast her a mock glare, all the time aware of the effects her naked body had on his manhood. "Woman, you annoy me. I'm accustomed to dictate my will, not to obey wenches."

Melusine stood near the bed but out of reach. She cut a lovely picture in the nude, with that smug smile, even while holding a dangerous sword. "Think of the power it represents... invincibility in battle for a knight certainly is worth a small promise!"

Indeed, if the sword could do what she said, and he'd seen enough to believe it, Sigefroi must consider taking that oath. With such a blade he could carve his future kingdom.

He sat up on the sleeping furs, crossed his legs, and faced her squarely. "What promise do you want from me?"

She held the sword up high, as if it weighed nothing. Was she threatening him? "The first Wednesday of each month," she said slowly, as if measuring her words. "From eve to sunset as we count the days, I will disappear from these walls."

The words registered in his mind. "What? You can't... This is ludicrous." Surely the little minx was trying his patience. "The lady of my domain has to be available at all times to run this household. You can't just disappear for an entire day each month!"

She leveled the point of the blade to his throat. "I am not asking permission, my lord." Her eyebrows knitted together. "I'm telling you I will."

Sigefroi swallowed hard. The sword point grazed the kin of his neck and he remained very still. He'd seen the blade in action and didn't want to repeat his shame.

Exerting control over his anger, he opted for diplomacy. "All right. But that's not an oath. What do you expect from me?"

Her arm remained steady as she kept the sword point to his throat. "I want your solemn promise that you will never try to find out where I go or what I do when I disappear."

This couldn't be. Sigefroi grabbed at straws. "It's not safe nor proper for a noble lady to run about day and night without an escort."

Melusine snorted but her sword arm did not waver. "I can take care of myself, my lord. Besides, for all you know, I could be reading ancient scrolls, praying at a nearby convent, visiting a relative, or simply taking a long bath. I just don't want to be questioned about it."

The little vixen was enjoying this. "You offer me power in exchange for one day of unrestricted freedom each month?" But even with a sword at his throat, Sigefroi found it difficult not to react. "What if I grow tired of your little secrets and break that promise?"

Melusine shrugged with a dismissive sigh and lowered the blade. "You have much to lose in the bargain, my lord. Your honor, your wife, Caliburn, the riches I brought you, as well as your zest for life."

Sigefroi knew that power always came at a price. Indeed, it must be paid, but he wouldn't give her the satisfaction of victory, not yet anyway. "How can I possibly explain my wife's regular disappearances to my vassals?"

"Doesn't a lord make the rules in his house?" The naked little witch chuckled. "I'll go along with whatever you choose to tell the others."

What she proposed could work, but Sigefroi kept quiet.

"Besides, why shouldn't a woman have a day of freedom?" Even in animated argument, even as she humbled him, Melusine remained oh-so desirable. "Mine is the first Wednesday, and I insist upon it... Or should I rescind our wedding arrangement?"

Jesu, how he wanted her right now. He sighed, letting his shoulders fall. "Is that why you made me change our wedding day?"

She flashed a devilish smile. "I could leave now and free you from our betrothal vows."

Did she know he valued her more than the riches and the power she offered? His voice came as a harsh whisper. "You're not leaving me."

"That is not for you to decide, my lord." She brought the sword point up to his throat again.

Sigefroi glanced down at the blade then gently pushed it aside, feeling no resistance. "I will abide by your conditions, but I want your assurance that this is the last of your unreasonable requests."

"Aye, my lord. It is the very last." She seemed elated as she presented him with Caliburn flat on her extended hands.

Sigefroi met her gaze. "Then I do solemnly swear, on my honor as a knight, never to try to find out what you do when you disappear on the first Wednesday of each month."

She slid the blade onto his open palms and a shiver spread from his arms through his entire being. The power of the sword. This miraculous weapon was his!

He bowed slightly but remained seated on the bed. "I thank you for the boons you bestowed upon me, Melusine. I am the luckiest man alive right now."

She smiled sweetly, fetched the bejeweled scabbard and handed it to him. "I hope this happiness lasts you a lifetime, my lord."

After sheathing the sword, Sigefroi rose from the bed and hooked the weapon to his leather baldric hanging from the bedpost.

Then he swept Melusine up in his arms. "We must seal this deal properly."

He took her mouth then dropped onto the bed with her. They rolled in the sleeping furs. When he came up for air, she chuckled.

He pushed away an unruly strand of hair and gazed into her eyes, the color of a clear stream in summer. "I want to hear you sing again."

Chapter Six

By the time Melusine awoke, the embers had cooled in the hearth. They had made love all night and spent the day in bed, dozing then reigniting their passion for each other's body. Lust had flared and waned in relentless waves, leaving them more exhausted each time.

A familiar pang tugged at Melusine's mind. Almost sunset! Soon Tuesday would end, and it would be Wednesday's eve. She had to leave now, before her body changed shape. She glanced at Sigefroi who snored softly, as vulnerable now as a sleeping babe. She regretted leaving him like this, without a kiss or a tender word, but she could not chance any delay.

Quickly, Melusine pulled on her gown then snatched her cloak from the peg. What about the guard at the door? Sending the guard a distracting thought, she unbarred the door and slipped out of the bedchamber, hiding herself under a veil of glamour, an old trick she'd learned as a child. To the casual eye, it made her look like a slight shadow, a mere trick of flitting light brushing the walls.

When she reached the main hall, servants readied the tables for supper. She was famished. In passing, she snatched a piece of bread and a chunk of cheese from a platter and took a few voracious bites.

The stronghold's gates would soon close for the night. She had to hurry. In the courtyard, soldiers walked the wall, and serfs hastened toward the gate to get back to the village. Under the glamour, Melusine slipped between the guards unnoticed then crossed the wooden bridge over the gorge to the village on the main plateau.

Lazy smoke rose from the holes in the many thatched roofs. Past the village fortifications under repair, she took the steep path down the cliff face. Dear Goddess! She had barely enough energy left to maintain the glamour and negotiate the trail. If her transformation happened before she reached the water, Melusine was doomed.

The descent seemed to take forever. Her foot slipped on a rock. Already, the first paralyzing webs impeded her footing. Her leg muscles ached. Just a little further down. Almost there. No one in sight. She must get rid of the gown.

Pulling the garment over her head, she stretched up to tuck it upon a rocky ledge where it would remain hidden from prying eyes. The last light waned in the sky, and the shadow of the cliff darkened the river. At sunset everyone returned to the safety of home. But once a month on Wednesday's eve, Melusine found home in the cool waters of the Alzette River.

Naked, she walked on the muddy shore with great difficulty. She tripped over her feet when sharp pain surged through her hips. Almost at the waterline. The cold flow soothed her itchy scales as she stumbled in the shallows then rolled into the swift current.

Within moments, a membrane stretched between her legs, sealing them together, then her serpent tail lengthened, round and thick, gleaming gray. Although she had experienced the transformation over a thousand times, Melusine still hated the degrading change. She prayed this unique chance to redeem the curse with Sigefroi would work.

Dear Goddess, allow him to free me from the curse!

As twilight turned to inky darkness, she let go of the glamour shielding her from mortal eyes and drifted toward the fast current. Then she flicked her tail and dove.

Until the next sunset...

She already missed her legs. Sigefroi had very much enjoyed the pleasures that lay between her thighs... and so had Melusine.

Sigefroi blindly reached for Melusine among the sleeping furs, but his hand only met a pillow. Sitting up in bed, he scanned the chamber and realized darkness had fallen, and no light filtered through the cracks in the shutters. He couldn't remember the last time he'd slept all day. The open dowry chests still sat along the wall, and Caliburn hung from his baldric. The delights of the night had been real.

"Melusine?"

No answer. Where was his betrothed? Why did she abandon him so soon? Had he disappointed her? A pinch of rejection squeezed his heart. No woman had ever treated him so lightly. Wenches usually clung to him even after he tired of them. Melusine's casual treatment wounded his pride.

The aroma of pork stew teased his nostrils, making his stomach growl. Perhaps Melusine had gone to the hall for supper. Hastily, Sigefroi pulled on his chausses and donned a fresh woolen tunic from his garment chest.

Melusine should have awakened him, but Sigefroi refused to give in to frustration. He had much to be thankful for... a sword of power, riches, and an incredible woman to share his bed. The heavy door was unbarred. It creaked as he pulled it open.

Sigefroi nodded to the rugged soldier with a droopy moustache who stood guard before his chamber. "Did Lady Melusine go to the dining hall?"

The trustworthy fellow, handpicked for his loyalty on the battlefield, stood at attention. "Nay, m'lord. You must be jesting. The lady is with you. I've let no one through this door all day, except the servant who brought your morning meal."

Tendrils of cold anger coiled around Sigefroi's gut. He felt the blood drain from his face.

"What day is it?" he asked between clenched teeth.

"Well, 'tis Wednesday's eve, m'lord." Concern narrowed the soldier's bloodshot eyes. "Are you well, m'lord?"

"Aye. Just ravenous." Hellfire and damnation! He'd forgotten Melusine's day of freedom, once a month from sunset to sunset. Sigefroi cleared his throat. "I now recall the Lady is praying in the seclusion of my alcove before the wedding. She won't join me for supper."

"Aye, m'lord." The soldier's blinked several times as if confused. "Should I have the lady's supper carried to your bedchamber?"

"Nay!" Had Melusine stolen out the window? Impossible. The bedchamber was on the second floor of the villa, and the shutters were locked closed. How did she slip past the guard unnoticed?

Uncomfortable about pushing the issue, Sigefroi sighed. "Lady Melusine wants to see no one. I'll bring her supper myself. Guard this door with your life until I return."

The soldier straightened, puffed up with new pride. "Aye, m'lord."

* * *

That night, Sigefroi couldn't find sleep. He paced his chamber by the dim light of dying embers, unmindful of the chill from the open window. Stopping to gaze at the cloudy night sky, he breathed deeply. Where was Melusine?

Although his betrothed possessed everything he had always wanted in a wife, some sinister foreboding warned Sigefroi against marrying her. Was it a genuine omen from the Almighty, or just the fear of being chained to the same woman for a lifetime?

A small voice in his mind told him something was very wrong with his future bride. How could she disappear so completely and escape the guard's notice? He couldn't stand not knowing where she was. He cursed himself for letting the little hellcat make a mockery of his authority.

But he had sworn on his knight's honor, and he must keep his word.

Sigefroi expected his friend the emperor might feel slighted by his choice of bride. Marrying against Otto's wishes could damage his laboriously earned privileges at court. But honor-bound by his oath, Sigefroi couldn't afford the risk of the emperor prohibiting his marriage.

A quick wedding would not allow time for an interdict. Sigefroi hoped there would be no unpleasant reprisal. Otto had a legendary mean streak.

All that for a woman.

He wondered where Melusine would spend the night. Or with whom? A noose tightened around his gut. Probably wounded pride, or could he possibly be jealous? The discovery unsettled Sigefroi. He'd never experienced that nasty twinge of the heart. He'd always considered it a sign of weakness.

Making a conscious effort to let go of the unwelcome feeling, he turned his gaze to the night sky.

The third full moon of the year rose over the eastern wall through a veil of clouds that formed a blue halo. At dawn, he planned to go hunting with Gunter and Thierry. The long ride might calm his nerves. Besides, the cook needed fresh venison for the wedding feast.

Away from Melusine's bewitching presence, Sigefroi now questioned everything she said. Yet, he could not ignore the silver and the gold sitting in his chamber, neither could he doubt the miraculous sword he'd seen in action. Besides, how could he deny his attraction to the wench, or the divine completion he felt in joining with her? If a higher dominion bound them together, who was he to object? In any case, she seemed to fit his master plan, and that mattered enough to indulge her strange whims.

Sigefroi never considered himself a devout Christian. So why would God reward him with such an opportunity? But what if Melusine's dowry came from unholy sources? He shrugged away the thought. Nay. He didn't believe in witchcraft or in Pagan gods... although he wasn't so sure about the devil.

He attributed his many successes to skill and determination. He alone had brought about this providential boon. When the bishops asked, however, he would prudently state that his bride was most likely chosen for him by God.

After all, he hadn't sold his soul or sealed a pact with the devil. He'd only promised to take the bride and give her one day of freedom each month. How could that tarnish his immortal soul? He couldn't refuse power offered at such a small price, and just when he needed it the most. After all, Sigefroi strongly believed he had a great destiny ahead. So he silenced the warning voice in his mind.

Dropping to the bed furs fully dressed, Sigefroi tucked both hands under his head and stared at the bed canopy. Funny how he'd slept alone all his life, then suddenly couldn't find peace without the lithe body of his betrothed beside him. It took an effort to close his eyes. Fitful sleep came at last, ridden with disturbing dreams of water serpents slithering into his bed.

Sigefroi awoke in a cold sweat. A loose shutter banged against the outside wall. The night sky paled, close to dawn, and the fire had long died in the hearth. He rose and lit a candle, then closed the noisy shutter, trying to conjure away the vague unease left by the dissipating nightmare.

After pulling off his tunic, he threw cold water on his face and armpits from the washing basin. Not bothering to dry himself, he donned a warm tunic, a pair of chausses, and a leather jerkin. Sigefroi reached for his baldric, from which hung Caliburn next to his poniard, and buckled on the belt. After smoothing his hair under a hunting cap, he retrieved from a trunk his crossbow and arrows then plucked his spear from the wall rack.

Sigefroi stalked out of the bedchamber carrying his gear, and reminded the guard to let no one inside. Then he made his way quietly down the stone stairs, toward the kitchen.

There, by the light of a single candle, Gunter, poniard in hand, sat at the massive table, in front of a fat wedge of cheese. Sigefroi carefully laid his hunting gear against the wall, but it rattled a bit, startling one of the scullions who slept around the embers of the main fire.

Gunter rolled his eyes. "How can you leave a warm bed with a sweet wench?" he whispered, shaking his dark head. "You truly prefer hunting in a cold, damp forest?"

A twinge of guilt twisted his gut. Sigefroi had never lied to Gunter until Melusine came into his life. But he'd sworn to tell no one of her monthly escapades.

He sat on the bench, next to his friend. "Some men grow weak when they marry, but I intend to stick to my soldiering ways. No princess will take the warrior out of me."

When Gunter chuckled, a scullion stretched and rubbed his eyes, bewildered at seeing his lord at the kitchen table.

Gunter's black beard came alive as he chewed thoughtfully, nodding in appreciation. The cook who fussed about the kitchen brought more bread and ale for Sigefroi, as well as dry sausage to complement the cheese already on the table.

The two men ate quietly. Sigefroi wasn't hungry but needed strength for the hunt. Outside, a rooster crowed... almost dawn.

The cook wrapped more food in a thick cloth, tied the corners together, then slid the bundle on the table toward the two men. "For your midday snacks, m'lords."

When Sigefroi rose, Gunter picked up the food bundle. Both knights gathered their gear. As an afterthought, Sigefroi grabbed another handful of bread, cheese, and sausage from the platter for Thierry, who had probably skipped breakfast to saddle the horses.

The two men stole silently through the dimly lit hall, stepping around the womenfolk who still slept. Outside, in the dusky courtyard, fresh soldiers prepared to relieve the night guard.

Near the stables, Thierry, sleepy-eyed, his blond hair tousled, waited with the three horses. The lad barely controlled in one hand two braces of eager hounds pulling on their leashes.

"Did you eat?" Sigefroi asked the youth.

When Thierry ignored him, Sigefroi shoved the food in the lad's free hand.

Thierry mumbled his thanks but kept his eyes downcast. The boy's sullen attitude bordered on disrespect, but Sigefroi didn't want to address the delicate matter in front of Gunter. He'd made the lad swear never to mention his defeat to the maiden.

Sigefroi hung his gear to the saddle then vaulted onto his mount. When he took the hounds from Thierry, the panting dogs calmed somewhat under their master's firm hold. The guards opened the gate for their lord's private hunting party, saluting as Sigefroi passed them by.

As they crossed the bridge, the damp mist that bathed the valley below enveloped them and the village beyond in a gray cloud. The thick veil muffled the cries of early birds and the sound of hooves on the disjointed planks. Through streams of fog, the three hunters crossed the village in silence, the hounds pulling on their leash, tails wagging fiercely.

While Thierry lagged behind, Gunter brought his steed abreast of Sigefroi's destrier. "I'll go for a short gallop. Care to join me in a race?"

Sigefroi shook his head. "Nay. I've much on my mind and would rather meditate upon it."

"As you like." Gunter spurred his horse and galloped ahead along the fields, disappearing in the thinning mist.

Acutely aware of Thierry lagging behind, Sigefroi entered the forest of the western plateau as the damp haze melted into dew under the first rays of sunrise. He released the hounds, who scattered in a sniffing frenzy.

He stopped his destrier to allow his squire to catch up. When Thierry reached his level, Sigefroi rode alongside him. "Life isn't always fair, Thierry, even for a knight. You'll soon learn that God throws obstacles in our way, and we must make the most of it."

The youth cocked his head. "Aye? So what happens to honesty and trust, then? Not only did you lose the fight, m'lord, but you lied to your people, even to Gunter."

Sigefroi smiled sadly. At least he'd broken the boy's apathy. "Aye, that I did, and I regret it, but there was no other way."

The lad shook his head. "I don't understand!"

"I'm only a man and far from perfect, but I need the respect of my people. I'd risk my life for Gunter anytime, but he's suspicious enough of Melusine as it is." Sigefroi kept his gaze on the trail ahead, unable to face the boy. "The knowledge of the incident would burden his mind and spread doubts about my ability to rule. I can't afford to show any weakness."

"But you told me yourself that I should always tell the truth."

"Aye, that's what I expect from you." Sigefroi sighed "But sometimes, truth and courage alone can't win the battle. It takes intelligence and strategy. And some battles are meant to be lost. Life is a battle, lordship is a battle. Even love with a woman is a battle."

Thierry stared at his lord questioningly. "Love?"

"Aye." Sigefroi stared back into the boy's eyes. "When you find the lady of your heart, the terror of losing her will be worse than the fear that grips a warrior on the battlefield. God only knows what a man does for love."

Thierry blushed and offered a timid smile. "Really?"

"Aye." Sigefroi chuckled. "You'll find out soon enough."

"But you don't love Lady Melusine, you only pretend." Thierry glanced up, suspicion narrowing his eyes. "Don't you?"

"Things are... complicated, lad." Damn the boy for being so direct. "Although at first I was bound by honor alone, my feelings for Lady Melusine have grown deep and strong. She is very courageous, smart, and quite beautiful."

"I never thought you of all people would fall under a woman's spell, m'lord."

"The best of us do." Sigefroi caught sight of Gunter waiting ahead in a clearing. "Can I trust you to keep my secret?"

Thierry straightened in the saddle. "Aye, m'lord. Your secret's safe with me."

They caught up with Gunter who had halted his steed. The dark man smiled, patting the horse's neck, then he resumed riding with them. "As you suggested during the banquet, I had homing pigeons sent to the neighboring lords to announce your wedding. Lady Melusine was clever to push it back a few days. We'll have a better turnout for the feast."

"Aye." Sigefroi realized with annoyance that Gunter wouldn't let him forget about the wedding, even during a hunt. "Any word from my brothers?"

"Nay, but they should have received the message by now. I also sent for musicians, storytellers and jongleurs from Trier." Gunter would never waste an opportunity for drinking, feasting, entertainment, or wenching.

Sigefroi smiled. "I never envisioned something so grand. You did well beyond my wishes."

"Someone had to make the decisions around here." Gunter sounded almost petulant. "You were too busy plucking the lady night and day, not even leaving your chamber at mealtime."

"And I appreciate your taking over my castle so quickly while I was otherwise occupied." Sigefroi wondered whether Gunter could hear the slight sarcasm in his tone. "I noticed the guards didn't slack off a bit."

Gunter raised a dark brow. "I see the lady didn't have the usual effect of bettering your mood! Was she less than satisfactory in the furs?"

At Gunter's worried tone, Sigefroi exploded in laughter and tightened his hold on the reins to steady the warhorse. "Nay, my friend. No problem lies there."

Gunter relaxed. "Is she to your liking, then?"

"Aye, quite." Damn the ever inquisitive bastard! Always fishing for gossip. Sigefroi recalled with delight his sweet Melusine rutting under him. "Beyond anything I could have imagined."

The big man guffawed. "I'm relieved. What is it, then? Wedding jitters, like a blushing bride?"

"Don't push your luck, my friend." Sigefroi fought to sound menacing. "I'll have your hide if you ever dare call me a blushing bride again."

Gunter's brown eyes twinkled with mirth. "I wouldn't dare provoke a war hero." His gaze lighted on Caliburn. "A new blade? Fine weapon, judging by the scabbard."

"A present from my future bride," Sigefroi declared smugly.

"Ahhh!" Apparently, Gunter was having a grand time. "And what present will you give her before the ceremony? A bride bringing such a dowry deserves an extravagant gift."

"By St Peter's balls!" Sigefroi felt a stab of shame. Caught in the suddenness of the events, he'd forgotten the most elementary rules of nobility.

"Don't tell me you forgot!" Gunter roared.

"Aye," Sigefroi admitted sheepishly. "I'll think of something..."

"You had better, because the emperor will hear about everything that transpires at your wedding, and he might take offense and forget that you are his favorite knight if you ignore basic etiquette."

Damn Otto and his many rules. He would certainly take umbrage at such a faux pas from one of his generals.

The dogs sniffed the underbrush, tails wagging as if they found some game. Sigefroi signaled his friends. As one, he and Gunter reached for their crossbows, while Thierry swiftly loaded a sling and whirled it overhead.

In a sudden drumming of wings, a flock of partridge took flight, startling the horses.

* * *

By sunset, Melusine was a shivering mess. Wet strands of hair clung to her face and drenched the back of her dress. While she enjoyed frigid waters in serpent form, as a woman she preferred warmth.

Although she marveled at how easily she had tricked everyone so far, she couldn't play this dangerous hiding game every single month. Beside depleting her energy, casual magic often led to inadvert discovery. And discovery of Fae powers would mean death. Mortals usually destroyed what they feared or did not understand.

As she climbed up the cliff trail under her concealing glamour, Melusine realized she would need a safer escape route.

She didn't remember seeing water carried up from the river. The stronghold must have its own well. Perhaps she could carve stairs down the shaft as a shortcut to the bottom, then excavate a horizontal tunnel from the shaft to the Alzette River. It would take a great deal of Fae powers to accomplish, but then she could reach the river and return to the fort unseen. The plan sounded practical enough.

In the twilight, under a glamour of invisibility, Melusine re-entered the fort before they closed the gate. Once inside the villa, she slipped past the guard, distracting his attention to some noisy sparrow nesting in the rafters while she opened the bedchamber door. As she closed it behind her, she willed it not to creak.

The dark room stood empty. Leaning against the heavy tapestry, she listened for a few moments then let out a sigh of relief. Safe!

The fire had died. She should have some embers brought in from the kitchen fire, but calling servants in her disheveled state would raise too many questions. Better to rely on herself, as she'd always done before.

Using kindling and logs that lay beside the hearth, Melusine built a fire then struck the flint with trembling fingers. When sparks flew on tinder, she cupped her hands and gently blew. A vivid thought on her part, and bright flames flared up. Soon, the crackling blaze generated a welcome heat. With a firebrand, Melusine lit several candles that bathed the chamber in a pleasant glow.

After slipping out of her wet garment, she donned a simple gown of undyed wool, loosely woven for softness and warmth. At the waist, she cinched a wide leather belt, the ends of which fell low on the front. The soft fabric clung to her curves. She hoped Sigefroi would find the dress attractive.

She checked the effect in her hand mirror, a small oval of polished silver. The light, natural shade of raw wool enhanced her creamy complexion. She pushed back plastered hair from her high forehead, revealing wide eyes of the deepest river gray. Her nose was rather small, compared to the women of the area, but Melusine liked it just so.

Turning the mass of her hair toward the fire, she sat by the hearth to brush out the tangles. She let the heat lift off the moisture and dry the long strands to a lustrous sheen. While she enjoyed the familiar ritual, the fresh scent of the river spread throughout the chamber, mixing with the smoky smell of the fire.

She was almost finished when heavy footsteps rang in the hallway outside the door. Sigefroi! Melusine stopped the brush in mid motion.

By the sound of his steps and the angry edge in his voice as he spoke to the guard, Sigefroi seemed in a foul mood. Melusine hoped the guard wouldn't get in trouble on her account.

The door swung wide then slammed back shut, almost extinguishing the wildly flickering candles. The flames in the hearth leapt and the blaze popped under the sudden draft. Sigefroi took a few steps into the room then stopped, taking in the scene.

Melusine finished brushing her hair, then pushed back her thick tresses and faced him, but she did not rise.

Confusion flickered on Sigefroi's face, but only for an instant. He came forth, holding crossbow and quiver in one hand, a spear in the other. He looked as formidable in the firelight as Achilles before the walls of Troy. Melusine cringed at the intrusion of the faraway memory.

"I knew it was you!" Sigefroi's voice rumbled like a brewing storm. "I saw light through the cracks in the shutters."

"Aye, my lord." Melusine rose, bracing herself to meet his wrath. "I said I'd be back after sunset. I always keep my word."

"Hellfire and damnation!" Marching to an open chest, Sigefroi threw his hunting gear inside in a clatter, slammed down the lid then faced her again. "Is it not enough to make me swear ludicrous oaths?" He glared at her like a lion with amber eyes. "I won't have you corrupting my guards! How did you get the simpleton to lie to me? Did you give him gold? Promise him special favors?"

Stunned, Melusine couldn't think of a benign answer that wouldn't betray her Fae powers.

"Speak, wench!" he boomed.

Despite the tremor that shook her, Melusine managed a cool smile. "I didn't do anything of the sort, my lord. Your guard is loyal. He couldn't possibly have seen me leave or enter through this door."

Crossing both arms on the leather jerkin, Sigefroi planted his feet apart and glared at her. "Nay? Don't you lie to me, wench! How else could you get out and back in? The shutters were locked!" His gaze followed the clay conduit that led the smoke through the tiled roof then he gazed at her dubiously. "I don't like to look like a fool in front of my men! Where, or with whom did you spend the night and the entire day?"

With a calm she didn't feel, Melusine returned the brush and mirror to a stool beside the hearth. "My lord, you promised not to inquire, remember?" She glanced at Caliburn hanging on Sigefroi's hip. "Unless, of course, you wish to relinquish the sword."

Anger and uncertainty battled across Sigefroi's stern face.

Melusine kept her tone even. "Good. Then we have an understanding."

Sigefroi dropped onto the bed, took his head in both hands then rubbed his stubbly jaw. It sounded like parchment under his fingers. "Can you tell me why a woman of your standing, who enjoys the best the world has to offer, needs such unreasonable freedom? I don't like it. It's unnatural!"

"Truly?" Shocked at his unfairness, Melusine repressed a smarting retort. "My lord, you go wherever you please, anytime you chose. Like all noblemen, you take your freedom as a given, don't you?"

"Aye. And anyone would be ill advised to contest me that right!"

"Then how can you blame me for wanting to enjoy the very same thing, only once a month? Is it asking too much?"

"It goes against decency!" Sigefroi rose from the bed and paced in front of it, one hand wrapped around Caliburn's hilt. "Even I defer to my brother the Duke! And to the Emperor!" His expression softened. "I do understand the need... but why the secrecy? Why not tell me where you go and what you do?"

"It would be a restriction of my freedom, my lord." Melusine drew confidence from his wavering. "But that's not my point. I thought we had an agreement."

"Aye, we do." Their gaze met. The scowl upon his brow wrinkled into a frown and his mouth opened, but he only shook his head then threw up his arms in surrender. All hostility faded from Sigefroi's face.

Melusine rejoiced at her victory "Then let us both honor our word and never mention this again. Agreed?"

She offered a slow, seductive smile. Sigefroi's eyes roamed over her shapely body, and Melusine congratulated herself for the choice of the gown.

His gaze fixed on her face. "How is it that, when I am with you, my anger always vanishes?"

"Perhaps, for the same reason I can't look at you without remembering the feel of your hands on my skin," Melusine said huskily, steering his mind along a safer path.

Sigefroi reached for her and pulled her close. "Woman, you drive me wild with lust."

Melusine weakened into his unyielding embrace. His piercing amber eyes gazed into her soul. When he stared at her lips, she parted them slightly in invitation. Sigefroi

100

smelled of the forest, smoke, and leather. Gently at first, he took her mouth, then his demanding kiss stole her breath. Suddenly, he broke all physical contact, leaving her wanting.

Sigefroi's smug grin infuriated Melusine, but two could play that game. A delicious aroma drifted from the kitchen.

"Will you take me to the hall for supper, my lord? I'm famished," she said lightly, as if his kiss had not affected her.

His smile faded away. "Aye, but I will satisfy my need of you later. Make no mistake about it. And this time I won't let you out of my sight."

Melusine took his offered arm, reveling in his uncommon strength. "I promise not to escape, my lord. This night will be ours to enjoy."

Chapter Seven

Since Sigefroi had left the bedchamber at cockcrow to brief the guards about the arriving wedding guests, Melusine had some private time before the servants brought her bath. In the absence of a divining basin, she had to improvise. After pouring fresh water in the wash basin of the bedchamber, she lit a row of candles around it.

In the chilly down, she tightened the green woolen shawl about her shoulders.

Bending over the basin, Melusine called softly, "Palatina?"

The water rippled. "Melusine? Is that you? Where are you?" The young face in the basin looked like Melusine's own reflection. Same creamy skin and wide gray eyes. The girl, however, wore white silk and kept her darker hair in a tight bun, which made her look older.

Melusine's heart leapt with joy at the sight of her triplet sister. "Palatina! Finally. I'm so glad you answered. Are you well?"

"As well as one can fare while condemned to remain secluded under a mountain, away from worldly pleasures." Bitterness hardened Palatina's clear voice.

"I'm so sorry, sister." Melusine swallowed hard on a clenched throat. "I never meant for you and Meliora to pay for my mistake."

"It took me a long time to forgive you..." Palatina's eyes clouded over. "But I realized no good would come from blaming you. Still, my cave is a very lonely place."

Tears rolled down Melusine's cheeks at the thought of the harm she had caused. "I've often felt lonely, too."

Palatina offered a half smile. "Only one significant mortal dared visit me in fourteen decades, an adviser to the king of Aragon. He never returned, though. Since the man was already old, he must be long dead by now."

Remorse stabbed Melusine's chest. "I feel terrible."

Palatina shrugged. "I have my books, of course. A few shepherds know of my existence and provide me with food, medicinal herbs, and books from a nearby monastery. They call me the hermit. Once in a while they bring me a child or an animal in need of healing. But what good is all my knowledge if I can't share it with the rest of the world? I miss the sky, the colors, the beauty... I can run in the wind through a water basin."

Melusine swallowed a lump of guilt. At least, she was free to roam. "How can I ever atone for embroiling you into this? I was misguided to seek revenge against our father. I now understand human weakness. Love can alter anyone's judgment."

"You revised your opinion of mortals?" Palatina sounded intrigued.

"Aye. Manipulated by his heir, blinded by love, our father never meant to betray our mother and bring about her curse. I should have consulted Aunt Morgane before making such drastic decisions." Melusine wiped away a tear. "After we locked him into the Crystal Cave, our father must have died of solitude and despair. But he was only a victim, not the monster we believed him to be."

Palatina nodded. "I, too, changed my mind about our father, but only because I understand how he must have felt... just like me in my cave. At least, I know one day I'll walk out of here, still young enough to enjoy life. All he had to look forward to was a slow and lonely death."

The same sad images haunted Melusine's nightmares. "All because of me. I deserve my serpent curse."

"It was not your fault alone, sister. Meliora and I went along willingly. It's only fair we all paid for the deed."

"Still... it was my idea." Melusine trembled under the burden of her guilty conscience but took hold of herself.

"How is Meliora? She still ignores my summons. It's not like her to hold a grudge for so long!"

"I fear her punishment is the harshest for her sensitive soul. Being forbidden to love or be loved must be the worst torment. She pours her affection onto an enchanted hawk and leads a reclusive life in her castle on Mount Ararat."

"I'm glad you two still talk."

Palatina smiled as if to some private thought. "She developed a taste for honeyed sweets and looks rather plump these days. It becomes her. But she never let go of the rage that kept her alive all these years. Better hatred and resentment than no feelings at all, she once told me."

Melusine couldn't control the sobs shaking her. So many lives ruined by her foolish desire to avenge her mother. "Poor Meliora. I wish I could comfort her."

"Her wounds will take a long time to heal, if they ever do." Palatina straightened and set her even gaze upon Melusine. "Enough sad stories. Why did you summon me, sister? You sounded almost joyous."

Wiping her eyes, Melusine managed a smile. "I'm getting married today!"

Palatina's face glowed with genuine joy. "Married? I can't believe it! What happened to the cynical girl who deemed mortal men unworthy?"

Melusine chuckled. "I guess I grew wiser."

Dimples punctuated her sister's smile. "How wonderful! Do you love the man?"

"Aye." Melusine suddenly realized it was true. "Although I seduced him solely to obey the Goddess, I think I do love him. He makes me feel all warm and soft inside."

Palatina's face turned ashen. "What about your curse? Does he know?"

"Nay. He's a Christian. He can never know I'm Fae. If I can keep it a secret until his death, the Goddess will lift my curse."

Palatina's features froze, her eyes wide in surprise. "The Goddess can do that?"

"Aye, the Goddess can do anything."

"I wish you luck. Should I tell Meliora? I can only imagine her despair. She'll be upset and resent you even more if the Great One lifts your curse. All she wants is a man to love and children to nurture, and her curse forbids it."

Melusine shook her head slowly. "I shall not add to her distress."

"Then let it be our secret. But you will tell me everything. I miss the world so much. Who is your betrothed and how did you seduce him?"

"Well..." Melusine searched for words.

Ignoring her attempt to answer, Palatina went on with her usual volubility. "And you'll have to tell me which nobles will attend the banquet. Will there be jugglers, storytellers, dancing? I don't want to miss any of it. I'll be watching through the divining basin. How I envy you!"

Melusine laughed good-heartedly. "You haven't changed a bit, Palatina. All right. I'll tell you everything... But promise to keep me informed about Meliora."

"Aye. Don't worry, I'm not angry at you anymore. I miss you so much."

"I miss you, too, Palatina. I really do."

* * *

The blast of trumpets startled Melusine. Her fingertip caught on the opal broach she was pinning to her soft yellow gown. "Ouch!"

She berated herself for being so nervous and sucked the tiny drop of blood while a servant girl hurried to secure the jewel on her wedding gown.

"I'd also like you to wear this!"

Melusine jumped at the familiar voice. "Sigefroi? How long have you been standing here?"

Holding a lovely box with inlaid mother of pearl, he stared at her in unabashed wonder. She did the same. His clean-shaven cheeks invited a kiss, but she refrained in front of the servants. Years of solitude had made her shy about public displays of affection.

The white silk tunic and red chausses looked regal on Sigefroi's muscular frame. He opened the box for her.

Melusine gasped at the precious jewel laid on the crimson silk lining the case. The exquisite gold crown shone with emeralds, blue lapis, amethysts, topaz, and rubies in a pattern of entwined wild flowers.

"How beautiful and delicate! I wager this is the masterpiece of a famous goldsmith, my lord."

"Aye. It was once the crown of a French queen," Sigefroi announced with pride. "My late mother, Princess Kunegonde of France, trusted me to pass her family keepsake to my chosen bride."

"Chosen?" Overwhelmed by the solemnity of the gift, Melusine felt her throat clench. Finally, she managed in strangled voice, "I couldn't accept such a priceless memento."

"Of course you can, and you will." With a rueful smile, Sigefroi took the crown and handed the box to the servant. Then, facing Melusine, he grew serious. "Had we met in normal circumstances, my lady, I would choose no other in the entire Christendom."

Melusine swallowed hard. "Even with all the promises I exacted from you?"

"Aye. I couldn't have chosen any better, my little hellcat!"

"Hellcat?" Although given in tenderness, the pet name struck too close for Melusine's comfort. Despite the fact that her kind strived to serve humanity, most mortals would consider her evil. She frowned.

With infinite care, Sigefroi adjusted the small crown on her head. The way he touched her hair reminded Melusine of their passionate night. He smelled of soap and scented bath water. She couldn't resist laying her hands on his hip.

Sigefroi stroked her shoulders and gazed into her eyes. "The royal trinket suits you."

The soft kiss that brushed her lips made her forget the servants hovering nearby, and she wondered whether she'd ever get used to such a crowded place. Melusine now wished for more than a kiss, but it was all circumstances would allow. The reluctance in Sigefroi's eyes at letting her go warmed her soul.

Then he offered his arm. "Are you ready to marry me?"

"Aye, my lord. I would like nothing more." In that instant, Melusine believed that Sigefroi would make her very happy indeed.

They walked out into the late morning sunshine. A colorful crowd of well-dressed lords and ladies in bright silk and velvet chatted in front of the villa, but Melusine's yellow gown eclipsed them all. She congratulated herself for following the advice of the cloth merchant.

Families of serfs and servants had gathered by the guardhouse and the fencing yard. Delicious smells wafted from the kitchen. As they passed the kennel, even the hounds in their enclosure barked and wagged their tails to their own festive tempo.

The white square tents of noble guests, sporting multicolored pennants, lined the inside perimeter of the fort. Banners hanging straight down from the top of the ramparts, fluttered in a light breeze. Except for the black boar on red field of Ardennes, Melusine knew none of the coats of arms and made a mental note to learn them all in the near future.

As the nuptial couple crossed the bailey at a stately pace, nodding at friendly faces, Melusine suggested, "You should design a coat of arms for yourself, my lord. You are no longer a son of Lorraine, or just lord over the vast forests of Ardennes, but the new military might of Lucilinburhuc."

Sigefroi raised one eyebrow. "True enough. The thought occurred to me, but I haven't made up my mind about a crest yet."

Without missing a step, Melusine cast him a sidelong glance. "Looking at you today, I see a crimson lion, standing on its hind legs, clawing the air on a field of white. The lion symbolizes strength, nobility, valor, and the white field represents purity, a virgin land ready to be impregnated and tilled."

As he nodded right and left to familiar faces, Sigefroi chuckled. "Is that how you see me, my sweet? As a rutting lion?"

Easy laughter escaped her throat. "Your victory cry in the furs certainly sounds like a lion's roar, my lord. If I remember well, so does your battle cry."

A shiver swept over Melusine at the recollection of Sigefroi's mighty charge. Even with Caliburn in hand, she had cringed in fear. She also recalled her first impression of the knight, a great cat with feral eyes and a red mane, bloody from hacking off a thief's hand.

Walking at her side, Sigefroi smiled appreciatively. "I like the red lion. Far better than anything I have considered so far. Can you draw?"

The question brought a joyous spring in Melusine's steps. "I have a rare gift for the art, my lord."

"That's settled, then," he said seriously. "I officially request your services to design my new coat of arms."

Melusine congratulated herself. After impressing Sigefroi with her design for the coat of arms, she would have an easier time making him accept her ideas for the improvements of the fortress. Women didn't usually participate in military projects. She would have to use persuasion, and since Sigefroi seemed immune to her gifts, she would have to prove herself.

The crowd parted to make way as the couple slowly advanced toward the tall linden tree under which a dais had been erected.

"And another thing, my lord. About Lucilinburhuc, or Lutzelburg..."

Sigefroi gave her an inquisitive glance. "Aye? What about it?"

"The name sounds light and small. It even means little fort. Why not give it the grandeur you are striving for. A name that will inspire respect in France, as well as in Italy, and throughout the German empire."

Amusement played in Sigefroi's amber eyes. "Something tells me you already have a name in mind."

"How did you guess?" Melusine chuckled. "I would call our country Luxembourg, my lord. Lux for light in Latin, and bourg for the thriving city that will one day spread far around your fortress."

Sigefroi stopped walking to gaze at the light clouds overhead. "Luxembourg. It sounds noble and grand. Luxembourg... It evokes a safe haven for the righteous and a fearsome place for our enemies. A good name for a military stronghold, a fortified city, or even a kingdom. Aye, I like it." He grinned at Melusine. "By the saints! You are a surprising source of great ideas, my sweet. Luxembourg it shall be!"

They reached the dais and Melusine lifted her hem to climb the few steps leading to the wooden platform where an altar stood, covered with embroidered white linen. On the tablecloth sat a bouquet of early spring flowers, and incense burned in a metal dish, releasing a cloying scent.

To the side of the altar, a bishop in gold vestments over his purple robe spoke in confidential tones with a man in black and red silk. The bishop loomed tall from the added height of the golden miter on his head.

Melusine struggled to hide her aversion for clergymen. For centuries they had persecuted her kind. But she must not panic. As long as they didn't suspect her nature and there was no holy water at hand, she would be safe enough.

Smiling, Sigefroi took Melusine toward the two men. "Brothers," he called, "Allow me to introduce my bride, Princess Melusine of Strathclyde."

Both nobleman and bishop turned toward Melusine. She noticed the family resemblance among the three brothers. But despite similar height and various degrees of red in their hair, she also noted major differences. The frail nobleman looked soft, older than Sigefroi, while the bishop's thick brow made him look stubborn and inflexible.

Sigefroi's bearing loosened and warmed in his brothers' presence. "Melusine, meet my brother and Liege

Lord, Frederick, Duke of High Lorraine, and my brother Adalberon, Bishop of Metz."

Melusine curtsied demurely and kissed Adalberon's offered ring that sparkled above gloved fingers.

Tall and wiry, Bishop Adalberon nodded then shrewdly scrutinized Melusine through faded brown eyes. "You must enlighten us about the genealogy of your illustrious family, young lady. I hope we get a chance to discuss it."

"I hope so, too, Your Grace." The truth be told, Melusine fiercely hoped to avoid the subject altogether. Fortunately, there should be enough excitement to make the bishop forget.

The Duke of Lorraine smiled sweetly, as if beholding a holy vision. "Welcome into the fold of our family, Princess Melusine." He held and kissed her hand. "Be assured that my brothers and I are delighted to see our favorite knight finally betrothed. We are counting on you to tame his maverick heart and keep him safely here, away from Otto's battlefields."

Melusine froze. She hadn't thought of Sigefroi going to war anytime soon. "I'll try my best to remind him of his duties at home, Lord Duke."

Frederick chuckled. "Please, little sister-in-law, call me Frederick."

"Aye." Melusine offered a wide smile. "Thank you for the warm welcome, Frederick. Are there other siblings here today?"

"Nay. Gosselin probably didn't get the message, and Gilbert is fighting in Italy. As for our sisters, both are close to giving birth and can't travel."

Trumpets blared from the ramparts, heralding the beginning of the ceremony. All conversations ceased. The crowd turned to the makeshift altar under the tall linden tree.

Bishop Adalberon barely glanced at Melusine. "Are we ready?"

Melusine was rudely reminded that in the eyes of the Church, a woman had little value other than her dowry, her genealogy, and the sons she could bear.

The mass enunciated in Latin seemed to last forever, punctuated by awkward hymns, badly sung by the enthusiastic crowd. At the bishop's prompting, the assembly genuflected and made the sign of the cross.

Standing in place for so long, her back to the crowd, Melusine focused on the Bishop's purple robes billowing in the breeze as he turned and performed elaborate ritual gestures. Her mind wandered as she studied the precious gold chalice and saucer.

The aroma of roasting meat, fish, herbs, and fresh bread drifted from the kitchen, overpowering the penetrating smell of incense. While all the eyes focused on the unfolding ritual, Melusine, although apparently bent in prayer, directed her inward eye to the ongoing preparations for the feast.

Just now inside the hall, the servants spread white linen on the trestle tables for the noble guests. More tables outside would accommodate the families of serfs, craftsmen, servants, soldiers and entertainers. Gunter directed the operations quite efficiently, she noticed.

At one point, the bishop stopped the ritual for an austere discourse, where he reminded women of their duties of obedience, faithfulness, and childbearing. He made no mention of a man's duty regarding marriage, as if all men were above sinning!

Adalberon offered Melusine and Sigefroi the Eucharist in the form of bread and wine, the most important part of the ritual. A short blessing of the couple followed the communion. No vows were exchanged, but since the Church had blessed their union, Sigefroi and Melusine were now bound in holy matrimony until death.

When Sigefroi and Melusine finally faced the crowd as husband and wife, the trumpets announced the end of the religious ceremonies and the beginning of worldly festivities. Clutching her husband's arm, Melusine stepped down from the platform. A cheer rose among the guests, punctuated by hoots, good wishes, and friendly jibes.

Through the throng of congratulating guests, they made their way to the villa. Melusine smiled as a group of excited children showered them with flower petals. Between the tables set outside, Melusine walked proudly along Sigefroi and they entered the main Hall.

Inside the villa, the decorated hall dripped with banners and ribbons floating down from the rafters. A tumult of excited voices bounced off the walls. Melusine let Sigefroi guide her to the high table, on a low platform, at the far, narrow end of the hall. The delicious aroma of fresh bread and venison made her stomach growl. She hadn't had anything to eat all day.

She and Sigefroi sat at the center of the high table. Duke Frederick took his seat by Melusine. Bishop Adalberon, who had removed his miter and golden vestments, now only wore purple robes. He sat by Sigefroi. The bishop looked so thin, ascetic and rather pale, but Melusine suspected that his wiry frame could handle a sword, and the determination in the set of his jaw made her wish he never became her enemy.

Further down the high table, Gunter cast wistful glances through the wide open door. She followed his gaze to the maids sitting outside in the courtyard with the soldiers. Melusine presumed he'd rather sit with them than share a silver cup with the bishop. On both long sides of the hall, trestle tables accommodated the lesser nobles, leaving the center space open for servers and entertainment.

Melusine smiled to Frederick on her right. She sensed in the older brother a kind and fair lord, devoid of ambition.

"Where is your lady wife?" she inquired while a kitchen lad poured the wine.

"She doesn't care for travels." Frederick frowned slightly. "But she asked me to convey her best wishes." His eyes twinkled. "I see my mother's crown suits you well. She would be very pleased."

"Thank you." Melusine's insides melted at the thought that Sigefroi's family accepted her so easily... but only because they didn't know what she was.

Rising from his chair, Sigefroi gently knocked on his silver goblet with the blade of his poniard. When the surrounding noise hushed, he raised the goblet.

"Let us drink to the new House of Luxembourg," he enunciated clearly. "With the emblem of a crimson lion standing on its hind legs against a field of white, may the House of Luxembourg prosper, rule, and protect our good country."

Frederick turned to Melusine, arching a brow. "The House of Luxembourg, did he say?"

She simply nodded, but her heart beat faster as Sigefroi went on.

"Aye, I have great plans for Luxembourg. As you probably saw on your way here, I have already started new fortifications on the Rham plateau. Next, I will build my stone castle on the Bock, and soon I foresee a thriving city with a free market, shops, crafts of all kinds. Let our new town prosper and our enemies tremble at the roar of the Lion of Luxembourg! Long live Luxembourg!" He drained his goblet, then smacked it down on the table and sat.

A serving lad hurried to refill his cup.

Gunter then rose, goblet in hand. "Long Live Luxembourg!"

Following his example, lords and ladies at the trestle tables stood up and cheered.

"Long live Luxembourg!" they repeated three times in unison, then the men drank while the ladies waited to partake of the wine from the same goblet.

Duke Frederick grinned and leaned behind Melusine to address Sigefroi. "My coffers will profit greatly from a prosperous town in these parts, little brother. Besides, the project will keep you busy here, away from the empire's borders."

Adalberon nodded gravely. "You also need to build churches and monasteries to insure the salvation of the souls in your charge. Prosperity without God's guidance leads to eternal damnation."

As Sigefroi didn't respond, Adalberon turned to Melusine. "Don't you think so, my lady?"

Melusine felt the blood drain from her extremities. Churches meant priests, bishops, holy water, baptism, all dangerous threats. "We must see to basic necessities first," she said with a neutral smile. "Safety and survival of our expanding population are the most pressing matters right now."

Sigefroi glanced at Melusine with a look of surprise on his face then turned to his bishop brother. "I already support several churches and monasteries on my other estates."

Adalberon frowned. "I understand, but..."

"I will not have Roman prelates dictate the rules in my own home, as I've seen it happen too often." Sigefroi downed more wine. "As much as I love you and I support Holy Mother Church, I hope you'll forgive me for wanting to be the only master in my house."

When Adalberon gave a non-committal shrug, Melusine sighed with relief and gave Sigefroi a grateful smile. He picked up her hand from the table and brought her fingers to his lips.

"I'm impressed." He chuckled, tickling her fingers. "I didn't picture my little hellcat as such a shrewd politician. Wenches usually stay clear of political debates."

"I guess I'm not your average wench, my lord." Melusine smiled.

Sigefroi rolled his eyes. "I couldn't agree more."

Young servants ladled on the bread trenchers a first remove of thick pea soup and ham with soft cheese and applesauce. Meanwhile, lads refilled the wine goblets. Controlling her appetite, Melusine ate moderately, knowing that many other removes would bring more delicious foods.

After so many years of solitude, all this activity around her made Melusine dizzy. Soon, the insistent pounding of a small gong quieted the din of conversations. Lively music of reed flutes and tambourines accompanied bouncing acrobats, contortionists, and jongleurs in bright red and yellow costumes, tumbling down the center of the hall.

Tiny bells at the ends of their long pointed hats and at their ankles jingled in rhythm as they vaulted and twisted in mid air. As if by miracle, they landed back on their feet then bowed, only to start a new round of cartwheels and somersaults. The wedding guests watched with fascination.

Among the entertainers, a mischievous dwarf imitated and missed the most difficult moves, tripping over himself. Knocking down an acrobat, he stole the jongleurs' balls, tickled the contortionists, and ended up getting chased by his companions.

Running like a hen chased by the cook, the tiny jester screamed in a piercing voice all the way to the high table. There, he stole Sigefroi's hand-water bowl and spilled it over his own head. Uproarious laughter and tears of merriment erupted from the delighted guests.

Bishop Adalberon remained stoic during the entertainment. Melusine noticed that he barely touched the food and didn't drink the wine, leaving the run of his silver goblet to a delighted Gunter.

Next came a remove of fresh fish with boiled dandelion greens and viper's grass roots, followed by the breathtaking performance of a tattooed man who swallowed swords and daggers without apparent injury.

Each partridge and pheasant in wine sauce came with smoked mushrooms and hazelnuts. Melusine did enjoy more than her share.

"I see you like my catch," Sigefroi teased with obvious satisfaction.

"Aye, it is delicious, my lord," she managed between bites.

A strange man with black skin, wearing only white silk pantaloons and a turban, exposed his hairless chest to the appreciative stare of the noble ladies. A few men looked unhappy about it. The rest, already in their cups, exhibited a jolly mood. The Moore, as the ebony man was called, came from faraway Spain. Melusine wondered whether her sister Palatina had seen any of these black Moores while spying on her southern neighbors.

After juggling with fiery torches, eliciting cries of admiration from the crowd, the black man swallowed a foul-smelling liquid then belched fire from his mouth, like a dragon. His performance received a standing ovation.

During a lull in the entertainment came the roasted goose stuffed with sweet chestnuts, served with honeyed oat cakes.

By the time the sun set, the chill of early spring nights intruded on the festivities. The guards lit the torches in the hall and closed the doors. The villagers returned to their homes, the servants to the kitchen, and the soldiers to the guardhouse. Only the noble guests went on feasting.

Soon Bishop Adalberon excused himself. "This is more excitement than a prelate should experience in an entire life. I will return to my tent and pray for my sins. I expect to see all of you at morning mass."

After Adalberon left the table, Sigefroi turned to Melusine and Frederick. "I wish he would loosen up. It's not as if he'd earned his position through sainthood. He wasn't even religious until our father purchased the Bishopric of Metz for him."

Frederick sighed. "Aye, he changed a lot in the last few years. He has strong ideas about reforming and regulating the monasteries. He started a crusade against corruption and complacency among the clergy."

By the light of bright torches, the festivities continued late into the night, with an abundance of wine, ballads, and dances, to the melancholy strings of the lute.

Gunter had left the high table, but Melusine spotted him at the far end of the hall, in romantic conversation with a lovely lady. The woman's noble husband had passed out on the tablecloth and snored from too much wine, leaving his turtledove easy prey for the swarthy knight.

Restless at sitting all this time, Melusine glanced sideways at Sigefroi, wondering how long she'd have to wait to savor the pleasures of his hard body. He caught her look and smiled devilishly, his liquid amber eyes full of promise.

After the last of the entertainment, Duke Frederick rose. "You'll have to excuse me now. I must leave at dawn for the return journey."

Sigefroi rose to give Frederick a brotherly hug. The easy love between the two men filled Melusine with longing for her sisters.

Frederick then kissed Melusine's hand. "Have a wonderful night, young lady." He winked. "If my brother's reputation holds true, you should have a lovely time of it."

Frederick chuckled and walked away, waving as if he knew they both stared at his retreating back.

Heat crept up Melusine's cheeks. Even the most charming men could sometimes lack delicacy. In the hall, the revelry now escalated. Soon, as the custom allowed, the drunken men would defy all decency. Gunter was nowhere to be seen, neither was his lovely turtledove, although the abandoned husband still snored soundly on the table.

Sigefroi grinned. "Well? Shall we follow Frederick's advice? I ordered a fire in our chamber and a ewer of wine. Our bed should be pleasantly warm by now."

"I thought you would never ask, my lord." Melusine wondered whether her radiant smile betrayed the sensual thoughts that made her body tingle with anticipation.

They made their way to Sigefroi's chamber under the hooting calls of a few young nobles who noticed their escape. Never in her life had Melusine felt so right about anything. Gone was the anguish, the frustration, the bitterness that had plagued her since the curse. She now felt loved and accepted. She had a place in society.

The Goddess had blessed Melusine with a capable husband, a promising house, and the opportunity to serve a worthy cause, all beyond her expectations. But most of all, Melusine had proven her mastery by fulfilling her mission so far. Tonight, in Sigefroi's furs, she would savor the fruit of her remarkable success.

Chapter Eight

Six moons later - Michaelmas Day, September 963

Afternoon sunlight flooded the chartroom through the western window on the second floor of the new castle. Serene and content, Melusine shifted in the chair, one arm instinctively protecting her belly.

She glanced up at Sigefroi across the parchment rolled out on the table. "Now that the walls around the village are completed, I think we should start on the drawbridge."

"Aye, something we can finish before rain, fog, and snow keep us indoors. The towers will have to wait until spring." Sigefroi rarely wore his mail inside the fort anymore but favored white tunics embroidered with the red lion of Luxembourg. Melusine was proud of the pattern. Despite the flatness imposed by the fabric, the beast looked fierce, almost alive and breathing on Sigefroi's chest.

"This winter we could dig the tunnels." Melusine's heart beat faster. She couldn't help the eagerness in her voice. The secret passages would mean multiple exits for her monthly flights, and less chances to be discovered.

Sigefroi rubbed a smooth chin. "A long siege could deplete our food supplies. The main fields lie far outside the walls."

"True enough. So, the underground passages should run in different directions." Pleased that he followed the desired reasoning, Melusine indicated several points on the map. "At the bottom of the cliff by the river, toward the plateau with a shaft up to the village, and from the village far into open country, behind potential enemy lines."

While Sigefroi studied the chart, Melusine pretended to survey the bailey through the open window. Her keen interest in the question at hand might raise suspicion.

From the bailey, the happy chirping of sparrows filtered in through the now familiar sounds of construction, weapon practice, loud commands, and the creaking of loaded carts. The swallows gathered in the linden tree before their annual flight south.

She feared it might upset her husband to think she valued her days of freedom above him. He probably considered her request as a whim. How could he suspect that his destiny and hers, maybe even their lives, depended on such a trivial matter?

Sigefroi lifted his gaze. "Only a handful of loyal men should know about these passages, lest our last resort escape be leaked to a possible enemy. Many people flock to Luxembourg nowadays. Not all can be trusted."

"I agree." Melusine looked away. How could Sigefroi trust her, with all the secrets she kept from him? "There could be underground vaults as well, a safe place to keep the treasury. The sandstone makes it easy to carve an entire network of rooms and passageways."

"And in the spring, we can use the stone excavated from the tunnels to build the watchtowers and the new battlements."

Melusine bent over the open trunk of rolled parchments at her feet. She pulled out another chart where she had sketched the details of the complicated mechanism of weights, ropes, and pulleys that would set the new draw-bridge in motion.

Sigefroi helped her unroll and spread the scroll then turned it to get a better look. He studied the sophisticated drawing for a moment. "How you concocted this infernal piece of machinery on your own, I don't know, but I have to admit it is the most ingenious contrivance ever imagined."

Of course, Melusine couldn't tell him where she'd learned about castle defenses and war machines. How could she explain such familiarity with Trojan and Roman warfare from a former life. As a Christian, Sigefroi believed he only lived once. How she wished to banish all secrets between them! Unfortunately, Melusine couldn't share with him her very nature.

She allowed a regretful smile to touch her lips. "I studied Roman machines in my youth. A simple matter of logic when you put your mind to it, my lord. Just a little improvement on ancient archetypes."

"You are too modest, sweet wife." Sigefroi's happy grin made the amber in his eyes twinkle.

At a sharp kick from her unborn child, a surprised cry escaped her lips. Melusine flinched.

Sigefroi rushed to her side, a worried look on his stern face. "Are you well?"

"Aye, my lord." She laughed. "It's just a kick." Taking his strong hand in hers, she laid it on the side of her belly and marveled at the warmth of his touch through the stretched blue gown. The baby kicked again.

The awe on Sigefroi's face turned to fatherly pride. "I wager it's a son. He has a mighty foot."

Melusine only smiled. She didn't have the heart to rob him of his hopes. Noblemen wanted sons and Sigefroi was no different.

She knew a little girl grew in her womb, but telling anyone would bring suspicion upon her. Only devils and saints could foretell the future with any accuracy. She didn't care to find out in which category the good people of Luxembourg would cast her, given a chance.

Rising from the chair, Melusine banished a shiver of unease to declare in a cheery tone, "The afternoon sun is still warm for the season. Shall we take a walk on the ramparts?"

"Anything to please the mother of my future heir." Sigefroi took her widened waist to lead her out of the chartroom. "I shall call him Henri. Henri of Luxembourg. What do you think?"

"But what if our child is a baby girl, my lord? What name shall we give her? There are no guarantees of a son."

"It will be a boy." The finality in Sigefroi's tone forbade any further comment.

Melusine smiled to hide her unease. Sigefroi would be disappointed by a daughter. "Will you make your first son your only heir, then? This prosperous domain you are building one town at a time should not be divided among many children as the custom demands. It destroyed the might of your father's house."

Sigefroi eyed her curiously. "A very cunning thought, my lady. That's what Emperor Otto plans on doing with his first son as well. He may even have him crowned by the Pope as a child, to avoid any contest."

They crossed the solarium where young girls and ladies stopped chatting at the sight of their lord. Melusine had spent long hours with them in the past months, decorating the guards' uniforms with the coat of arms, teaching them to sew and embroider new winter surcoats for the men.

Melusine nodded at the familiar faces smiling above their needlework. She now truly belonged among her people in the House of Luxembourg. A comfortable life, surrounded by those she loved, in the new residence she had designed and built.

Then there were the dreaded Wednesdays...

Her arm on Sigefroi's, she passed the treasury room, locked and guarded at all times, then several private chambers destined to house occasional noble guests. Watching her steps, Melusine followed Sigefroi down a narrow flight of stone stairs.

When they reached the knights' hall, light flooded the vast room. It stood almost empty at this time of day, although a small army now resided there. The soldiers trained hard, participated in the daily chores, and helped in the construction work, leaving little time for idleness.

Melusine glanced up with pride at the mixture of German and Roman architecture. She had designed with precision the wide rounded arches of the vaulted ceiling and the two rows of tall columns that supported the edifice.

Through the line of high windows on each side, sun rays played on the flagstone.

With a monumental fireplace at each end, the long hall made a grand place for gatherings and formal celebrations. At one extremity, an entire room was reserved to the armory. The other end opened upon the old Roman villa, transformed into a vast kitchen.

When Melusine and Sigefroi stepped out into the bailey, a young uniformed guard snapped to attention. In his eagerness, he bumped into children with sticks, who prodded protesting pigs and cattle toward the shed that served as a temporary slaughterhouse. The sickening smell of fresh blood and guts made Melusine's stomach lurch. She stifled a moan.

"Are you all right?" Sigefroi's concern warmed her.

"Aye." She forced a smile for him. "Being with child makes me squeamish." Even the squeals of the beasts being butchered bothered her more than usual, but she closed her mind to the disturbing sounds as they walked away from it.

Sigefroi squeezed her hand. "There will be plenty of food for the winter. The meats will be smoked or salted for the larder, blood sausage prepared, livers, kidneys and hearts set in lard and preserved in clay pots."

Although familiar with the process, Melusine had never prepared for the winter on such a large scale. "I will ask the cooks to prepare the heads, tongues, and tripes of the animals and serve them at Sunday's feast after mass."

Next week, they would slaughter most of the drakes and ganders, cook them, and preserve them in lard. She observed the orderly row of serfs unloading baskets of golden grapes into huge wooden vats. Tomorrow, they would trample the fruit to make the new wine.

"The year's wine must be stored as well."

Sigefroi nodded. "After paying the food tax to my brother Frederic of High Lorraine, there will be plenty left to feed everyone for many months."

Baskets of apples on a cart spread their sweat smell. Melusine hoped there would be enough of the fresh green fruit from the old orchard to last the winter. The newly

122

planted trees would take several years to produce. But since the fields had brought a bountiful crop, they wouldn't lack wheat and oats.

The smell of eel from the smoking shed whetted Melusine's appetite. Despite morning sickness, she ate five meals a day, and still felt ravenous most of the time.

Sigefroi supported her to climb the stairs to the ramparts. "Just like this place, you are blossoming, my wife."

"Aye. You like it?" Her feeding frenzy and round belly made her plump, just the way that appealed to men these days.

"You look irresistible." Sigefroi playfully kissed her neck. "I'll have to keep you with child at all times. It suits you."

"You think so? I feel good, too." She breathed deeply as they reached the rampart walk over the main gate.

Being with child was a wonderful experience. Melusine didn't mind at all that it was an essential part of her mission to the Great Goddess. Her hand rested on Sigefroi's arm as they gazed toward the village, across the gorge, on the plateau.

The panorama from the ramparts had changed in the past months. Recently harvested fields and young vineyards now graced the surrounding hills. Huts, houses, and working sheds spilled outside the town walls and at the base of the cliff, along the river below. The sun's reflection upon the water reminded Melusine that she must leave at sunset.

As he studied her, Sigefroi's expression turned serious. The western sun set his leonine mane aflame. "I have a favor to ask, my lady."

Melusine shivered despite the warm afternoon. "What kind of favor?"

Sigefroi surveyed the ramparts, as if to make sure they couldn't be heard. "Now that you are with child, I want you to cease your monthly escapades."

The blood drained from Melusine's face and a fist gripped her heart. She choked on the words. "You want me to what?" A trickle of cold sweat slid between her breasts under the blue gown.

Sigefroi considered her coolly, but Melusine could feel cold fire behind his composure. "I've indulged your fancy long enough, dear wife. My heir growing in your womb must not be weakened or endangered by such childish whims. I want him safe in the castle at all times."

This couldn't be. If her secret were discovered, Melusine would lose everything, maybe even her life and the life of her child. Sigefroi would lose his lands, and his descendants would be cursed for nine generations. She couldn't let that happen.

As panic settled in, Melusine breathed faster. "My lord, do I need to remind you of your oath?"

Sigefroi scoffed. "Obtained under duress if I recall correctly."

"You vowed nevertheless." She groped for the right words. "My lord, a knight never betrays his word."

"And as a knight, I'm ashamed for giving in to your ruthless blackmail."

Dear Goddess, she had to think fast, or his new attitude would bring disaster to everyone involved, including the good people of Luxembourg. "Are you ready to give up Caliburn, then?"

"In your condition, I doubt that you can take it from me. I am the lord of this castle, and I order you to behave like a responsible wife, not a spoiled maiden." He stared straight into her eyes. "I forbid you to leave."

"You forbid me?" Shocked by his sudden show of authority, Melusine didn't attempt to hide her outrage. "Lord Husband, I have never taken orders from anyone." She'd almost said from a mortal, but stopped the word before it passed her lips. That, too, was dangerous knowledge. "And certainly I will not obey a knight who breaks a sacred pledge. You can't prevent me from leaving at sunset."

"Even if I lock you up under guard? Are you insinuating you know witchcraft?"

Paralyzed in the face of such a perilous accusation, Melusine only stared at her husband. "If you insist on this, I'll refuse to share your bed."

"Do not fear." His words sounded more like a threat than reassurance. "I can make you."

"You wouldn't dare!" Despite her dread, Melusine forced herself to laugh. For his sake as well as hers, she had to win this argument, and to win she must keep a cool head.

His tone remained daunting. "Do not try my patience."

"I warned you of what will happen if you don't keep your promise. We'll be lost to each other forever." Melusine didn't dare enunciate the full extent of the curse, but it made her shudder inside.

"You don't really believe such tales, do you?" He watched her intently. "No Christian would."

"But God will punish a knight for not keeping his word."

As he stood there, cold and unmoved, icy ribbons of fear slid across her skin.

"Aren't we happy the way we are now?" she heard herself plead. "What more do you need?"

"Happy?" His wry tone cut deeper than his wrath. "How can I be happy, not knowing where you are for an entire day each month? I do not care for that feeling."

"But it has nothing to do with us. You know I love you and would never betray you."

"I know that!" His palm slammed the flat rock of the rampart ledge. "But I want my wife and child to remain within these walls. I can't see to your safety outside the castle without an escort."

When he paused, she said, "I do not need protection."

Worry etched the hard lines of his face. "I heard today that an ondine was sighted in the river a month past... an evil omen. I fear for your life and that of our future son."

Dear Goddess, so that's what it was all about? How could she have been so careless as to be seen? Melusine sighed in an attempt to ease the pressure building in her chest. "Perhaps I carry a daughter."

"Nonsense. Since when are you an oracle?"

Fear pushed her to argue. "Oh! And I reckon you are?"

The anger in Sigefroi's face receded further in the face of logic. "Stop answering questions with questions."

Their eyes met and Melusine held his glare.

"Stubborn woman! I swear, sometimes I feel bewitched by you."

That dangerous accusation again... Melusine had to diffuse it. "But you don't believe in such evil things, do you?"

She suddenly wondered, why would a Christian think her evil? She was only trying to survive and save their happiness as well as his beloved Luxembourg.

Confusion flooded Sigefroi's features. "I know you'll do just as you please, but I beg you to stop vanishing like that. It can't be good for you or our son. Our people are noticing your absences. I'm out of excuses and it undermines my authority. This ridiculous secret is festering, and for both our sakes it needs to stop."

"It cannot stop, ever!" Melusine immediately regretted the strength of her reaction and looked away from his drilling gaze.

He turned her around, forcing her to face him. "Why? At least tell me why."

The earnestness in his eyes made her cringe. Temptation ate at Melusine's gut. Here was a man in love with her. He wanted to know her. She should give him a chance to love her for who she really was.

"Well?" He glared at her, waiting.

What was she thinking? No righteous Christian knight would ever condone what she represented, the old gods, the ancient curses. He would see her as the very evil he was sworn to crush. Even if he could live with such a lethal secret, it would destroy him from inside, as a man, and as a ruler.

Assailed by regrets, Melusine took a deep breath. He might understand religious language. "I guess you can tell your people I have a sacred duty, a pilgrimage I vowed to make each month to a secret holy place. On my life, I must keep my word or perish in eternal flames."

126

"Is that it? Why didn't you say so? I can ask a bishop to relieve you of your vow."

"Please, don't. This vow is beyond any bishop. Such practices have caused great harm in my family. Believe what you must, but I warn you, do not involve the Church, or it will be the end of us."

His shoulders relaxed a bit. "I can't really go against God, but I find this vow strange and unsettling."

"I will be safe, if that's what you fear. God will protect me." Inwardly, Melusine hoped the Goddess would. The area was getting too populated. She would have to hide in her cave or go further away, far from her favorite cliffs.

The sun now dipped toward the western plateau, and a flutter of warning rippled through Melusine's body. "I must go."

She laid a gentle hand on Sigefroi's shoulder and kissed his cheek, but he remained still and unresponsive. How she loathed having to leave him like that. The look of powerless despair on his beloved face would remain etched in her memory, like a sad reminder of how fragile their happiness truly was.

She turned and hurried down the stone steps of the rampart, but she didn't look back for fear that he would see her cry.

Chapter Nine

Three months later - December 963

Sunset came early on these midwinter days just before yuletide. Seized by a chill as soon as she regained human shape, Melusine splashed awkwardly out of the freezing water and stood in the shallows on lead feet, holding her cumbersome belly. She stumbled toward the shore, clutching frosted boulders for balance. A skim of ice thickened at the river's edge and cracked under her bare feet. She had to get warm fast, or the cold might kill her.

A violent tremor shook her naked body as she stepped onto the snow-covered bank. She leaned against a boulder, holding her ample belly. Teeth chattering out of control, she peered furtively through the twilight rendered luminous by the white blanket draping the surrounding hills. She still couldn't sense or see anyone watching her. Too exhausted to shield herself with a glamour, she hoped everyone was indoors, warming by a fire.

Overhead loomed the cliff of the Bock, crowned by the new ramparts. At the sight of the light burning inside Sigefroi's square tower, Melusine wondered whether her lord awaited her return in anger. For the past three months, his temper had flared, increasing to barely restrained violence each time she returned from her escapades.

Dear Goddess, please soothe his impatient spirit.

Eyes closed and jaw clenched, Melusine struggled to control her shaking. She made a clumsy dash in the direction of the newly completed tunnel, leaving tracks in the virgin snow among the rocks strewn along the shore.

Slowed by her girth, Melusine reached the boulder concealing the opening at the bottom of the craggy cliff.

She squeezed behind it to slip into the cave-like entrance. The door further in the shadows creaked as she pushed it open. She quickly donned the sheep-skin slippers and fur-trimmed mantle she had left there on her way out. But even the thick garment didn't melt the chill in her aching bones.

Too exhausted to use magic, she struck flint to tinder. It took several attempts with frozen fingers to make a spark and light the torch in the sconce. Finally it flared. She closed and barred the door. Lifting the torch from the wall she reveled in its warmth. But she needed to hurry home, just in case that tremor was the baby coming.

Water dripped from the carved stone ceiling, and small night creatures scuttled underfoot as Melusine forged ahead. The torch flame flickered, barely penetrating the gloom. Soon, she reached the foot of a narrow snail-like stairwell that spiraled its way straight up to the castle's underground cellar.

A flash of pain through her swollen belly bent her over. Melusine cried out, momentarily blinded. A kick? Or a contraction? She remembered to breathe as she waited for the pain to recede.

Dear Goddess, please, not now.

She couldn't make any noise for fear of revealing the secret passage. Hundreds of stone steps rose inside the shaft above her, carved through the cliff. Like so many tests of her endurance... but the torch only lit a few of them. If her childbirth was near, more contractions would follow. She must hurry before the next onslaught.

At least, she no longer felt cold. Rivulets of sweat trickled down her back as she began the difficult ascent. Sudden warmth whooshed down her legs. Steamy liquid drenched her slippers and cascaded down the steps. Light-headed, Melusine hugged the wall for support.

One high step at a time, over and over, she kept climbing, focused on her goal. She must control the fear gripping her chest. She couldn't give birth alone in this rat-infested shaft. For the sake of her child, she had to reach the safety of her bedchamber.

A third of the way up, the next contraction caught her, but this time the intense pain made her crouch and grip her mid-section with a muffled cry. In her agony, she let go of the torch. It bounced down and down the steps in a flurry of sparks and echoed long after its light had sunk into the spiraling pit.

Complete darkness enveloped Melusine. Panic threatened to overcome her, but she controlled her breathing and eventually recovered from the harrowing contraction. She couldn't possibly go back all the way down to retrieve the torch in her weakened condition. She would have to manage without it.

Feeling her way in the dark along the roughly-hewn stone wall, she struggled up the steps. Another onslaught, then another, sapped her waning stamina. Gasping from the pain, she gritted her teeth and kept climbing, now crawling, panting and moaning like a wounded animal. Finding strength in desperation, she did not relent, even as her fingers and knees, raw from the rough stone, grew wet and sticky with blood.

"Hold on, little one," she murmured. "Don't come out quite yet." In such a state of fatigue, Melusine couldn't summon magic, but she could pray. "Dear Goddess, I beseech you, protect your rebellious disciple, but above all, protect my precious daughter fighting to come into this world."

Intent on her goal, Melusine lost track of time and contractions. When the stairs flattened out to a landing, relief flooded her and she sat in darkness, her back to the stone, for a short respite. The door to safety was close at hand.

But the child inside her demanded to be born. Painfully, she rose and felt for the handle, then tugged at the heavy door with a grunt. When it swung on well-oiled hinges, she knew she was in the wine cellar, but darkness reigned here, too.

Pushing the heavy door closed, she leaned her back against it with a sigh, then she pushed the bar locking the door from the inside. Safe.

She let her hand explore the shelf where she knew sat a candle. When she found it, she groped for the flint and struck it. Then she blew gently on the sparks to light the wick.

She sighed as a soft glow spread, lighting a row of clay bottles corked and sealed with red wax, couched in square wooden niches. The shelving lined the stone walls and rose in straight rows up to the arched ceiling.

Glad for the familiar surroundings, Melusine scanned the area. The Goddess be thanked, no one had seen her. Clenching her jaw, she straightened her frame and walked erect across the cellar. She still had to climb the last excruciating steps that led to the castle above. After sunset, everyone would be gathered in the knights' hall for the evening meal.

At the top of the stairs, Melusine crossed a servant girl on her way to the kitchen.

It was Alyx. "M'lady?"

"Get my maids to my bedchamber immediately." Melusine's voice sounded calmer than she felt.

Alyx regarded her mistress with unmasked horror. "M'lady, you are unwell!"

Of course, Melusine must look a fright. She couldn't help a humorless chuckle that prompted another contraction. "The baby's coming."

Melusine flinched and leaned against the wall, this time giving in to her agony with a long drawn-out moan that ended in a full-blown scream.

"Get the midwives!" Alyx shouted hysterically above the other women's screams, bringing around a buzz of help, as if she'd disrupted a beehive.

Strong arms came to support Melusine, and she thankfully yielded in exhaustion from the latest onset. While soothing words drifted to her ears, she offered no resistance when the women carried her to her bedchamber.

* * *

By morning, Melusine lay in a clean bed, with her tiny daughter suckling at her breast. Swaddled in soft linen and wrapped in wool for warmth, the child made small contented noises. A blaze crackled in the fireplace, and the soft glow of oil lamps lit the bedchamber on this gray winter day.

When the servants retreated toward the door, Melusine knew Sigefroi had arrived. She braced herself for his reaction.

The ring of his boot steps stopped at the edge of the thick rug covering the chamber floor. He stood there for a moment, imposing, as he took in the scene.

Melusine smiled feebly, but Sigefroi's gaze was riveted upon the gluttonous child feeding at her breast.

"A lady of your rank shouldn't be nursing," he said roughly.

"I know, but I so enjoy the feel of it." Melusine modulated her voice on purpose, shamelessly using her gifts to soothe his disappointment.

Curiously enough, Sigefroi calmed somewhat. At least, her powers seemed to be working fine. She remembered that her mother had lost her Fae gifts while in childbed, but it must have been part of her particular curse.

Sigefroi's expression softened. "I'll find a wet nurse."

Melusine offered an apologetic smile. "Sorry, it's not an heir, my lord, but a beautiful daughter to marry away and make alliances."

Sigefroi grunted. "So I heard."

The strong planes of his face relaxed a bit more as he approached the bed. The baby stopped suckling and stared up at him. Unlike most just born babes, this one didn't seem blind but wide awake.

Sigefroi peered into the innocent face. "Is she whole?"

"Aye, my lord." With one of her hands supporting the baby, Melusine closed her camisole with the other. "She is perfect in every way, strong and healthy, with much patience and grace... most unlike her father."

His laughter burst across the room. "Amen to that."

Although fathers rarely cared to name a daughter, Melusine offered. "What shall we name her?"

The tiny hands grappled at empty air and Sigefroi extended a stout finger to the baby's grip. "I haven't a name for a girl." He chuckled as the child strained to grasp his finger. "Do you?"

The sight of this fierce warrior charmed by an innocent babe prompted Melusine's smile. "I've been considering Liutgarde, a strong and noble name for a wise woman."

As if approving, the baby burped.

Sigefroi laugh softly. "Liutgarde of Luxembourg. It sounds regal. Liutgarde it will be, then. And since my brother Adalberon is coming to celebrate Yuletide with us, we should have her baptized at Christmas midnight mass."

Melusine swallowed hard and shivered despite the warm bed. Baptism meant holy water, the scourge of all Fae folks. It had been known to kill pure-blooded Fae. Even if Liutgarde survived baptism unscathed, it would deprive her of her Fae gifts, and longevity.

"So soon?" Melusine's throat constricted, strangling her voice. "It's only two days away."

Pride shone in Sigefroi's eyes. "What better occasion to present our newborn to our gathered vassals?"

He freed his finger, kissed his daughter's feathery head then brushed Melusine's lips. After a slight hesitation, Melusine returned the kiss. How she missed him. It had been weeks since they had spent any time together.

"You need your rest, sweet wife." Judging by the sheen of desire in his amber eyes, he had missed her, too. Sigefroi cleared his throat. "But you must be hungry. Fatherhood has left me famished, too! I'll have food brought to you from the hall."

He smiled to mother and child then retreated toward the door.

The babe in Melusine's arms now stared at the door, as if trying to understand. In her confusion, Melusine hadn't contested Sigefroi's decree of having her baptized, but panic now settled in.

133

"Dear Goddess, protect my child. I couldn't bear losing her to the baptismal font!"

Have no fear for your daughter. Melusine welcomed the reassuring voice of the Great One in her mind. Unlike you, Liutgarde can survive the ordeal. Only her longevity and her powers are at stake. Let her make her own choices. She is fully aware and wiser than you were as a child.

"I made my mistakes and I'm still paying for them." Melusine couldn't help the bitterness in her voice. She understood the cruelty of her past actions, and the guilt over punishing her father made her angry at herself.

Ask your daughter... the voice whispered, then silence filled the room. The Goddess had departed.

"Liutgarde," Melusine said softly, gazing into the baby's blue eyes. "Would you ever forgive me if I condemned you to a short life in a limited realm? Would you judge me harshly for depriving you of your Fae gifts?"

The child only burped in response.

"For you, baptism would mean no foreknowledge, no reading others' thoughts, no supernatural powers to help you out of dangerous situations, no centuries of experience accumulated in a single lifetime."

The child stared at her as if she understood.

Could Melusine subject her daughter to such a punishment? On the other hand, it also meant no abuse of power in childhood as it happened for Melusine and her sisters, no Fae curse, and no persecution by the Church. Liutgarde would live at peace among mortals, and hold a rightful place in this new order that now flourished in and around the Western Empire.

Do not fret, mother.

Surprised at the intrusion of another voice in her mind, Melusine stared at her daughter. The dark slits of the baby's eyes stared intently, as her tiny hands moved forward. She worked her lips, forming bubbles as if she struggled to speak, and the voice in Melusine's head rang clear and true.

I do not need immortality to serve the Goddess, mother. I can worship her as the Madonna if that's what

134

She wants. And you should know that we come back and live again. I'm not afraid of mortal life.

Tears rolled freely down Melusine's face. "Is it what you really want, little one? We will lose this wonderful link between us."

A sacrifice to make. Do not fear, mother. Whoever I become, as a Christian, the angel blood that flows in all Fae folks will still course in my veins. And so will it flow in my children, who will guide humanity on the path of wisdom.

"Aye, little one, I know that. Still, it's a great sacrifice to ask of a Fae."

Not so great as you think, mother. Liutgarde yawned and closed her dark blue eyes. I am tired and need to sleep.

As the baby's eyelids closed with long chestnut lashes, Melusine heard a contented sigh, then Liutgarde's breathing slowed to a peaceful rhythm while the small body relaxed in total abandon and drifted off to sleep.

Joy bubbled inside Melusine's chest. For once in her life, something felt right. "Thank you, Great One, for the gift of this wonderful child."

* * *

Christmas Eve 963

Melusine slipped into a gown of fur-trimmed green velvet, a pricey fabric imported from the southern reaches of the Empire. It would suit the formal ceremony. She shuddered with apprehension. Since Sigefroi had forbidden regular mass inside the castle, she had so far eluded contact with holy water. But today, even childbed confinement hadn't been excuse enough in Sigefroi's eyes. Everyone expected to gaze upon their noble mother and child on the Christian God's birthday.

Well, a few educated bishops probably knew that the Christian savior had been born in the spring to herald the age of Pisces. The Church marked the event at Yuletide only to prevent the Pagans from celebrating Saturnalia around the solstice, or the ancient Roman holiday of

December twenty-fifth, celebrating the birthday of the unconquerable sun.

Melusine checked herself in the small oval silver mirror. She had recovered quickly and presented a perfect image of health. Color had returned to her cheeks. By the glow of many oil lamps, she looked even prettier than the maiden she had been a year past.

The remaining plumpness also suited her. Only swollen breasts betrayed her recent ordeal, for she had insisted on feeding the child against Sigefroi's wishes. She wasn't ready to abandon her daughter to be raised by a stranger with the other castle children. She wanted little Liutgarde to remain at her side as long as possible.

Lovingly, Melusine looked upon her child dressed in embroidered white linen. The baby watched her every move in silence from inside her wicker basket. "No regrets, little one? Are you sure that's what you want?"

Do not fret, mother, I shall be fine.

Although Liutgarde's Fae blood was thinned by Sigefroi's ancestry, Melusine couldn't help imagining that contact with holy water must be painful still. Despite the many assurances that Liutgarde would be fine, her mind rebelled at the idea of subjecting an innocent babe to potential harm.

But she must comply. The Goddess ordered it, and it was her daughter's explicit will. The old soul in the baby's body had decided her own fate.

She pinned on her head the white veil that concealed her long flowing hair. "Ouch."

She'd pricked herself with the pin. Why was such a contrivance a requirement for women at high mass? She licked the drop of blood then she plucked the child from the basket.

Holding Liutgarde in her arms, she proceeded with trembling steps toward the council chamber, where the ceremony would take place, while the servants prepared the knights' hall for the lavish feast to follow.

* * *

Sigefroi repressed a smile as Adalberon's cool gaze scanned the council chamber, decorated with holly boughs and transformed for the occasion into a temporary place of worship.

"This arrangement is not acceptable for a knight of your stature." Adalberon, in purple robes and full ceremonial vestment, spread a parchment on the table that would serve as an altar. "This room, however spacious, is not properly consecrated for a baptism."

Sigefroi had anticipated his brother's comment. "We do have a small chapel dedicated to the Virgin Mary... a special request from Lady Melusine. But it wouldn't hold all the guests."

"You ought to build a decent church on the castle grounds, brother, even a cathedral. I know you can afford it." Adalberon paused, as if to give weight to his words. "His Holiness would be glad to place a bishop in residence here as a spiritual guide. God knows you and your flock need one. I could recommend a friend."

"No, Adalberon." Sigefroi considered his brother coldly. Although he loved his sibling, he would not tolerate religious interference in his affairs. "No bishop will flourish in my lands to dictate how I live my life and rule my domain. And I'll certainly not have one in my home. I thought I made myself clear on that matter."

"Such sacrilegious words!" The tone could be misconstrued as a jest, but Adalberon was not smiling. "Were you not my brother, I might take umbrage and report you to the pope in Rome."

"Since when does a brother of mine take religion so seriously?" Sigefroi searched Adalberon's familiar face. They had a lifetime of brotherly trust behind them. "You would never dare betray me."

"Of course not... unless it is for your own salvation. After all, it is my responsibility to see my brothers in the fold of Holy Mother Church." Adalberon returned to his parchment and wrote in a fluid and regular script. "For the proper recording of your daughter's baptism, what is your wife's Christian name, and the name of her godparents?"

Taken aback, Sigefroi masked his confusion with practiced assurance. "It never came up. She only mentioned Melusine of Strathclyde."

"I know of no Christian saint by that name." Adalberon arched a questioning brow. "Could it be possible that she was never baptized?"

"How could you entertain such a notion?" The thought had never occurred to Sigefroi, but deep inside, it bothered him not to know. "A woman of her education, who speaks fluent Latin and Greek and has read all the sacred texts, couldn't possibly be a heathen."

"Aye." Adalberon's unsettling gaze fixed on Sigefroi. "Yet, I heard of stranger happenstance. We live in a world where all is not always as it appears, brother. Remember that Lucifer once was God's brightest angel. He can still radiate great light to seduce the best among us."

Heat rose to Sigefroi's face. "Don't you dare compare my wife to the devil!"

Arriving Yuletide guests gathered and stood in polite conversation, only a few steps away from the altar.

From the back of the room, Gunter in full knight regalia, wearing his father's coat of arms, motioned to Sigefroi, catching his attention.

Sigefroi nodded in understanding and turned to Adalberon. "Here she comes with the baby. She can give you the answers you seek."

Among the crowd of guests, Sigefroi watched Melusine make her way toward him, displaying the baby for the growing crowd of curious guests, answering good wishes and compliments with her most charming smile.

When she reached the two brothers, Sigefroi elbowed Adalberon's arm. "Go ahead, ask her!"

"Ask me what?" Melusine set her precious load on the altar table, next to the Bishop's miter, then, as if having an afterthought, she took the child back into her arms.

Adalberon remained silent. Was he shocked by Melusine's casualness at the altar?

"Melusine," Sigefroi cleared his voice. "Adalberon wants to know your Christian saint name and that of your godparents. I could not remember you ever mentioning them."

Did he imagine it, or did Melusine pale at the simple question?

"Oh, that?" Her disarming smile erased any doubt Sigefroi might have had about her innocence. "We have so many local saints in Strathclyde, Your Grace, I'm not surprised you never heard of Sainte Melusine. Her humble deeds probably never reached all the way to Rome. And the tradition of giving godparents is just starting in my native land, a hundred years behind the times, I'm afraid. I never had any godparents myself."

"Really?" Adalberon's superior attitude poisoned the warm ambiance. "Then, who saw to your religious education, my child?"

"My mother, my aunt, and the congregation of holy women who raised me." Melusine sounded candid as a young maiden.

"A convent?" Adalberon looked her over with subtle disapproval. "No wonder you are too educated for a woman."

Sigefroi chose to ignore the derogatory comment. "There, are you satisfied, brother?"

"Aye... for now." As if avoiding Sigefroi's gaze, Adalberon dutifully recorded on his parchment the information imparted.

* * *

Toward the end of high mass, after communion, the Bishop motioned the nobles to come to the side of the room where a deep stone basin stood on a pedestal. It was full of holy water, an abomination by Fae standards.

The contrivance scared Melusine more than slow painful death. She'd heard that on rare occasions, holy water had been said to melt the flesh from the bones of Fae

139

folks. She shuddered at the thought then reminded herself the Goddess had promised Liutgarde would be fine.

Melusine was glad she wouldn't have to hold her daughter over the baptismal font. Traditionally, Liutgarde's godparents would.

Hiding her growing dread, she handed her daughter to Gunter, the child's godfather, and followed at a safe distance while the guests formed a wide circle around the baptismal font.

Since the godmother, the Duchess of High Lorraine, wife of Frederick, could not attend, Lady Alyx, of Melusine's entourage took her place at Gunter's side. Melusine and Sigefroi stood behind them, but Adalberon motioned the parents to come closer.

Melusine resisted Sigefroi's pull on her arm and held back.

"What's the matter?" Sigefroi raised an eyebrow.

"Nothing... I just feel faint." Melusine forced a weak smile.

"You look a little pale. Come here, I'll support you. You don't want to miss our daughter's baptism." Firmly supporting her arm and her waist, Sigefroi led her to the edge of the basin, much too close for Melusine's comfort.

In an effort to master her fear, she concentrated on her daughter's face.

Liutgarde seemed serene and unafraid. When Adalberon dropped a grain of salt on her tongue, she grimaced, to the delight of the assembled guests. Then, the bishop dipped one hand in the water basin, reciting the Latin ritual.

Among the flames of the tallow candles reflecting in the still water of the baptismal font, Melusine perceived movement. Suddenly, the water came alive, as when she consulted her divining basin, and a scene of pure horror overwhelmed her vision.

The din of battle assailed her senses. Weapons clunked, men screamed, horses shrieked and pounded the wet earth. Melusine smelled smoke, sweat, and the sweet sickening scent of blood. Among the carnage lit by a blazing village, Sigefroi in battle gear rode his destrier like a bloody demon, hacking off hands, ears and noses.

Riveted, Melusine watched as crimson swirls tainted the waters of an unknown river. On the strange shores, the Knight of Luxembourg wielded Caliburn, mercilessly massacring and maiming unarmed men, women, and children! The victims begged for mercy, but Sigefroi showed none. His cruel face exuded pure hatred, as if he were possessed by the dark angel himself.

"No!" Melusine gasped when Gunter dipped Liutgarde's crown of soft chestnut hair into the blood bath of the baptismal font where the battle raged. The child looked like a white lamb sacrificed to her father's unholy wrath. The baby struggled and cried, splashing Melusine's left hand with a tiny drop. Melusine jerked her hand back. Her flesh sizzled briefly, and she cried out at the searing pain.

Sigefroi turned to support her, but Melusine stepped back. All she could see of her husband was the bloody face of a ruthless killer. Her muffled scream barely reached her ears as she slowly collapsed to the flagstone, blind and on the brink of losing consciousness.

Chapter Ten

Luxembourg castle, Easter, 964

Melusine shivered in the embrasure of her open window. The unusual activity in the bailey down below attested to her imminent departure for Trier with Sigefroi. Servants loaded the carts with Melusine and Sigefroi's personal effects, and with the heavy chests containing the gold to purchase their new domain and build their second castle.

Uniformed guards wearing Luxembourg's coat of arms formed the columns that would escort their convoy. Melusine stroked the tiny white scar above her left thumb where holy water had burned a small hole. It still hurt on cold days. The chilly dawn matched her state of mind. She had no desire to travel.

Since Liutgarde's baptism, Melusine had kept to her bedchamber, weak and exhausted all the time. Everyone attributed her weakness to the birth, but she knew better. She left her bed only on the days when she stole to the river through the extended secret passages. She had been too weak to supervise the construction, the digging, or even the day to day running of the castle.

One tiny drop of holy water at Liutgarde's baptism had sapped her strength and damaged her powers. They'd become faint, erratic and unwieldy. Melusine wondered whether or not they would ever return to their past brilliance.

And what of her immortality? The Goddess had remained suspiciously silent on the subject. An opportunity to explore your own humanity, she'd suggested.

Ever since the fated baptism, Melusine's life had been miserably dull and lonely.

After the vision in the baptismal font, nightmares of the same bloody massacre had haunted her sleep. When the dreams finally relented, she could have returned to her husband's bed but didn't have the heart to try, afraid to see blood on his face in their most intimate moments.

How she missed him, though. Sigefroi had respected her reluctance to share his bed on account of her weakened state. After the first refusal, he had chosen to ignore her. Now she felt sorry for rejecting him.

Melusine couldn't possibly explain to this man who loved her the aversion brought by a vision of his senseless slaughter of innocents. He would deem her deranged... or worse. While avoiding her, he kept busy with construction, overseeing his estates, riding out to annex a neighboring village, or defend his new lands from pesky warlords and roaming brigands.

Over the past weeks, however, Melusine's repugnance for Sigefroi had faded away. She reasoned that not all visions of the future came true, and she fervently hoped this one wouldn't. In any case, it wasn't fair to hate him for a crime he hadn't committed yet, and might never commit.

Little Liutgarde provided no comfort. The baby had shunned her mother's breast since her baptism and now thrived on the nursemaid's milk, throwing a fit whenever in Melusine's presence. Could Fae milk poison a mortal child? Could the baby hate her mother's very nature, like the rest of Christendom? Or did her daughter resent the loss of her own powers?

Isolated from those she loved, Melusine had lost her happy disposition. She felt hollow, like an abandoned husk after the threshing, useless, dejected, and utterly alone. Perhaps a change of scenery would rekindle her interest for life.

"Are you ready, my lady?" Alyx, the smart young girl who had become her personal servant, didn't seem affected by Melusine's morose mood and had insisted she wear a bright yellow riding dress. "Our lord master is awaiting you at the stables with your mare."

The mention of the white mare brought a sunny thought. Was it only a year ago that Melusine had thundered down the hillside in full armor to give Sigefroi his first defeat? The memory awakened a passion for life she hadn't felt in months. She had enjoyed the fight, wielding the magic blade and winning.

In those carefree days, the future lay full of promise. Now, she feared she would never feel that way again. She missed her baby so much... Melusine could only imagine the torment her own mother had suffered in banishing her three daughters.

As she followed Alyx outside, Melusine noticed the red and white banners fluttering in the pale dawn from the top of the new battlements and square towers. Sigefroi had followed her drawings perfectly in finishing the ramparts. She was proud of him for recognizing superior design and completing the task to perfection.

"Be careful with that, don't hurt your back!" Melusine told the menservants carrying the heavy trunk full of silver and gold for the purchase of the new estate.

"Not to worry, m'lady," one puffed, then they hoisted the oak coffer onto the cart.

Surveying the bailey, Melusine spotted the wet nurse bringing Liutgarde to say farewell. Her heart filled with timid hope. Grateful that the woman had risen early to see her off with the baby, she smiled, then changed course to meet them half way.

The wet nurse walked toward her slowly, her head bent under her hooded mantle, as if not to awaken the child. As she neared them, Melusine saw the face of the little bundle the woman carried. Liutgarde slept peacefully, like the angel she truly was.

It had happened many times before. The child looking peaceful as long as she didn't detect her mother's presence. Melusine bit her lips. Did she dare wake the baby? Maybe just this once, the little one wouldn't reject her? With a mother's tender touch, she brushed a finger to the child's cheek.

Liutgarde's eyelids flew open. Something akin to fear flashed in her blue-green eyes, then she fussed and her mouth contorted.

"No, please, little one, don't be afraid of me." But Melusine's words faded with her hope.

The child squirmed in the nurse's arms and bellowed, struggling to escape on her own. Heads turned around them. Melusine felt ashamed by her child's rejection. Was she an unworthy mother?

There was no point in denying that Liutgarde refused any dealings with her mother. Melusine had already tried to impose her presence on the child long enough to wear out her protests, like when taming wild animals... to no avail.

On those instances, Liutgarde had cried herself to exhaustion, only to fall asleep and wake up to more screaming. The baby also refused to feed in Melusine's presence, even from the wet nurse, and would have let herself die of starvation rather than remain close to her mother.

Melusine regretfully gestured to the wet nurse to leave. Her throat constricted as she swallowed the lump in her throat. Her eyes filled with unshed tears, and a familiar sadness tugged at her chest. As much as she loved her daughter, she must let her go, for the child's sake.

It was unseemly for ruling families to raise their own children anyway, but Melusine would have liked a chance at knowing her daughter. Longingly, she watched the nurse walk away around the corner of the guardhouse.

Alyx, who now reached Melusine, gently took her arm. "Come, m'lady. Babies don't know what's good for them. She'll grow out of that phase, you'll see..."

"Thank you, Alyx, for your kind words. I fervently hope she does."

With some reluctance, Melusine let herself be led. When the two women reached the stables, Sigefroi straightened and dismissed his captain with a brief command. Standing beside the white mare, he eyed

145

Melusine warily, as if expecting trouble, and she wondered whether he had seen what had just happened. Then again, how could he have missed it?

His gaze softened, and other emotions flooded his face. Compassion? Love? Longing? A warm smile etched his strong features. Immediately, Melusine felt a little better and attempted a smile of her own.

The effect on Sigefroi was instantaneous. His grin widened as he gave the mare's reins to a lad to help her mount. Pleased by the attention, Melusine nevertheless let out a sigh upon noticing the side-saddle.

"I know you'd prefer to mount astride, dear wife." Sigefroi winked then hoisted her unceremoniously upon the mare. "But the Bishop of Trier would look upon it as a serious breach of etiquette, and we don't want to upset him before he sells us Saarburg."

His hand lingered on her thigh. Melusine wanted him to keep it there, but he let go when Thierry approached, leading Sigefroi's black stallion.

The squire had grown in the past months and looked gangly. His clear gaze strayed toward Alyx as he handed the warhorse to his master. Melusine smiled inwardly. How could she have missed the budding attraction between these two? Even her keen sense of observation had slipped. The two youngsters looked happy, in the early stages of falling in love.

Sigefroi vaulted onto his stallion with the agility of a feline. Melusine admired his skills with the horses. What a formidable rider, an invincible warrior, and a great lover. It had been too long since they'd joined in a tender embrace. She fiercely missed him.

Gunter rode toward them, flushed and excited as usual at the prospect of new adventures. "All is ready!"

Sigefroi nodded then turned to Melusine with a confident smile that warmed her heart. "Are you certain you want to come along? Trier is only the first step... Once we acquire Saarburg, we'll have to make it flourish like we did Luxembourg. We won't be home again for at least a year."

"I'm ready for a change." She kept her voice light. "I need to forget the past months and make a fresh start. Organizing a new castle will remind me of our early days. It should help me heal." So would his tender ministrations, if he were so inclined, but she didn't voice the thought.

The long day trek proved uneventful, punctuated by the barking of hounds, the creaking of heavy wheels, the clicking of harnesses, chain mail, and weapons. Messengers ran to and fro along the convoy. The constant bantering of Sigefroi and Gunter about past battle feats reminded Melusine of the haunting vision of carnage she was trying to forget.

But once in a while, as she rode behind Sigefroi, he turned in the saddle and ventured a grin. Despite his daunting looks, there was a winning warmth to him, a charm she could not resist. These moments of intimate exchange compensated for the discomfort of the side-saddle.

The convoy reached Trier just after sunset. While the escort found lodging in town, Sigefroi and Melusine boarded for the night at St Maximin, the abbey where they would seal the deed two days hence. Travel weary, Melusine sought her private cell and had supper brought there.

A knock on the door much later that evening surprised her, since Alyx had retired for the night. Melusine slid the thin plaque covering the knot hole in the door and peeped through. Sigefroi stood there, smiling.

Uncertain what to expect but glad for the visit, Melusine opened the door wide.

He hesitated on the threshold. Never had she seen him so unsure of himself. "I grew bored with the monks' conversation."

Melusine invited him in then sat on the hard pallet. "Lord Husband, do I detect a lie in the tone of your voice?"

Sigefroi dropped into the only chair in the small room and drummed long fingers on the armrest. "Aye? Well, truth be told, your company is more entertaining." His tone regained some of its natural confidence and his gaze roamed shamelessly over her night chemise. "This yellow dress you wore today got me thinking we neglected our nuptial duties."

Melusine perked up, teasing. "Duty, is it?" Her attempt to breach the distance between them felt gauche, inadequate. "It has been a while..."

"We need sons, remember? And you look to me way too thin." He propped a booted foot up on the prayer stool and grinned wolfishly. "I must keep my promise to keep you with child at all times."

The mention of another child made Melusine wince. On second thought, however, the Goddess had ordered it. Perhaps it would make her feel whole again... a child who, unlike Liutgarde, would love his mother.

Had Sigefroi anticipated her need? His insight frightened her sometimes. Did he manipulate her like a young maid? Why did he remain so distant if he weren't playing a game? Her weakened powers since the baptism had left Melusine defenseless. She had to rely on human senses, blind to others' thoughts and intents. Not that she'd ever read Sigefroi's mind.

He regarded her intently but remained in the chair. "I remember our early love-making, wild and passionate, hot as an inferno."

Melusine flushed at the thought. Was he waiting for her to make the first move? Tentatively, she stood up and went to warm herself by the fire, closer to his chair but still beyond his reach.

"You chose a strange place to rekindle our flame." She smiled, matching his playful tone. "What would the holy monks think about using a friar's cell for our nightly pleasures? The pallet is small and hard as a board, and these walls have only witnessed silent prayer."

Sigefroi's amber eyes shone in the light of the flames and his voice grew husky. "We'll have to make do and be quiet, is all."

Anticipation rushed through Melusine. Although she felt stalked, she approached the chair like a willing prey then laid a light hand on Sigefroi's shoulder.

148

She bent to whisper in his ear. "I've never known our bed games to be silent, my lord."

Seizing her wrist, he brought her hand to his lips, pulled her in front of him, snatched her waist and sat her on his lap. Melusine gasped at the commanding strength of his hands but did not resist. The heat she felt owed nothing to the fire and everything to the hard fullness in Sigefroi's chausses.

"The devil with the friars," he whispered harshly, then sealed her intended reply with a passionate kiss.

Melusine gladly forgot her words and responded to his demanding kiss in kind. Her mind swirled at the urgency in his possession of her mouth... so willful, like a conqueror.

When he relented and trailed his lips along her jaw line and down her throat, she moaned with anticipation. The heat at her core could not be denied. How she wanted him.

He grabbed her tight and rose from the chair, lifting her up in his arms. Melusine purred as she hooked her arms around his corded neck. She leaned her head against his hard chest, and he carried her to the small pallet.

When he deposited her there, she didn't let go of him. She pulled him close on top of her, enjoying the weight of his body, his breath in her hair. She reveled in the possessive way he held her, as if he'd never let go. It didn't matter that the mattress was thin and hard. All she could think about was this magnificent lion in her bed, who wanted her as much as she wanted him.

* * *

The next morning as she walked the abbey's corridors at Sigefroi's arm, Melusine couldn't erase the blissful smile from her face. The monks diverted their gaze from her as they passed them by on the way to the refectory. Because she was a woman, or because of the unseemly sounds that had escaped her cell the night before?

Suppressing a giggle, she recalled how, when the bells rang for matins, muffled footfalls had passed their door on the way to the chapel, but Sigefroi, far from slowing down, had renewed his ardor and made her moan even louder.

At least, her husband wasn't a Christian zealot afraid of breaking the rules. Perhaps, one day, Melusine would confide in him after all. Sharing her Pagan secret would certainly alleviate some of her burden and possibly strengthen their love.

In any case, she felt much better this morning. There was hope in her life again. The horrible visions of Sigefroi killing children had faded farther in her memory, and perhaps, in time, Liutgarde would even learn to love her.

Over breakfast, the abbot regarded Melusine suspiciously but wouldn't dare reprimand his overlord over such a personal matter. Despite the severity of monastic rules, exceptions had to be made for valorous knights. After all, Sigefroi was the abbey's noble champion and protector.

The sealing of the deed giving Saarburg to Sigefroi would take place on the morrow in the abbey's great hall, so Melusine and her lord had the day to themselves. They enjoyed the morning at the Roman baths, like newlyweds, as Sigefroi had promised long ago. After the midday meal, they recruited laborers and purchased supplies for their future castle.

As they returned to the abbey in the afternoon hours Melusine didn't have the heart to remind Sigefroi that the morrow was the first Wednesday of the month. She refused to spoil their fragile reconciliation. She hoped he'd remember the day of the week as soon as he realized she was gone, and concoct a believable story for the abbot. After all that was their arrangement.

* * *

Before sunset, while Sigefroi sampled wine with the abbot in the hall, Melusine discreetly left the monastery. She hurried along the Roman fortifications and passed the Porta Nigra, the imposing Roman gate of Trier, then walked briskly toward the setting sun, in the direction of the Moselle River.

150

As she surveyed the unfamiliar shores, the smell of the tar coating the boat hulls drifted from the pier, where the activity had slowed. The river flowed lazily, wide and deep, unlike the Alzette. Hoping the shaky glamour concealing her would hold long enough, Melusine walked north along the bank, away from the bridge, toward a flat strip of land that formed an island off shore.

As soon as she found a secluded area, she disrobed and hid her clothes in a hollow tree trunk, then she entered the chilly waters. Although she could tell her glamour still held, she glanced around, acutely aware of the added dangers of unfamiliar surroundings.

Just as the sun disappeared behind the rolling hills across the river, Melusine drifted into its cool dark depths. Within minutes, her serpent tail responded as she flicked it, then she propelled herself upstream to reconnoiter her future estate.

Nervous at the idea of swimming through such a populated area, Melusine remained deep underwater while passing the pier and the bridge. It wouldn't do to let the good people of Trier surprise an ondine in their midst.

Several miles south, Melusine came to the confluence of the Saar River, took a turn and swam up river, until she smelled the strong acrid stink of the tannery described by the abbot that morning.

By moonlight she saw a waterfall cleaving the hill in a silvery shower where the turbulent stream of the Leuk joined the Saar River. Most importantly, she wanted to see Mount Chumberlum where her future castle would stand.

As she scanned the hilly banks, her eye caught the highest point to the south, not a sheer cliff like the Bock of Luxembourg, but just as high and very steep. From up there, one could survey the entire valley, and the boat traffic on the river.

A strategic location indeed. Once again, Sigefroi had chosen well. Melusine could already envision hilltop towers facing the river, a high wall lining the crag on all sides. The castle would also need a moat at the base of the hill. Possibly the Leuk River could serve to fill it.

Digging the well might present a challenge, but Melusine could convince Sigefroi to do it. Every castle needed its own well.

Melusine smiled. today she'd experienced a new surge of energy, the likes of which she hadn't known since the ordeal at the baptismal font three moons past. And today, she had conjured her glamour easily enough. She now believed her powers would flourish again.

* * *

Sigefroi resented Melusine's absence at the signing of the deed. Damn the little hellcat! She'd done it again, leaving without warning on her ridiculous pilgrimage.

"Sorry, Lady Melusine is slightly indisposed today." Sigefroi hope they would think his prowess in bed had exhausted his wife.

The abbot smiled from across the table. Did he have reason to doubt the lie?

"What a pity." Archbishop Henri of Verdun commiserated. "I so wanted to make her acquaintance."

"Well, she is sorry to miss such an important event." Sigefroi struggled to remain calm, but he seethed inside.

In truth, Melusine would have enjoyed the bargaining and appreciated Sigefroi's political skills. Despite his rage, he managed to smile at the right time to the right people. He looked genuinely concerned when notified of a potential problem, while all along he was playing their game of intrigue.

The deliberations lasted longer than Sigefroi anticipated.

"I added this clause." Quite the old fox, Archbishop Henri had waited until everything was settled to make further demands. "Within the year, a castle must be built on Mount Chumberlum to oversee and protect the Saar valley, and Lord Sigefroi must man the fortress with a capable garrison at all times."

Sigefroi sighed. Although the prelate was receiving a fair price in gold, Saarburg now came with an added responsibility to the Church and to the people of Trier. Still, The Church constituted a valuable ally. But Sigefroi wouldn't let the archbishop get away with his sneaky maneuvers. "This costly condition demands compensation."

Archbishop Henri smiled. "I knew you would say that, so I'm adding to the bargain a large vineyard on a well exposed hillock."

Sigefroi nodded. The archbishop knew him well after all. "How can I refuse a vineyard?"

* * *

The signing of the deed had gone mostly according to plan, and Sigefroi rejoiced as he ambled along the cloister. Pleased with his acquisition, he turned into an alcove and pushed open the door to St Maximin's library.

As he entered, a monk cleared his throat, breaking the studious silence. The place smelled of polished wood, parchment, and ink. Bent over pulpits fronting the windows of the scriptorium area, friars, quill in hand, copied and illuminated sacred texts on parchment with elaborate and colorful designs.

All around them, precious books and scrolls covered the walls up to the Roman arches. Around the thick pillars, cabinets and coffers overflowed with ancient scrolls, some dating from antiquity.

But the religious books were not what Sigefroi sought this afternoon. He was after something more mundane, the genealogy of the rulers of Strathclyde. Since the baptism and Melusine's indisposition, many questions had sprouted in his mind, from his bishop brother, Adalberon, and from Sigefroi's desire to understand his wife. Learning about Melusine's family might clear the mystery.

The friar bibliothec displayed an ingratiating smile. "How may I help your visit to our humble library, my lord?"

"Just point me in the direction of genealogies of royal dynasties." Sigefroi didn't want to say too much or arouse suspicion. "I need to refresh my memory on some remote family members."

The old friar bowed then glided quietly on leather sandals across the flagstone, motioning Sigefroi to follow. They negotiated a path around pillars and long tables loaded with scrolls. Then the friar halted in front of a wall lined with books and rolled parchments from floor to ceiling.

"This is our genealogy section." The monk motioned toward the shelves and the tall ladder. "The books are arranged by country and locality. The parchments on the top shelf are piled in a jumble, I'm afraid, and not all in good condition."

Sigefroi nodded his thanks, and the friar glided away as quietly as a wraith.

The search for the dynasty of Strathclyde proved more frustrating than Sigefroi anticipated. He found nothing in the books. Finally, climbing the ladder to reach the upper shelves, he sorted through the rolled parchments in hopes of finding something... anything.

His perseverance was rewarded in the form of a very old skin, gray and brittle with age that said only Strathclyde. Blowing the dust off the scroll, Sigefroi unrolled it on a nearby table and sat. The document, poorly scratched in bad Latin, emanated from a Benedictine monk sent to Strathclyde by the emperor Charlemagne himself.

The monk's account stunk of legend and sorcery. According to this doubtful record, King Elinas, whom Melusine claimed was her father, had disappeared a century and a half ago, after retiring and leaving his crown to a son named Conan, who could not prevent the famine and disease that afflicted his reign and eventually destroyed his kingdom.

An even more unbelievable tale related that the old king's Pagan queen, Pressine, was spirited away on a cloud with her three baby daughters, shortly after giving birth, never to be seen again.

What did this mean? Head in his hands, Sigefroi could feel a headache coming.

On further search, he found a small book that included a less than complete list of rulers of Strathclyde mentioning Elinas and his sons, one of which, Mattacks, was burned at the stake upon Charlemagne's order, for triggering a Pagan curse. To Sigefroi's dismay, the genealogy confirmed the dates implied by the Benedictine monk's scroll. Either Melusine was a century and a half old, or she was an imposter.

Giving way to a flare of frustration, Sigefroi slammed the massive oak table, jolting the precious documents.

Alerted by the sound, the friar bibliothec rushed toward Sigefroi, shifty eyes darting right and left. "Anything amiss, my lord?"

Sigefroi couldn't contain his anger. "These old records are less than complete."

The monk considered the badly damaged skin. "I'm afraid many documents of that time were destroyed by Viking raids, my lord. That's all we could salvage from that collection."

"That's not enough!"

"My lord, zealous friars incurred great dangers to preserve these precious testimonies." The friar bent his head. "I apologize for their incomplete and damaged state."

"So you should."

The old monk crossed himself and retreated quickly.

Sigefroi exerted all his control not to rip the scroll and book to shreds. Did the little hellcat play him for the fool? Who was she, and what did she want with him? He felt used, manipulated. Sigefroi couldn't stand being played.

Should he believe dusty records, or the woman he loved? For he knew now that he had fallen hopelessly in love with her. She occupied his mind so completely that he couldn't imagine bedding any other. He'd remained chaste while she was indisposed and had only her well-being in mind.

He hadn't imposed his personal needs upon her. Until last night, which had proven particularly rewarding, when Melusine had come to him of her own volition. He never felt happier than when he was with her.

Melusine had brought him wealth, given him a family. She supported his ambitions and spurred him on to become powerful and respected. She'd even designed his fortress. How could he doubt her against a dusty scroll? She had great personal wealth and beauty and didn't need him. Did she do all this for love? Or did she have darker motives? But he couldn't imagine what these other motives could be.

Sigefroi always suspected that Melusine had lied to him in some measure. Did he dare confront her with his discovery? His blood cooled at the idea that he could lose her in the bargain. No. He would rather face the fiercest enemy on the battlefield than endanger this fragile happiness. After all, what did it matter if she wasn't a princess? As long as no one else found out...

Besides, Melusine had already gone through so much. Her recent malady proved her vulnerability. And the fact that her own child rejected her must be a terrible ordeal. He'd seen how the brat's tantrum in the bailey had saddened her.

Aye, Sigefroi would keep quiet and find the answers on his own, or wait until she chose to tell him the truth. Knowing her shrewd and uncompromising character, she must have good reasons to keep secrets from him. Even when, like today, her escapades placed him in a difficult situation.

But if Melusine wasn't a princess, where did all the riches come from? A more sinister thought entered his mind. What if she truly were King Elinas' daughter? Didn't she say her mother's name was Pressine? Could it be the Pagan queen of the Benedictine's tale?

And what powers really lay inside Caliburn? Sigefroi touched the bejeweled hilt of the miraculous sword she'd given him. He felt the familiar tingle, as if the blade wanted to reassure him. He couldn't imagine not wearing that sword. He'd feel exposed and vulnerable carrying any other blade.

Not bothering to look around, Sigefroi tucked the incriminating scroll and the small book under his arm. The scandalized monks didn't dare stop the irate and armed knight who marched away with the abbey's archives. After all he was their champion and protector.

Sigefroi barged out of the library, slamming the heavy door behind him.

An inexplicable shiver coursed between his shoulders as he headed for his cell, but he refused to give in to fear. Only weaklings believed in Pagan Fae curses, making excuses for their shortcomings. Whoever she was, Melusine pleased him. She also served his ambitions, and he wanted her near. Soon, he would extract the truth from her, but all in due course. For now, he would bide his time.

* * *

When Melusine returned after sunset, to her surprise, Sigefroi didn't berate her. As a matter of fact, he seemed very understanding, but this sudden change of heart made her wonder. What game was he playing now? She knew how charming he could be when he put his mind to it. What did he want? This new behavior made her uncomfortable. She didn't know what to make of his pondering watchfulness.

Over the next few days, they gathered supplies to start building the new castle and they oversaw the loading of the goods on barges at the pier. Melusine had seen the heavy boats during her escapade and knew how sluggishly they would travel under oar against the current. Still, it would carry the supplies on a smoother ride than ox carts on rutted trails through hilly terrain.

After Sigefroi sent off the barges, Gunter rode ahead with Thierry and the escort to wait for the boats at their destination. They would prepare temporary quarters in Saarburg and unload the barges upon arrival.

Sigefroi and Melusine remained at the abbey a few more days, enjoying the comforts of the Roman city of Trier, and shocking the monks with their nightly love games. By the time they left St Maximin, Melusine had fully recovered from months of apathy. She looked forward to riding through the rolling hills with only Sigefroi for companion. He'd even agreed to let her mount astride.

Laughing like newlyweds, they raced through the woods and along the green slopes fragrant with lily of the valley. The sun glinted off Sigefroi's mail as they rode on, making plans for the castle they would build. But besides the love she saw in his startling eyes, Melusine detected unusual keenness, as if he watched her every move.

Could he have guessed she was with child again? No, it was too early... but this time around, Sigefroi would enjoy fatherhood, for Melusine's returning powers told her the baby growing in her womb was a boy.

Chapter Eleven

The new castle of Saarburg, two years later, spring of 966

In the festive bailey, Melusine directed the servants carrying baskets of fresh lettuce and eggs to the kitchen. Looking toward the stables, she spotted her maid in an intimate embrace with Thierry in the doorway.

"Alyx!"

Thierry's head came up. He grinned and let go of Alyx then quickly ducked into the stables. Alyx blushed as she walked toward Melusine and wiped her mouth with the back of her hand. She flashed a radiant smile and smoothed a strand of blond hair. "M'lady?"

Melusine had to force a serious tone. "You are spending too much time with this gallant of yours. Today of all days, leave the boy alone! Or I'll tell Lord Sigefroi to give him more chores."

Alyx curtsied. "Aye, m'lady. What can I do for you?"

The lass now looked like a grown woman, and Melusine suspected a baby grew in her belly. The two lovers would have to be married soon. The Church would frown at a child out of wedlock in Sigefroi's castle. They made a cute couple, though. Thierry had developed into somewhat of a hot head, but Alyx would temper his excesses with common sense and reason.

"Young Thierry better straighten up before the emperor arrives." Melusine remembered Sigefroi mentioning how strict Otto could be regarding neat appearance and etiquette. "The great man frowns upon disheveled subjects, especially on such an important day."

Alyx blushed some more. "Sorry, m'lady."

"Right now, I need you at the nursery with my babes." Melusine said my babes with pride.

She smiled as she watched Alyx hurry toward the keep. She considered herself blessed. Little Henri already walked and played with the castle children. Frederick, only two months old, was Melusine's greatest joy. Of course, her oldest and only daughter, Liutgarde, still threw tantrums at her very sight, so she remained away at Luxembourg castle, where a nun saw to her education. That child hated her, and Melusine knew she always would.

"Gunter," Melusine called as she saw the brawny knight inspecting a guard's red and white uniform. "Did you check the cellar for Otto's favorite wine?"

Gunter straightened his green silk tunic as he glanced up and grinned. "Aye, m'lady. I picked the perfect wine for today's feast. It will be just ripe to go with the lamb and the honey cooked apples."

"Thank you, old friend." Now, Melusine needed to get dressed before the emperor arrived.

As she gazed up, she saw Sigefroi atop the battlement, surveying the road. He fidgeted slightly as if he were nervous. Of course only Melusine could detect it.

As if he'd sensed her eyes on him, Sigefroi turned and looked down at her from afar. Melusine melted under his stare. Sigefroi had been wonderful of late. Never again had he challenged her dreaded Wednesdays, even when Melusine had grown heavy and close to birthing, and she loved him for it. He seemed more attentive to her needs and often asked for her advice.

Only once in a while did she catch him watching her, like now, a serious expression on his face. Did he suspect something of her secret? She fervently hoped he didn't, but if he did, he never mentioned anything to her, and she saw no other sign of it.

* * *

From the battlement, Sigefroi watched Melusine enter the keep. He turned toward the road as the convoy of his most important guests slowly ascended the hill.

Around him, the white and red pennants of Luxembourg hung from the ramparts, fluttering in the light spring breeze along with the blue and white imperial banners. Battle horns announced the noble visitors come to perform the knighting ceremony. Although the emperor would only stay the day, it was the first time Sigefroi hosted his illustrious friend. Would everything be to Otto's refined taste?

More familiar with the battlefield than with the niceties of high society, Sigefroi had relied on Melusine to supervise the preparations for the festivities. She had proven a great organizer. This marvelous woman of his kept his castles and domains well supplied and in good working order. She gave everyone a task, and even the most vindictive men contributed with enthusiasm whenever she asked. Sigefroi congratulated himself for such an efficient wife.

Only one thought marred his bliss. Last week, a merchant boat reported an ondine in the Saar River. Sigefroi didn't believe in ondines, but from the description, he suspected that Melusine might have been the woman bathing nude in the chilly waters. The sighting happened on the first Wednesday of the month, when his wife should have been praying to the Virgin Mary.

Although Sigefroi didn't quite believe Melusine's story about her monthly devotions, he couldn't come up with a better explanation. Briefly he had her followed, but she had eluded his best spies.

In time, Sigefroi had resigned himself to the fact that his wife harbored a secret and he left it at that. If he pushed the issue, he might discover she wasn't fit for him, and he couldn't afford to lose the best asset of his financial, political and emotional life.

In three short years, Melusine had become indispensable to his holdings and to his bed. So what, if she wasn't exactly who she claimed. She fulfilled all his needs and had carried his heirs.

As Sigefroi climbed down the stairs into the bailey to meet the first guests at the gate, he waved to Thierry. Dressed in a white tunic, the squire made his way to the area delimited by ribbons and flowers. Now nineteen, the lad had bloomed into a strong young man and Sigefroi had declared him fit for battle. "Are you ready?"

Thierry grinned. "Aye, but the smell from the kitchen is making me hungry. I spent the night in prayers, and didn't eat for two days... I even abstained from my lover's bed."

Sigefroi chuckled. Thierry was courting Melusine's maidservant, and reports of their noisy lovemaking in the stables delighted the men. "It's not every day Emperor Otto himself bestows knighthood upon our deserving young nobles. Better be on your best behavior. Now be on your way."

"Aye, m'lord."

When the horns sounded again from the battlement, all activity in the bailey slowed and all eyes turned to the open castle gate.

At the head of the group of riders entering the fortress, Sigefroi recognized his bishop brother, Adalberon. At his side, Emperor Otto rode a magnificent white stallion harnessed in gold and silver. The Imperial guard in blue and white surcoats flanked the procession, and many colorful guests rode sedately behind the two eminent personages.

* * *

Melusine walked out of the keep, wearing a peach satin gown cinched at the waist by a heavy silver belt hanging down the front. A gay fanfare of discordant horns announced the start of the ceremony. Fortunately, the mass would be performed in the fencing yard, turned into holy ground for the circumstance. So, Melusine wouldn't have to get close to any baptismal font or other basin of holy water.

She had easily evaded the baptisms of her last two children, pretending to be too weak to attend and still in childbed. Now that her Fae powers had fully returned from the incident at Liutgarde's baptism, Melusine intended to stay away from holy water at all cost.

Recovered from Frederick's birth, she now felt whole and wonderful. She joined the first rank where benches had been set for the most noble guests, as it might be a long ceremony. The arrangement reminded her of her wedding three years past. It felt like so long ago.

As she sat, Sigefroi nodded and smiled his approval. "I see your favorite gowns fit you again. It might be time to get you with child again, my sweet."

Melusine emitted a soft laugh. Not only had she regained her svelte figure, but she felt safe and loved. She turned and waved from a distance to Alyx who stood several rows behind, holding little Henri's hand while carrying the newborn, Frederick.

The crowd hushed when the emperor, dressed in a dark blue silk robe and wearing a sable cloak, walked to his imposing chair, set to the side of the altar. When the powerful man's green gaze stopped on Melusine, he smiled with white teeth under a curly blond beard.

Melusine shivered at the predatory grin and the cruel glint of his eyes.

The emperor then took his seat, and a young body servant rushed to arrange his blond ringlets over the collar of the fur cloak.

The four young men to be knighted walked solemnly through the central aisle and came to stand in front of the altar. They went down on one knee, heads bowed.

Emperor Otto motioned to Sigefroi's brother. Adalberon, in purple robes, nodded then faced the faithful, extended his arms, and enunciated a Latin litany. Alternately facing the four cardinal points, Adalberon closed his eyes, lifted his gaze to the heavens, and genuflected in rhythm with the words lost in the spring breeze.

After the bishop genuflected for the hundredth time, he nodded to the emperor who now rose and pulled his ceremonial sword from the golden scabbard.

"By the holy powers Pope John XIII invested in me," Otto scanned the audience like a skilled orator, "I declare these young men worthy of knighthood. May God guide their swords in defense of Christendom, the empire, and their liege. May God make them strong and fair, respectful of their betters, and magnanimous to their inferiors."

After presenting the blade to Adalberon, who anointed it with holy oil and blessed it with the sign of the cross, emperor Otto walked to the first young man kneeling in front of the altar. It was Thierry.

Holding the hilt with both hands, the emperor brought the sword one inch from his own nose then gently, mumbling Latin words, tapped the lad's left shoulder with the flat of the blade. After a pause, he tapped the right shoulder, then the top of Thierry's head.

Melusine could see the pride in the young man's bearing. Never had Thierry looked so radiant. After the emperor repeated the symbolic ritual for each of the benighted, he called his manservant who went to a coffer behind the emperor's chair and retrieved four swords in silver scabbards then carried them to his master, holding them on both extended arms.

Otto took one of the offered swords from the man then went to Thierry

"Rise, Knight Thierry." The emperor hooked the sword to the young man's empty baldric. Then he offered his ring for the boy to kiss in sign of fealty. He repeated the same ceremonial for the three other knights.

When Otto returned to his seat, the crowd cheered the new benighted.

Finally, the faithful approached the altar in orderly ranks to partake of the communion, the new knights first, then the assembled nobles. Melusine mentally said a prayer to the Goddess, and left the congregation unnoticed in the general movement of the guests toward the altar and back.

* * *

Although it was still early spring, Melusine had planned the feast outdoors. The hall could hold hundreds, but not thousands. Of course, she'd asked the Goddess to provide balmy weather. From the kitchen, scullions and servants hurried, carrying the best foods the domains of Luxembourg and Saarburg had to offer.

At the U-shaped high table, Melusine and Sigefroi sat in the middle, Emperor Otto at Sigefroi's right and Bishop Adalberon at Melusine's left. Further down the table, Gunter beamed when the guests complimented the wine as they sampled removes of lamb and white beans, pork and cooked apples, carrots in red wine sauce, fresh fish from the river and spring greens.

Entertainers had come by boat and acrobats and contortionists as well as dwarfs juggled and danced to the rhythmic melody of reed flutes and tambourines.

A gypsy fortune teller in crimson veils curtsied in front of Melusine. "Would you like your fortune told, my lady?"

"Nay." Melusine paled at the very thought. She couldn't risk having a gifted Gypsy divulge her darkest secret, especially in such dangerous company. "Find another who will enjoy it more."

As the girl moved closer, Melusine glanced to Sigefroi for help, knowing he did not believe in supernatural powers. On her left, Bishop Adalberon frowned, his eyes reduced to slits as he studied the fortune teller.

Inspired by the bishop's bigotry, Melusine said, "A good Christian does not dabble in such things."

Sigefroi shrugged and smiled at the fortune teller. "My wife is a mysterious creature. She has many secrets. Why don't you tell me about her?"

Melusine's heart stumbled in her chest. What game was Sigefroi playing now? "My lord, I must protest."

165

On the other side of Sigefroi, Emperor Otto leaned over the table, watching Melusine intently, a lurid smile on his rubicund face. "Do I have to order you myself, fair lady? Should I remind you that open disobedience to the emperor is punishable by a swift beheading?"

Even Adalberon cast down his gaze at the emperor's comment, surrendering to his cruel authority.

Defeated, Melusine extended a trembling hand.

The Gypsy girl took it and stared as if through it for a while. Her eyes veiled and she whispered softly for Melusine alone, using an ancient trick so others could not hear. "An old soul, you are, my lady... and you know from whence you come." She dropped her hand but kept her voice to a whisper. "But do not be so bold as to tempt fate. Beware those who love you... that they do not betray or disappoint you."

An icy sluice drenched Melusine, although she didn't let it show. Had she been negligent? Too comfortable in her life among mortals? Had she tempted fate and would pay for it?

"So, tell us, girl!" Otto blurted out, and pounded the table.

The girl curtsied respectfully to the emperor then straightened and faced Sigefroi. "You are fortunate, m'lord to have such a good wife. She will bear you many children and keep your bed warm and your estates thriving." She paused and her face froze into an unreadable mask. "But never betray her, or your fortune will wither and your life fall into despair."

The closest guests fell silent and Melusine felt the stilling of the breeze. Her heart paused in her chest, waiting.

Sigefroi gave a raucous laugh. "Who are you to tell me what to do with my wife?"

Sudden fear flashed in the dark Gypsy eyes, and the girl flew away, her crimson veils floating behind her. Sigefroi and Otto laughed and toasted her departure with wine.

Bishop Adalberon cleared his throat. His benign smile alarmed Melusine to imminent danger. "Last time I saw you, my lady, you fell very ill. But you certainly look dazzling today."

"Well, thank you, Lord Bishop."

Adalberon's smile widened. "Please, call me Adalberon. After all we are family."

"Of course." Confused by such a display of affection from the prelate, Melusine still did not trust Adalberon. He watched her too closely, and unlike Sigefroi, he did believe in her kind and considered Fae folks to be evil.

Adalberon caressed his eating dagger. "We never had this conversation about your family line, dear sister. I sent for the scroll of Strathclyde from St Martin's monastery, but it disappeared from the library. The friar bibliothec seemed upset about it but could not or would not reveal what happened to that scroll. Would you happen to know where the document is?"

"I never heard of such a scroll in these parts." Melusine's heart raced. If a scroll existed of her family line, she could be in great danger. And Adalberon's persistence indicated that he suspected something amiss.

Emperor Otto slammed his goblet on the table. Red wine dripped from his lips down his curly blond beard. "Sigefroi, my friend, were you hiding your delicious wife from me all this time? I understand now why you refused my previous offers for a bride."

Although offended by the emperor's lewd behavior, Melusine appreciated the interruption and seized the opportunity to turn away from Adalberon. "And where is your lovely wife, sire?"

Otto wiped his beard with the tablecloth. "She likes our peaceful residence in Memleben. She grew tired of my incessant travels and war campaigns long ago."

And probably of your incessant wenching and vulgar demeanor. Melusine smiled politely. "Convey her my deepest respect."

"I shall." Otto glanced up at the square tower in the center of the bailey "Sigefroi, my friend, I have to compliment you on this splendid fortress."

"You should congratulate my wife, sire. She designed it and supervised most of the work."

Melusine found the grace to blush at the compliment. "I only utilized the natural defenses the terrain offered and took advantage of it, sire."

Sigefroi nodded. "All her ideas made this castle stronger and I had to agree."

Melusine smiled. Sigefroi had also authorized the convenient tunnels and escape routes that allowed her to get away each month.

"Indeed? What a talented woman." Otto winked. "And she still found the time to give you children?"

Sigefroi raised his silver goblet. "Aye. Two sons in two years. I'll drink to that." He took a sip and picked at the food again.

Melusine enjoyed being recognized. "But you should have seen the castle during the construction, sire. Soldiers and masons camped in tents everywhere, it was quite a sight!"

Otto nodded and pointed with his dagger to his surroundings. "But now I see garrisons and stables, an armory, and a spacious kitchen. How many men do you keep here?"

Sigefroi seemed to enjoy impressing his powerful friend. "Two scores of guards and a hundred soldiers in the lower levels of the keep. My lady and I occupy the top floor, our children and Melusine's ladies the floor below us."

"This fort looks every inch as impenetrable as that of Luxembourg."

Sigefroi glanced at Melusine and smiled. "Quite."

Otto turned to Melusine. "Impressive work, my lady. I also like the banners and the fine linen. My compliments on the feast, too. You know how to entertain the most discriminating guests."

168

"Thank you, Sire." Melusine bowed slightly. "I do my best for my lord husband."

Adalberon picked a piece of fowl from his trencher with delicate fingers. "How is it that such an accomplished woman as you, lady Melusine, finds the time to design fortresses?"

Melusine controlled her impatience with the prelate. "How do you mean?"

Adalberon took the juicy morsel to his mouth and chewed as he spoke. "It seems your children and the running of your husband's estates should keep you more than occupied." He daintily dabbed at his mouth with the hem of the tablecloth and gave Melusine a questioning look. "Don't you enjoy the role of chatelaine?"

"Aye, Adalberon, I do." Thinking fast, Melusine returned the false smile. "But even a woman can get bored on long winter nights, when the light is too feeble for needlework and all the spinning and weaving is done."

She hoped the bishop would not question her blunt lie. In a castle, the spinning was never done.

"Where do you find the strength, my lady?" Adalberon's shaven face remained impassible. "I also hear you do not attend church. Of course my brother will not tolerate a church in this fortress, but the town does have a priest. You could invite him to say mass at the castle on Sundays."

Sigefroi dropped his bone and licked his fingers with quick, irritated movements. "Adalberon, for the last time, I do not want priests to meddle in my affairs."

"Still, your lady wife should worry about your eternal soul, brother." Adalberon turned to Melusine. "You would not be one to worship the old Roman gods, dear lady?" His eyes stared in strong disapproval. "This would be akin to worshiping the devil."

Relieved, Melusine emitted a nervous chuckle. The Goddess she worshiped was much more ancient than the Roman pantheon. "Be at peace, Adalberon. I do not. But I often pray to Our Lady."

169

Closing his eyes briefly, the bishop smiled. "Aye, the Virgin Mary can give a woman strength. But she would not approve of your dallying in architecture. God meant women to breed heirs for their lords, not build fortresses. Matters of war should only concern men."

A cheer rose from the tables of guards and soldiers near the kitchen building. In brand new uniforms, the men joyously welcomed the wine brought by servants. A kitchen maid came to the high table and ladled wild mushroom stew on top of the emperor's meat. He caught her hand and stared into her eyes.

When she did not lower her gaze, Otto laughed and let her go. Returning to his meal, he winked at Sigefroi. "I heard an ondine was sighted in the Saar River last week. Found anything more about it?"

Melusine's heart faltered for a beat. Far from missing the Alzette where she had bathed for centuries, she now enjoyed swimming in the Saar. On the cursed Wednesdays, she frolicked in the wide stream that carried merchant boats. Of course, she had to use a glamour, and swim further behind the hill in order to hide from the villagers, but she didn't mind. Had someone seen her through her magic veil?

Sigefroi frowned and hesitated just for a moment. "Sire, if you were not my friend, I would think you are spying in my territory." The light tone belied the accusation, but Melusine could tell her husband was upset.

Otto shrugged, picked up his goblet and sipped his wine. "So, was it a mermaid or not?"

Sigefroi sighed deeply then offered a diplomatic smile. "I sent my men to investigate, but they found nothing. Not even a naked lass bathing. Sailors have a vivid imagination, sire."

Otto raised a blond brow. "What did the sailors see?"

"They described an ondine of legends with a long serpent tail." Sigefroi shrugged. "You know I do not believe in such ridiculous beings." He chuckled. "But Adalberon will tell you the Church considers them spawns of Lucifer."

Waving the comment away, Otto grunted. "Too bad." He burped. "In any case, we appreciate your keeping the river safe for merchant boats. The roads, too, are now free of highway robbers, thanks to your vigilance."

Sigefroi smiled. "Thank you, sire."

Otto nodded toward Adalberon. "The princes of the Church and I only want the prosperity of our towns and markets."

Adalberon offered Sigefroi a strained smile. "We are grateful for your loyal services, brother."

Otto winked. "Without peaceful trade, I would need to raise new taxes to finance this year's military campaign."

"War again?" Sigefroi's amber gaze twinkled with interest.

At the mention of war, Melusine felt as if a lance had struck her chest. Why hadn't she seen this coming? Of course, Otto had come to recruit Sigefroi for his unending wars.

"This is spring, is it not?" Otto raised his gaze to the sky, took a deep breath of cool air and released it slowly. "The Byzantines are a thorn on the Eastern borders of Italy. Pope John asked me to squelch the rebellion. I could use your help. I need an army of knights and horsemen to kill some Greeks... like old times."

Sigefroi's face lit up at the mention of battle. "No foot soldiers?"

"You know I don't believe in foot soldiers." Otto took a sip of wine. "An army of well trained horsemen constitutes an unstoppable war machine. This is how I win all my wars."

Melusine winced at the excitement, not only in Otto's voice, but in Sigefroi's eyes. He caught her staring at him and flashed a quick, reassuring smile. Had he read her mind?

Sigefroi calmly sliced a piece of the roasted boar in front of him and dropped it on his bread trencher. "Since when are you doing favors for the pope? You put him on St Peter's throne, isn't that enough?"

Otto tore a piece of boar for himself and bit into it then spoke through a mouthful. "In exchange for my military help, Pope John XIII will obediently crown my son as the future emperor of the Holy Roman empire."

Sigefroi whistled. "You didn't waste time, my friend. How old is Otto Junior? Nine?"

"Aye. I want the pope to crown him while I still live. That way, if anything happens to me in battle, no one will contest his right when his time comes to assume my throne."

"That is highly irregular, sire." Sigefroi chewed reflectively.

Otto waved away the comment. "I do not want my empire to be divided among my children upon my death. Charlemagne was a fool to split his lands between three sons."

A slight shadow crossed Sigefroi's brow. "Careful, sire. Charlemagne was my ancestor. But I tend to agree. His empire did fall apart after his death." Then he thought of Lorraine. "So was my father's duchy weakened by its division."

At a loss, Melusine realized she could not keep her husband inside fortresses forever. Sooner or later, he would leave to do battle, and she feared her long ago vision of Sigefroi's bloody massacre of innocents might come true.

* * *

A month later, Melusine watched from the battlement and forced a smile as she waved her white scarf in farewell. Outside the gate, on the steep road to town, Sigefroi on his warhorse flanked by forty knights, waved in return. In the knights' wake, four abreast, rode several hundred horsemen, many from the castle and others provided by the bishopric of Trier.

Barking hounds ran circles around the horses in their excitement at following their masters on the road.

"Death to the Byzantines," the riders sang as they raised their shields in rhythm to the battle cry.

172

Melusine shivered at the dreadful sound.

A few supply carts closed the train. At the junction of the Via Romana, Sigefroi's army would meet with the troops from Luxembourg castle, and within a few weeks, they would reach Italy, then the Eastern border where the Byzantine Greeks stirred trouble.

Melusine wished Sigefroi didn't have to go, but Otto's wishes were law throughout the empire. She thoroughly disliked Otto, a lecher and a cruel man under his blond ringlets and curly beard. Even Sigefroi recognized it. But Sigefroi must obey his emperor.

What bothered Melusine the most was the happy light in Sigefroi's amber eyes at the idea of new adventures. Had he grown tired of being a husband? Did three years of peace make him long for his former carefree life as a warrior?

Next to Melusine on the rampart, Alyx sobbed disconsolately. Thierry in his brand new armor, rode with Sigefroi and Gunter at the head of the column. The lad's first campaign would keep him away for months. For the lovebirds' first separation, he was going into battle. Worse. There had been no time to marry the two lovers in the hasty preparations for war.

Melusine hoped Thierry would return before Alyx gave birth, so they could get married in time to prevent the girl's public shame.

Chapter Twelve

Two weeks later, on the Roman road

After three years of castle life, Sigefroi relished the ride with his cavalry through the German empire. Following the Via Romana straight south toward Rome, the imperial army rode for two weeks without ever leaving the ancient road. They camped near rivers and lakes, requisitioned food from the towns and villages they passed, requested hospitality from monasteries and local lords.

Although their hosts received compensation in tax exemptions, Sigefroi could see in their eyes the burden this service would bring on their annual food reserves. But it was spring, and they could work harder this summer to grow more crops to survive the winter.

Sigefroi marveled at the Romans who had built the wide fare cutting straight through Saxony, Franconia and Swabia. With most of the stone bridges still intact, only once did the riders have to ford a shallow river. Centuries ago, the Romans had come this way to conquer the wild German tribes.

But Sigefroi wagered that their pedestrian armies would have been no match for Otto's mighty cavalry, half of them knights or seasoned warriors who had seen many campaigns. They fought not for silver or gold as most Roman soldiers did, but for their motherland, for God, honor, and for their families. These fierce and loyal men never questioned an order and would rather die than surrender.

As the troops entered yet another forest, the birds stopped chirping at the sounds of the army on the move. The high boughs echoed the creaking of leather and the clink of swords and scabbards. Barking hounds ran along the ranks.

A few riders armed with bows and arrows broke away from the column and whistled for the dogs to lead their hunt for fresh meat. The rays of the sun through the new foliage warmed the leather leggings and glinted off the chain mail and the polished brass decorating the shields.

Sigefroi held the reins loosely as he rode abreast of the emperor and his nine-year-old son Otto Junior, followed by Gunter and Thierry. Behind them stretched a wide column of over four thousand horsemen.

Still reveling in his new knighthood, Thierry laughed, puffed up with pride at being part of the emperor's chosen companions. While Sigefroi and Gunter enjoyed a high rank from birth, Thierry was the son of a landless knight, and this campaign would elevate his status, perhaps even grant him some lands for services rendered.

By the time the sun lowered in the western sky, the army emerged from the tree line into a vast meadow bordering a wide river.

Sigefroi recognized the stone bridge that crossed the expanse and knew they had reached the Danube River. On the other side, majestic mountains promised a challenge. He looked forward to crossing the Alps.

Otto raised his arm to halt the column.

Immediately, standard bearers galloped back along the ranks to relay the order. The column came to a stop. The horsemen behind them broke the ranks and dismounted on the grassy bank along the river.

Sigefroi pulled on the reins then loosened the strap of the leather cap under his mail hauberk. His throat felt dry from the dust of the road. "Water the horses!"

Squires took the horses to drink.

The clatter of a gallop on the stone bridge caught Sigefroi's attention. He squinted at a messenger riding fast toward them, carrying a gold and purple banner that floated in his wake. "An envoy from the pope."

Otto signaled for the imperial party to remain mounted as the papal messenger slowed his horse across the meadow and made his way toward them.

The messenger halted in front of the emperor, dismounted then bowed. "News from the insurrection, sire." He presented Otto with a scroll.

Otto motioned to Sigefroi. "You open it. What does it say?"

Sigefroi removed his gauntlets and bent down from the saddle to take the scroll. He broke the red seal, unrolled the parchment and read it. "This report makes it sound more like a farmers' revolt than a true military threat, sire... but we know better than that, do we not?"

Otto's clear green gaze turned to Gunter. "You've met these rogues up close. Tell us what you think"

"Aye, sire." Gunter pulled his horse alongside Sigefroi's. "Barbarian farmers who sleep with a sword and kill travelers for sport, or to steal their horses."

Otto sent a stern look to Sigefroi. "I wish I could lead the repression myself, but the pope awaits me. Politics..." Rays of the setting sun caught on his blond beard. "I am counting on you to end the insurrection swiftly. I do not want to wait in Rome too long for news of your victory!"

Despite his weariness from two weeks on the road, Sigefroi couldn't hold back a grin. "Your confidence honors me, sire."

He felt exhilarated at the prospect of battle. Born for the battlefield, he excelled at it. Besides, he wanted to try Caliburn against a real enemy. Would the sword make him invincible, as Melusine had promised?

The Emperor's face relaxed. "You are the best I have. My reputation lies with you. The Italian borders must be pacified before the rebellion spreads to more villages."

Otto glanced at his young son. The boy, who had ridden with the men without complaint, now fidgeted atop his slender mare. His light complexion, blond hair and blue eyes made him look like a girl, but the set of his jaw and the determination in the boy's steely eyes revealed a future leader of men.

Otto sighed. "I cannot afford to give Pope John a reason to refuse crowning my heir. The future of the empire is at stake."

Sigefroi grinned. "Don't worry, sire, Gunter and I will not fail you. After all, we learned from the best strategist in all Christendom."

Otto waved away the flattery. "Make camp for the night. We'll cross the river in the morning." He slid off his white stallion and gave the reins to his manservant. "It's too late in the day to start crossing the mountains."

When a squire offered to take Sigefroi's reins, he dismounted and let go of his horse. He rolled the scroll from the pope and handed it to Otto.

The emperor took the message. "Learned from the best, hey?" He grinned. "That would be me, would it not?" He pushed back the mail hauberk, letting lose a full head of blond curls. "But I'm giving you the best trained and best equipped cavalry in all Christendom. As I always say, heavy cavalry, when properly handled, is superior to any other military force known to this day!"

Sigefroi laughed. "Aye, sire. Trample them with horses, and they'll flee or die underfoot."

Otto slapped Sigefroi on the shoulder. "Do not forget speed, flawless discipline, and the element of surprise."

All around them the camp organized itself. The imperial tent was raised, and soon cooking fires spread the smell of meat stew. The dogs waited expectantly for scraps of food.

As darkness fell, a dozen privileged knights gathered around the campfire in front of Otto's tent to listen to their liege. With blood lust gleaming in his eyes, the emperor spoke ardently of the great battle fought just south of there, eleven years earlier, on the Lechfeld River.

Sigefroi remembered the place and the battle well. He was very young then. In the heat of summer, eight thousand horsemen from eight different kingdoms and duchies, including the Czechs from Bohemia, had descended on the Hungarians who had crossed the southern borders and besieged the town of Augsburg.

Otto's green eyes shone as he relived the battle and smiled as he described in details the capture and the interrogation of the Hungarian king. "And his face dripping blood, we finally dangled him on a rope from the town's postern gate, and the crows and ravens picked his empty eye sockets for days, in the stink of the decomposing carcasses of slaughtered men and horses lying outside the walls on the battlefield. These were the days..."

The knights laughed.

Sigefroi remained silent. He knew how men could get carried away in the heat of battle. Many friends had perished in that war as well, among them the Frankish king. While the troops of Lorraine had remained behind to guard the Rhine River, Sigefroi had followed Otto into battle. It had been a great adventure, a glorious victory forever imprinted on his young mind.

In the flickering light of the flames, Sigefroi met Thierry's gaze. The young knight's smile of approval looked forced, and Sigefroi understood Thierry's reservations. He reminded Sigefroi of his own youth. Given time, the lad would make a valorous knight.

Next to Thierry, Otto Junior nodded and stared at his father with unmasked admiration, obviously fascinated by the tales of such heroic feats. Sigefroi wondered what kind of emperor he would become. Would he have his father's political skills and cunning? Would he lead wisely or follow his passions? Under his rule, would the empire flourish or die?

* * *

Two days after crossing the Danube, the imperial army came to a fork in the road and Sigefroi parted ways with the emperor. While Otto followed the wide road south toward Rome with his son and fifty knights, Sigefroi led the rest of the riders along rough mountain trails, heading southeast through Bavaria toward the Byzantine border.

Riding at his side, Gunter laughed, retelling past conquests, while Thierry's eyes widened with admiration.

178

Sigefroi enjoyed the journey. It felt good to be on the road again, alive and free, among friends, and eager for battle.

The weather remained clement as they crossed the Eastern tail of the Alps. The mounted warriors lived on goat cheese and mutton foraged from local shepherds. Within days the sky became bluer and the land drier as they moved further southeast. The dense forests soon gave way to olive groves, vineyards, dry mud dwellings, and red dirt. The fine dust of the trail filtered through the mail and inside boots and garments.

The imperial cavalry encountered no army, no soldiers, no resistance as they depleted the larders of several abbeys and purchased wine and food from local landlords loyal to the empire. Everywhere gentle folk went about their daily chores.

As they crossed a small town, Thierry remarked, "The population looks peaceful. I see no sign of revolt."

Gunter grunted. "Looks are deceiving."

Sigefroi nodded agreement. "For the past two days, the peasants on the road stare at us with disdain and pride."

Gunter spit to the side of his horse. "The farther south we get, pride will turn to contempt."

Sigefroi rode slowly along the road crossing the town, followed by his imposing cavalry.

The eyes glaring at them were slightly almond-shaped above high cheek bones, and the locals' skin took deeper shades of bronze. The barbarians from the east, who had precipitated the fall of Rome centuries earlier, had mixed with the Greek population to produce a vindictive breed of warring peasants.

From then on, Sigefroi kept the bulk of his cavalry to the countryside, sending only food forays to the villages and towns. But the forests grew scarce and the trees too far apart to hide his troops. In order to water the horses he had to keep close to the few rivers. It made his camp easy to spot and vulnerable, but peasants would have to be harebrained to attack the best trained cavalry in the civilized world.

Sigefroi slowed his horse as he passed a decomposing cadaver covered with red ants on the side of the path. The stink also attracted vultures who circled overhead. "We are not far from the border."

Farther south, an arrow had split a sapling, a broken sword lay in the dust of the road, a tattered pennant fluttered high in the branches of a cedar tree. In a field, a peasant hammered a broken shield into a plow blade.

That night, Sigefroi made camp by the river. For a change, the supply team had found a large friendly village willing to provide abundant food and wine. They seemed relieved to see imperial troops and said they appreciated the soldiers' protection from border raids. They were willing to give up their prepared summer feast in exchange for a handful of gold coins.

The men celebrated with banquet food and barrels of wine, but Sigefroi worried about the darkness. There would be no moon tonight, and the border was only a few miles away. No doubt the enemy had spies and knew of his movements.

So, Sigefroi posted twice as many sentries as usual along the perimeter of the camp, just in case. Then he went to sleep to the songs of cicadas, under a summer sky full of stars. A warrior needed no tent in such balmy weather.

* * *

What woke him in the middle of the night must have been the silence. The cicadas and night birds had stopped chirping. Sigefroi at first thought he was still dreaming. His eyes and mind refused to focus.

Among the sleeping men glided furtive shadows, light as children, like thieves in the night. But their hands held curved daggers, and under the faint starlight the blades dripped dark blood. The murderous shadows ran noiselessly in every direction, like wraiths on the wind.

Sigefroi closed his hand on Caliburn's hilt and rose on unsteady feet. He drew the sword and yelled his battle roar, but it came muffled to his ears. Thunder rumbled inside his skull. His guts churned with unholy fire. How much wine had he gulped last night? No more than usual. Yet, his arm barely had the strength to lift a sword.

Was the food poisoned? The wine drugged? The sudden realization that his camp was under attack from a stealthy enemy made him yell louder.

Other knights responded with sluggish battle cries of their own, and soon the clink of drawing swords echoed into the night as the soldiers emerged from their stupor.

Sigefroi stumbled after one of the aggressors, but his wobbly legs couldn't run fast enough to catch the intruder who seemed to fly like a spirit.

"To the horses! Catch the bastards!" His head pounded as if crushed by the blows of a giant hammer.

But only a few horses remained. Sigefroi seized a frightened destrier by the mane and clumsily heaved himself upon its bare back. Raw lightning coursed in his veins. He could barely control his body, and the thought that he had been poisoned enraged him.

He galloped after fleeing shadows, some on horseback. His own horses, stolen by thieves! When a cloud veiled the stars, he lost sight of them as they vanished into darkness.

Turning his mount, Sigefroi returned to camp, where the soldiers who could still stand and walk had revived the fires and lit the torches. Ignoring the fire in his gut, he dismounted to inspect the damages. Many knights sat, heaving last night's food in obvious agony. The dogs lay dead, green foam on their fangs. The poison had killed them first. The remaining men would surely die next.

Sigefroi closed his mind to the twisting knots in his stomach. He realized with horror that most knights had not risen from their sleep. A few slumped, face down in a pile of vomit. Others lay on their backs, immobile, eyes and mouths wide open, in a pool of blood. Their slit throats gaped at the stars.

Gunter, deathly pale, rushed to Sigefroi. "Over two hundred dead, my lord. Some poisoned, others slaughtered like rabbits in their sleep, without a chance to fight back.

Those still alive are deathly sick. Few can stand, even less ride."

From the expression on his friend's face, Sigefroi realized something worse had happened. "Gunter, what is it?"

"It's Thierry!" The big man's face twitched. "This way... see for yourself."

By the light of a torch, two paces to the right, Thierry lay on a blood-soaked blanket, his neck gushing crimson under a ghostly face. His eyes opened wide as if he recognized his lord.

Sigefroi fell on his knees besides Thierry. No, not that innocent soul. It was not fair. "I'm here, lad."

Thierry's lips formed a word with no sound. Alyx! In his last agony he was calling his love, the mother of his unborn child. Then his face relaxed, and his clear blue eyes fixed on something beyond the black sky as he remained perfectly still.

A tear of frustration rolled down his cheek but Sigefroi let it drop as he raised his hand to close Thierry's eyes forever. Dipping his thumb in the boy's fresh blood Sigefroi drew a cross with it on his own forehead. "Your death will be avenged, my friend."

"How dare the bastards kill Thierry?" Gunter spit on the ground then he turned away, kicked a dead dog and sent it flying several paces.

A sudden calm seized Sigefroi. The spot in his chest where his heart used to beat turned to a block of ice. "Gather the horses. Take the torches. We are going to teach these peasants not to trifle with imperial knights."

Within moments, every able horseman had saddled up and now moved upriver, like an ominous ribbon of torch fire in the night, toward the village that had provided the tainted food. Behind them, horseless riders whistled in hopes of retrieving their mounts, stolen or let loose in the wilderness.

At the head of his troops, Sigefroi seethed. He'd lost two hundred men and might lose a thousand or more in the next few hours, but his guilt focused on that innocent soul he had taken under his tutelage. Thierry, his former squire, a young man he had taught from childhood, and who had become his friend.

How could he ever break the news to Melusine? And to Lady Alyx?

The blood rushing through his temples rumbled like a war drum. Was he dying, too? Would they all expire in horrible pain? Fueled by guilt, shame, and revenge, Gunter on his heels, Sigefroi yelled as he rode ahead on his destrier.

Ignoring the stabs of wrenching pain in his gut, he focused on the anger and the frustration of the men who followed him, and he drew strength from it. He would show these insolent traitors the cost of angering him.

When Sigefroi and his men reached the village, it stood empty. The riders touched the torches to the straw roofs and filthy hide curtains serving as doors, then they threw the torches inside the dry mud homes. Several villagers ran for the river, trying to reach their boats.

Sigefroi cut off their retreat and drove them back. "Burn the boats. Let no one escape!"

The horsemen spread out through the countryside and rounded up men, women, and children who had fled their homes at the first sounds of approaching horses. The soldiers dragged them back screaming with wide, frightened eyes.

A woman produced a knife from under her skirt and threw it at Sigefroi's head. In the split second as he ducked, Sigefroi recognized the dagger. It was Thierry's, a present from Melusine. With one stroke of Caliburn, he decapitated the culprit. A man rushed him with a spear but fell from a knight's arrow.

The warriors gathered the murdering villagers on the muddy river bank. The prisoners had not expected the soldiers to be able to fight after ingesting the poison. Now they pleaded with their aggressors. Kneeling in surrender amidst the dust and the smoke, they cried and sobbed, begging for mercy.

By the ominous glow of the burning village, Gunter, his red face covered with sweat and grime, rode toward Sigefroi. "We found many of our horses penned behind the hillock. What should we do with the prisoners?"

Sigefroi wanted to say kill them all, but these were women and children, not warriors, and as a knight he was bound by honor to let them live. Still, he would not let them get away with slaughtering his men.

They had killed Thierry. Hell and damnation, all his warriors might be dying from their poisoned food or wine. Sigefroi himself might not survive the night. He must instill fear in the other villages to prevent them from striking again in the future. "Make an example, but let them live to tell their tale!"

"Aye! So, what do we do?"

Sigefroi could feel the impatience in Gunter and in the men. The horses pranced, as if feeling the tension in the air.

"Cut off their right hands like the horse thieves they are. And also their ears and noses, so they remember never to plot against the empire."

Gunter frowned. "All of them?"

"Aye." Sigefroi surveyed the many faces staring at him. "Do not let their innocent airs fool you. These underhanded foes killed your friends. We may all be dead in a few hours from their cowardly poison. They wielded the blades that slit our valorous knights' throats!"

A cry rose from a few horsemen who recognized the prisoners as the very assassins who had slaughtered their friends.

"Obey your orders," Sigefroi shouted. "And if they resist or try to run, kill them without a thought. They deserve no mercy."

The knights uttered their battle cries and broke the circle as they advanced upon the prisoners. A woman screamed. She grabbed two children and pressed their heads to her chest. A male prisoner started to run and even reached the river, but a knight rode after him, splashing into the water and hacked him open from shoulder to midriff.

Children sobbed, old men stared. From a burning abode came a newborn's cry.

But Sigefroi could not forgive. Clenching his stomach against the pain rending his gut, he yelled his battle roar, rode forth, and sliced off a woman's hand. She screamed and raised her bloody stump to her head. Sigefroi then dismounted, and in one easy stroke sliced off her nose then hacked off her ear before she crumpled to the slippery ground. In his frenzy, he still marveled at the sharpness and precision of the miraculous sword.

Pushing aside all feelings, Sigefroi systematically picked one trembling victim after another and sliced off ears, noses and hands. Soon he couldn't remember what he was doing or why, but he kept hacking and slicing. Blood splashed his surcoat and stained Caliburn. Red rivulets ran across the mud and swirled into the river.

By the time the pink sun rose on the eastern horizon, there was nothing left of the proud village. Only a few bloody cripples whimpered as they crawled among fresh corpses on a crimson river bank, by a pile of smoking ruins.

While the knights gathered the stolen horses, Sigefroi slumped against a tree and heaved his gut. The pain of it mixed with the shame and disgust of what he had just done.

With the taste of bile, his revulsion for the bloody massacre grew as his head slowly cleared, and he realized he might survive the poison after all. But would God ever forgive him for what he had done this night? Suddenly, Melusine's face filled his mind and he began to sob.

* * *

Melusine awoke in the middle of a familiar nightmare she thought long forgotten. A river of blood flowed at the hand of Sigefroi wielding Caliburn. The sight of her beloved husband killing and maiming women and children by the glow of a burning village left Melusine shuddering with repugnance.

What had brought about the hated vision? The fact that Sigefroi had gone to war again? Had it happened? Would it

185

happen? No. She shouldn't be so quick to accuse him of such horrible deeds.

Melusine wished she could link her mind to Sigefroi's, but she had tried before and never could. She hadn't heard from him since he'd left for the war, and although she showed a brave front at the castle, alone in their chambers she missed him sorely. She knew Caliburn would protect his life, but war could be messy in more subtle ways.

When the first rooster crowed, Melusine pushed back the woolly blanket and rose from the bed. She opened the wood shutters to gaze through the window of the keep and shivered at the cool morning. Nestled on the hillside by the river, the town of Saarburg still slept. The moonless night now paled in the eastern sky.

Soon the rising sun would banish the nightmare that probably sprouted from unfounded fears. Sigefroi was many things, but not a cruel torturer of women and children. She knew him to be loyal and fair, harsh sometimes, but kinder than most, and always honorable.

She refreshed her face and hands with the cool water of the basin, refusing to look straight into it, for fear the dreaded vision would return. She dressed in a simple gown, intending to break her fast in the kitchen with the servants. They respected her for sharing the morning gruel with them rather than playing the haughty chatelaine. And after decades of solitude, Melusine enjoyed the company of her people.

As she crossed the bailey on her way to the kitchen, the guards extinguished the torches and hoisted the gate. The first villagers entered the castle walls, pushing hand carts full of victuals or walking a loaded donkey. At the sight of a rider galloping among them, Melusine's heart raced. A messenger. He didn't look like a soldier from Otto's army, however, but wore the surcoat of a man of the Church.

With his horse lathered with sweat from a hard ride, the messenger halted at the gate and addressed the guards in a solemn, booming voice. "A message from His Holiness Pope John, for Lady Melusine of Luxembourg."

Breathless, Melusine hurried toward the rider. "I am the lady of this keep."

The messenger glanced dubiously at her simple attire then looked to the guard for confirmation. When the guard smiled and nodded, the messenger saluted, dismounted, then handed Melusine a small scroll sealed in red wax.

Melusine took it eagerly. Such messages, carried in haste night and day from monastery to monastery, with fresh horses and new riders each time, reported only the most important news. In her impatience, Melusine almost ripped the parchment when she broke the seal. She read the missive.

An invitation to Rome? His Holiness and the emperor requested her presence for the crowning of young Otto II. Elated at the prospect of traveling and joining Sigefroi for such a grand occasion, Melusine laughed. Forgetting all about breakfast, she thanked the messenger, asked a passing servant to take his horse to the stable and pointed the robed man in the direction of the kitchen.

Melusine's mind whirled. She had to prepare for a long journey. She must also ensure that everything at the castle would go smoothly during her absence.

"Alyx!" Melusine called as she barged into the women's quarters. "Stop pining for your gallant and start packing. We are going to Rome."

The young woman opened wild eyes. "We are?" Her smile told Melusine how much she welcomed the news. "What about the children?"

"They will remain here. We must make haste. The crowning is in one month."

"A crowning? Will Thierry be there?"

"How could he not attend along with Sigefroi, and Gunter?" Melusine rejoiced for Alyx.

Later that day, in the midst of preparations, a disturbing thought assailed Melusine. She felt the tiny scar on her left hand throb. A Fae woman in Rome? Among bishops and prelates, in a city of many churches, holy water, and the Goddess knew what else?

Could she be so foolish as to throw herself into the maw of her worst enemy? What if she were discovered on a fated Wednesday? They would throw her in a dungeon and torture her before burning her alive.

She shuddered at the thought, but what choice did she have? None. The pope and the emperor had ordered it. Refusing to comply would raise grave suspicions. Already the bishops did not like her much.

Melusine must hide her fear and face the dangers in Rome. She took heart in the knowledge that Sigefroi would keep her safe. It had been a hundred and fifty years since she'd wandered that far from her home. The idea of warmer climates made her heart sing with anticipation.

Chapter Thirteen

The road to Strasbourg, three days later.

Invigorated by the exercise of riding all day, Melusine filled her lungs with the balmy summer breeze. She kept pace with the open cart, so she could converse with Alyx, who avoided the saddle in her condition. Despite the dust, Melusine thoroughly enjoyed the journey.

On the wide road, their retinue passed a merchant riding ahead of a slow train of loaded carts. A rich trader, judging by the quality of his clothing. Melusine wondered what he transported. Could it be spices from the orient, or Saracen carpets? Maybe Byzantine ceramics? Precious glass from Italy? Possibly olive oil, or rare silk? The handful of armed guards walking behind the merchant's train leered at Melusine with undisguised lust, making bawdy remarks.

The captain of Melusine's guard slowed his mount to let her catch up with him. "My lady, there is much traffic on this road." He bowed slightly. "I respectfully suggest you ride side-saddle from here on."

Melusine adjusted her wide riding skirt to hide a bit of leg above her riding footwear. "I will not switch saddle now. Do not worry, captain, your lord will not punish you for my reckless behavior when we get to Rome." She laughed at his sour face but took pity on him. "I will join Alyx in the cart as soon as we come into view of the town."

Alyx smiled from inside the open cart, where she sat wedged between two chests among furs and pillows. Her thickening waist bounced with each bump of the oak wheels on the uneven road. "My lady, what if one of these

189

merchants reports you to the abbey where we spend the night? Could the monks refuse us their hospitality?"

"Fear not, dear Alyx. We are still in High Lorraine, and Sigefroi's older brother is supreme overlord in these parts. Besides, abbots are easily swayed with a few coins." Melusine smiled. "Perhaps you should marry Thierry as soon as we get to Rome. It might avoid some awkwardness later on."

Alyx blushed. "Aye, m'lady. 'Tis a grand idea."

"I'll let you borrow one of my gowns."

The girl's green eyes lit up. "Aye?"

"Or, perhaps we can purchase silk or muslin veils with silver threads in Verona or Florence." The Italian names rolled like exotic pearls on Melusine's tongue.

As they negotiated the crest of a low hill, a walled city came into view a few short miles ahead, dominated by a tall Roman cathedral with three belfries, almost as imposing as that of Trier. Outside the golden Roman walls, a prosperous town spilled its many buildings in a wide crown surrounded by a gray fortification of more recent construction.

The captain glanced at Melusine as if torn between duty to his lord and obedience to his lady. "Strasbourg, m'lady, where we will spend the night. Tomorrow we cross the Rhine River and shoot east, toward Augsburg."

Alyx winked. "M'lady, you better join me in here, before the good captain dies of embarrassment."

"Soldiers do not get embarrassed, Alyx. Believe me, he's more worried about Sigefroi's reprimands." She motioned to the captain who stopped the small convoy. Melusine dismounted, gave the reins to a lad then climbed the steps into the open cart.

As the train resumed the ride, Melusine propped her back against a chest and arranged the furs and pillows around her. She glanced at Alyx who looked comfortable enough. "How can you stand such a bumpy ride in your condition?"

But Alyx didn't seem to hear. She frowned as she glanced up. "Why are we going east tomorrow? Italy is south, is it not?"

190

"Aye." Melusine smiled. "But south of us is the kingdom of Burgundy. Those barbarians would kill us all without a thought. It's safer to remain within the empire's borders, where people are civilized, and our local lords and abbots can provide food and shelter."

They entered the busy city through the Northern gate. Strasbourg was well named, the town of roads. No wonder it was a merchant's paradise. Four major trade routes ran through its center. Everywhere she looked, Melusine saw stone cutters and masons, building churches... so many churches!

The abbot of the new monastery where they stopped for the night received his important guests with enthusiasm. "My lady, you will be pleased to know that your eminent brother in law, Bishop Adalberon of Metz, is also visiting, along with Archbishop Henri of Verdun, and both are eager to meet with you."

"Really?" Melusine stiffened at the news. What was Adalberon doing here? But she refused to be intimidated by the presence of Sigefroi's brother. She forced a smile. "I'll be delighted to see them." Her hand flicked a dusty sleeve. "But only after I change into something more presentable."

"I understand." The abbot nodded.

"Would it be too much to ask for hot water?" Melusine smiled to soften the demand.

The abbot bowed respectfully. "That can be arranged, my lady."

Melusine didn't mind sharing the same cell as Alyx for the night. The girl had a happy disposition. After Alyx helped her scrub the grit from her skin and hair, Melusine let her use the bath water. Meanwhile, she donned a simple shift and covered her hair with a bonnet for modesty.

Moments after they finished dressing, the two women responded to the bell and followed the congregation to the refectory. Thanks to the rule of silence, Melusine did not have to speak to Adalberon, who sat with the abbot and the archbishop at the opposite end of the high table. The portly archbishop of Verdun looked like a sour man, and Melusine disliked him on sight.

The friars bowed their heads for the blessing of the food, then a monk stepped up to a lectern and read a sermon that echoed under the high-vaulted ceiling. Lay servants ladled steaming soup into the wooden bowls and soon the friars ate quietly.

Some broke the bread and soaked it in their bowl, others slurped the broth or munched on the bread thoughtfully. A meager fare to be sure, but such was monastic life for the Benedictines. Alyx frowned at the thin broth in her bowl. Melusine hoped the guards would fare better. Soldiers needed strength.

The sermon recited overhead warned of the evil nature of women, from the memoirs of a long dead archbishop now considered as a saint. Melusine shuddered. Such bishops had persecuted her mother in Strathclyde, and later set a price on the head of the ondine sighted in the Moselle River.

If they knew Melusine was that legendary ondine, these seemingly peaceful monks would throw her in a dungeon without a second thought. The Goddess be thanked, they suspected nothing of the sort.

Melusine wiped her bowl with the last piece of bread and, following the monks' example, sat straight and waited. At the end of the sermon, the reader clapped once. All the monks rose and filed out of the refectory. Imitating them, Melusine and Alyx returned to their cell.

A friar approached them. "Our Lord Abbot would like you to join him and the bishops to share a glass of wine in his study."

Melusine nodded. "Thank you, I will." She turned to Alyx. "You may go back if you like. I will join you later."

"Don't mind if I am asleep by the time you return, m'lady. I will fall like a sack of grain and not move until morning." Alyx curtsied and left.

Melusine followed the monk to the study. There, the two princes of the church and the abbot, ensconced in thick padded chairs around a sturdy table, already sampled the wine.

The abbot rose to meet Melusine. "Glad you came, my lady."

Adalberon nonchalantly offered his ring for her to kiss. "Dear sister-in-law, I am delighted to see you again."

Melusine genuflected as the custom demanded, hating the abasement of the gesture, and touched her lips to the gem.

Archbishop Henri of Verdun, who looked older, eyed Melusine curiously. He offered his own ring without leaving the chair.

"Your Grace." Melusine disliked his superior attitude but she controlled her anger, genuflected and lightly kissed the ring on the pudgy hand. Why did she, a noble lady, have to kneel before sitting bishops?

She rose and addressed her brother in law. "Adalberon, what a coincidence to be visiting the same city at the same time... and be staying at the same monastery while there are so many in Strasbourg!"

The abbot pulled a chair for Melusine and she sat at the round table.

Adalberon offered a condescending smile. "My presence here is no coincidence, dear sister."

Melusine's heart almost stopped. "How do you mean?"

"I am also on my way to Rome for the crowning of our German cousin. So is Archbishop Henri." Adalberon's thin smile widened but remained cold. "I shared his escort since Metz, but I have been wanting to know you better for some time. I thought I would join your traveling party. What better opportunity for us to get better acquainted?"

Archbishop Henri made a wry face. Decidedly a big man, he looked petulant as a child. "I should have known the house of High Lorraine would shun my company. What else can you expect from upstarts whose ancestors resorted to assassination as a means to ascend to power?"

Surprised and disturbed by the open attack on Sigefroi's family, Melusine did not respond. Wasn't one of Sigefroi's brothers liege lord of Verdun?

Adalberon snorted. "You can see why I would rather travel with a relative?"

Melusine froze. Adalberon's presence would certainly take the fun out of this journey. For a moment, she felt tempted to use her powers of persuasion to change his mind, but a bishop might be able to sense and recognize magic. She could not risk discovery.

"Wine, my lady?" The abbot smiled as he offered Melusine a silver goblet. Obviously he had known of Adalberon's plans and enjoyed her surprise.

Melusine took the goblet and thanked the abbot without looking. She must not give in to panic. Weeks on the road with a bishop? In a close proximity that did not allow for privacy? How would she escape Adalberon's scrutiny on her next fated Wednesday?

"I was expecting more enthusiasm on your part, my lady." Adalberon seemed amused by her shock. Did he suspect anything amiss?

Sipping the wine to hide her uneasiness, Melusine found it sweet and fortifying. "Forgive me, Adalberon, I had a long day. I feel a little dazed."

In her head, she already concocted a plan to escape the bishop on the road, but she didn't even know exactly how far her party would have traveled by Tuesday. Many delays could happen on such journeys.

The abbot returned to his chair and sat facing Melusine with a satisfied expression on his face. "I have sheltered your men in the stables. They are being fed in the kitchen as we speak."

Melusine nodded. "Thank you, Lord Abbot. I would appreciate if they were given a little more food than the monks. Perhaps some cheese or meat if you have it. I will compensate you generously."

The abbot nodded. "Aye, my lady. Your captain voiced the same concern. I already made arrangements to his satisfaction."

"Thank you." Melusine turned to Adalberon, struggling to sound casual. "It will be good to see Sigefroi after all these months, and Gunter, and Thierry..."

Adalberon stopped mid movement, his goblet not yet to his lips.

194

Archbishop Henri chuckled. "You haven't heard?" He sounded sarcastic, almost smug, as if enjoying his knowledge of something of importance.

Melusine decidedly hated the man but did not let it show. "Heard what?"

Sighing, Adalberon set down his cup and looked away. "Our victory on the Byzantines came at a high price. I thought you knew. Sigefroi lost over two hundred imperial knights."

Archbishop Henri scoffed. "Many of them from my personal guard. I wonder how he intends to compensate me for that loss."

A cold stone weighed Melusine's chest. "How many knights from Luxembourg did we lose?"

Adalberon stared down at the rushes covering the flagstone. "Too many." He raised his gaze to meet Melusine's. "I am afraid young Thierry, whom we just benighted in the spring, did not survive. I know Sigefroi took a liking to the lad."

"Thierry is dead?" Melusine barely breathed, hoping she had heard wrong.

Adalberon nodded sadly.

How could the Goddess have allowed such an injustice! The boy's roguish smile flashed in Melusine's mind. A vise crushed her chest. "Such a loss. Sigefroi had tutored him from childhood."

Adalberon sighed. "I am sorry, Melusine. But be certain your husband did avenge the young man's death. He buried Thierry under the ashes of the village responsible for his demise."

"Sigefroi burned a village?" Bile rose up Melusine's throat. The vision that had haunted her nightmares took hold of her once again.

"Aye, and killed almost everyone in it." Adalberon didn't seem to mind the bloodshed. "He made an example no one will soon forget. Thanks to my brother's efficiency, the rebellion is squelched, and His Holiness is immensely grateful."

Melusine's head swam. It had all been true. The senseless killing, the maiming, the massacre of women and children... and she had witnessed it all.

She rose to leave the room. "Excuse me, my lords. I feel unwell."

As the abbot walked her to the door, Adalberon followed them and touched Melusine's arm. "Will you join us for mass in the cathedral in the morning, my lady?"

Visions of baptismal fonts and holy water swirled in Melusine's mind, sickening her further. She instinctively covered the small scar on her left hand with her sleeve. "I will have to excuse myself, Adalberon. This trip is sapping all my strength. I will need a long night sleep. I hope you understand."

"Of course." Only Adalberon's tightly set mouth betrayed his disapproval.

From inside the study, Melusine heard the archbishop sneer at her excuse. But she didn't care. Nothing would make her get close to holy water again. Nothing.

Back in her monastic cell, Melusine found Alyx snoring softly on her pallet. She did not have the heart to wake the girl with the terrible news. Let her enjoy one more night of blessed innocence. Melusine had none left.

How could she face Sigefroi after that bloody massacre and share his life? How could she take a mass murderer to her bed? Although she did not know the details, she could never forgive him. What had started as a happy journey to Rome had just turned into a nightmare. Her anger flared, but with no other release than tears.

Falling upon her pallet, Melusine muffled her sobs in her sleeves. She wasn't sure whether she felt sorry for the loss of her illusions about Sigefroi, for Thierry who didn't get to live past nineteen, for Alyx who must face loss and unwed motherhood, or for the babe who would never know his father. She just couldn't stand all the grief and ugliness around her.

* * *

The next morning, Melusine delivered the news of Thierry's death to Alyx. The young woman wailed and heaved, and her morning sickness returned. Melusine comforted the girl as best she could, caring for her own servant, but she didn't mind.

Alyx had long become a friend. Melusine helped the listless girl climb into the cart, then the cortege left town. Now in a daze, Alyx reclined under a heap of blankets, rocked by the uneven road. She stared in the distance and silent tears rolled from her reddish eyes.

Melusine refused to ride side-saddle, even for Adalberon's sake. It was a long way to Rome, and she would not suffer more than she had to on this dreary trip. The bishop had frowned but did not fight her decision.

As the prelate rode ahead with the captain of the guard, Melusine noticed that he looked just as comfortable on a horse as in front of a church altar. She suspected him to be a fine swordsman as well and found the thought disturbing.

The convoy crossed several wooden bridges over the arms of a small river crisscrossing the town. The boat traffic looked as dense as the activity on the roads. Fishermen and traders sold their wares on the river banks.

Later, as they rode through cultivated fields, Melusine thought of Sigefroi and shuddered. She still loved her husband despite what he had done, but she could find no excuses for his cruelty.

Since she'd learned the truth, however, the nightmarish vision had fled her mind, as if the fear of the deed was stronger than the deed itself. Still, she refused to condone this kind of behavior and would confront Sigefroi in Rome. She intended to keep her anger alive and she would make him feel it.

Soon, Melusine's party came to the widest river she had ever seen. The majestic Rhine made her skip a breath. They dismounted as the road ended into a wide clearing. A number of small boats lined up onshore attested to the busy traffic on the river.

Along the towing path at the water's edge, Melusine watched as a team of hardy men advanced slowly to the

197

rhythm of a monotonous chant. Bending forward, as if into a strong wind, they pulled the ropes harnessed to their foreheads. Behind them, in the river, the loaded barge advanced slowly against the current. The ropes squeaked and groaned under the men's labored pull.

Melusine had to wait as her captain hired several flat boats to ferry her party to the opposite bank. Soon, they made their way across, among other boats ferrying merchants and travelers. Larger ships, some with a square sail, others with teams of rowers, went up and down the river.

Gazing through the deep waters, Melusine remembered legends of sirens and mermaids guarding ancient gold. Were these magic beings cursed like her, or from a different origin? In her monthly forays, she had never met a single one.

As she stood by the railing of the flat boat, Adalberon approached Melusine. "We missed you at mass this morning, dear lady." He looked almost like a knight in his elegant black and gold riding gear, with a sword hanging from his baldric.

"I had to comfort a friend." Melusine nodded toward Alyx who now dozed in the cart, probably exhausted from crying. "She and Thierry had plans to marry."

Adalberon raised one eyebrow, in a facial gesture that resembled Sigefroi's just enough to make Melusine flinch. There was no mistaking his contempt for lowly servants. "What did you think of the Benedictines?"

Taken aback, Melusine stammered. "Are you asking a woman's opinion? After last night's sermon in the refectory, I thought women were the embodiment of evil temptation and ignorance."

"I can recognize intelligence and education, even in a woman." Adalberon cast her a sidelong glance.

"Thank you." Melusine forced a smile.

"Although you do not behave like a proper woman... and I often wonder what sort of parents raised you to be so headstrong." Here it was again, in the tone of his voice. A barely veiled threat. Did Adalberon dig up her murky lineage? No. If he had, she would be dead.

Melusine struggled to sound light-hearted. "What about the Benedictines?"

Adalberon gazed away toward the opposite shore. "They seem to embody the kind of discipline and holy rule I would like to see in all our religious orders."

The snorting of the horses punctuated the sound of the oars fighting the might of the river.

Melusine followed the Bishop's gaze and scanned the opposite bank. "Why do you want to change the religious orders?"

"Too many monasteries are lax these days. Without tight supervision, they tolerate sloth and lust. Most monks are illiterate and only memorize shreds of Latin verses."

Melusine nodded. "I noticed."

"Holy Mother Church needs discipline in its ranks to overcome Pagan evil. Just like our armies protect our borders against the heathen tribes that would destroy us."

The Byzantine village Sigefroi had incinerated came to her mind, but Melusine pushed away the disturbing image. "Education might help. Why not teach them proper Latin?"

"Aye." Adalberon's thin smile flashed and disappeared. "I believe in education for the ruling class and the religious orders."

Nodding in approval, Melusine didn't want to antagonize Adalberon from the start. The prelate could be just as ruthless as a warrior. After all, he had been raised fighting like his brothers before purchasing the bishopric of Metz twelve years ago. If any chance remained to make him an ally, Melusine would certainly try.

She managed a smile. "We live in dark times and much of our past knowledge was lost for lack of records. Why can't we make pottery and glass as fine as that of the south? Why can't we manufacture our own silk? Or grow the spices we import from the orient at high cost?"

Adalberon clicked his tongue. "So many secrets to be learned. If you like knowledge, dear lady, you will love Rome with its fine artists and craftsmen. So many scholars, so many books and scrolls to study. Unfortunately for you, most of these libraries are in monasteries where women, even of high rank, are not allowed to tread."

"Women being lusty, evil and ignorant." She didn't quite manage to sound amused.

Adalberon's brow shot up. "Oh, there are a few exceptions among women of high rank."

"You mean like Jeanne, the woman pope over a century ago?" Melusine still remembered the shock among the clergy when it was discovered at her death that she had been a woman who had passed herself as a man all along.

"Nay." Adalberon shook his head. "That is pure legend. No woman could ever ascend that high in the hierarchy of Holy Mother Church. The weaker sex just does not have the intellect for it."

Melusine silenced a sharp retort. Adalberon's tolerance was only skin deep and full of contradictions. Such narrow-mindedness could make him even more dangerous. He might embrace the fanatical bent of the Church and its fear of Paganism. How could she escape his ever suspicious eye?

* * *

On Tuesday afternoon, Melusine's train reached the fortified city of Augsburg. Brand new walls and buildings, reconstructed after the Hungarian siege eleven years earlier, gleamed in the sun. Her plan to escape for an entire day still seemed sketchy.

As they dismounted in front of the monastery, she asked Adalberon. "I hear the good monks here have a well-preserved library. How would you feel about staying an extra day to study a few scrolls?"

Adalberon raised an enigmatic brow. "We still have a long road ahead."

"One day will not make a great difference. What do you say?"

"I hate to keep His Holiness waiting." Adalberon's features relaxed. He seemed to warm up to the idea as he removed his riding gloves. "I do enjoy a good read." He offered a faint smile. "In spite of your education, I did not picture you as a scroll worm."

Melusine patted her white mare's neck. "A woman's thirst for knowledge can be a driving force."

"Well, why not?" Adalberon relinquished his horse to a stable boy. "I will advise the abbot and see you at dinner time."

"I feel tired and will have supper brought to my cell tonight." She resisted the urge to lower her gaze as she lied. After sunset tonight she would be nowhere to be found.

"I'll see you tomorrow morning in the library, then."

"Aye." Melusine needed to speak to Alyx. Thank the Goddess, she could count on the girl's loyalty.

Later in Melusine's cell, Alyx asked too many questions. "Where are you going, m'lady? I know you are devoted to your monthly prayers, but isn't it dangerous to go about in a strange city without an escort?"

"Do not worry, Alyx, I will be fine. And no, I cannot tell you where I am going. Just tell Bishop Adalberon tomorrow that I am indisposed. Can you do that?"

Alyx sighed then smiled. "Aye, I can do that."

"And remember to unbar the garden door for me before supper."

With some misgivings, Melusine took her cloak and went out the door. Once in the deserted hallway, she hid herself under a veil of glamour and left the monastery through the garden door without attracting attention. She had just enough time to run out through the city gate and reach the Lechfeld River before sunset. She hoped her simple ploy would work.

* * *

The next morning, Adalberon wondered why Melusine, who had requested a full day to study, did not show up at the library. When her lady servant came to tell him that her mistress was indisposed and would remain in her cell all day, Adalberon observed the trembling of the girl's chin and the avoidance in her clear green eyes.

She was lying.

He also noticed that Alyx must be with child under her bulky clothes, and he immediately remembered her reaction to young Thierry's death and the fact that they were planning to wed.

Sin flourished in the empire at all levels, and Adalberon must crush all evil and cleanse the good people of God's kingdom for their own redemption. He had long nurtured the suspicion that Melusine was not who she claimed, but without tangible proof he had no case to present to Sigefroi, or to Pope John, for the annulment of their nuptials.

And now, she pretended sickness... but for what purpose? He must find out.

Waving away the girl, Adalberon returned to the study of a scroll on ancient legends. According to the scroll, some ondines only took mermaid form on certain days and lived as regular women the rest of the time. A fascinating premise, devised by one of Charlemagne's bishops who claimed to have observed the transformation on a river bank at sunset on a Tuesday, many decades ago.

Of course, who could see clearly at twilight, with the play of light and shadow? Adalberon had no doubt the bishop believed what he saw, but was it fact or distorted vision? Still, if such creatures existed they could threaten the very core of Christianity.

After lunch, he decided to pay Melusine a visit in her cell. It would baffle the monks to break their strict rules separating genders, but he was family, and a bishop of his rank could ignore a few rules.

When he knocked on the cell door and received no response, Adalberon let himself inside. It was empty. Where had Melusine gone? If he waited long enough, he could ask her when she returned. Adalberon believed in patience, a virtue often rewarded.

* * *

Shivering, her hair and body still wet under her clothes, Melusine hurried toward the city gate, invisible under her glamour veil. She had to reach the town before the doors closed. Although the sun had already set, a few straggling serfs drove the last carts heaped with today's harvest toward the safety of the city walls.

It took many fields to feed a large town, and Melusine took mental notes of what crops they carried, and what kind of tools hung from the side of the carts. Someday, Sigefroi's many towns would grow this large, and he would need her expert help to run them.

Melusine breathed easier as she crossed the gate with the last harvest carts, just before the guards would lower the doors and lock up for the night. Once in the narrow streets, she didn't feel the need to hurry. She watched as the shopkeepers closed the weather-boards on their displays. The smell of cooking fires reminded her that she was famished.

Melusine did not need to maintain her glamour all the way to the monastery. The less magic she used in proximity of the holy men, the less chances of raising suspicion. She entered the monastery through the garden door Alyx had left unlocked for her.

She encountered no one in the garden since it was supper time. Despite her hunger she did not dare appear at the table disheveled, so she quickly made her way to her cell to freshen up and change clothes.

Her heart almost stopped as she pushed open the heavy door.

"Ah, Melusine." Adalberon seemed to enjoy her surprise.

"Why are you here?" The presence of a man in a woman's cell was highly irregular.

"I was worried about your health, but I see you look quite recovered." He looked her up and down as if taking notes. "What happened to you? You look wet as a moat rat."

Melusine cringed inwardly. "I felt better, so I went to the public baths to cleanse my body from the remnants of fatigue. The monks' tubs are so small." She hoped Adalberon's nose would not pick up the scent of the river in her hair.

"I do not approve of public bathing." He shrugged as if shaking off sin from his shoulders. "The immodest practice is conducive to lascivious sins."

"How long have you been here? You are missing supper."

"I prayed here all afternoon." He narrowed his eyes on her. "Did it take you that long to bathe?"

All afternoon? Dear Goddess. What now? Melusine took a slow breath.

"First I went on a special errand I am not at liberty to discuss with you." It was all Melusine could think of in a cinch.

"Secrets?" Adalberon hovered over her, almost menacing. "One should have no secrets for God's representatives. Are you sure you are not hiding a more ominous sin?"

Melusine shuddered. "And what, pray tell, might that be?"

"A woman who rides like a man then disappears to wander in the town without chaperone might indeed have grave sins to hide." Adalberon's slow words sounded filled with menace. "Some might wonder about her virtue."

"You think I met a lover?" Melusine laughed at that and found it relaxing. "No, dear brother-in-law. I am perfectly content to love my husband."

That was the truth, although her love had recently faltered upon the news of Sigefroi's cruel streak.

Adalberon did not look convinced. "Who is your confessor, Melusine?"

"I have none. Our family does not need one."

"Well, I am family, too, so let me help you on this journey. Let me be God's forgiving ear for you."

Ice gripped Melusine's insides, but she remained silent.

Adalberon sighed. "Tell me all your sins so God can forgive you."

"You would be disappointed, dear brother-in-law. My sins are few and quite common. Another day, perhaps. For now, I am starving and I need dry clothes, if you do not mind giving me some privacy."

"Of course." Adalberon lowered his eyelids as if consulting a higher power. "Then I shall see you in the morning as we take the road again."

Melusine nodded and watched him leave. He reminded her of a patient fisherman baiting his next meal. The chill that seized her had naught to do with her wet hair or the cool summer evening.

Why did the Bishop enter her cell against the rule? Although she would not need to disappear again until they reached Rome, Melusine's insides swam with uneasy waves. Something had changed in the prelate's attitude... as if he held a dangerous secret.

Chapter Fourteen

Rome, three weeks later.

The priest in white robes escorting Melusine through the pontifical palace stopped at the imposing portal of a wide open door. A towering guard in Roman armor blocked the entranceway.

Melusine had hoped for Sigefroi's presence when she voiced her important request, but he was encamped with his troops outside of Rome and involved in a military council with the emperor. She had not seen him yet in the three days she had been in the holy city.

"His Holiness is ready to see you now." The priest bowed and left quietly on sandaled feet.

The guard hit the marble floor with the butt of his lance twice, then moved to the side to let her pass.

Drawing a calming breath Melusine walked through the open portal and crossed the expanse of mosaic floor. At the center of the dome-shaped room, Pope John sat on a high throne while talking to two richly adorned prelates seated on both sides of him on lower chairs.

To conquer her fears, Melusine reminded herself that the future of Luxembourg was at stake. Besides, the request was her idea and she must see it through.

At her entrance, the three princes of the Church glanced up from their chairs set on an elaborate Byzantine rug of blue, white and gold.

Framing the pope, Melusine recognized Adalberon and the fat Archbishop Henri of Verdun. While Adalberon remained unreadable, her keen senses detected fierce animosity from Archbishop Henri. As for Pope John, his smile seemed benign enough.

Although she had requested a private audience, Melusine understood that the pope's time was precious. He probably conducted several orders of business at the same time. She caught herself worrying the ribbons braided into her long hair as she walked.

Why would she be nervous? The pope, after all, would not last a week on St Peter's throne without Otto's support, and Otto favored her request.

A quick glance around the room revealed a bubbly water fountain off to the side. Holy water? A cloying scent of incense and Myhrr lingered in the air. In the center of the overhead dome, a round skylight brightened the vast room with sunshine.

Melusine halted in front of the pope and genuflected. When Pope John XIII touched the top of her head, she shuddered, wondering whether his hand held holy water. But when she rose she felt fine.

The pope's rotund face displayed only kindness. He rearranged his gold-threaded white robes. "You wanted to speak with me, child."

It had been a while since anyone had called Melusine child. She smiled. "Aye, Your Holiness. I have favors to ask."

Pope John raised both eyebrows and amusement danced in his small eyes. "More than one?"

"Aye." Melusine glanced toward Adalberon for help, but her brother-in-law kept a bland face.

Pope John straightened his sleeves. "Speak, child."

Melusine cleared her throat before reciting her rehearsed request. "Over the past few days, I have visited several monasteries and consulted their libraries. I found various useful documents and I would like to have them copied, so I can take them back with me to Luxembourg."

The pope scratched his smooth chin pensively.

"You see, Your Holiness, the abbots are unwilling to comply without your approval. So, Emperor Otto suggested I come to you. Of course, I will make generous donations to the monasteries concerned."

The pope narrowed his small dark eyes. "What kind of documents?"

"Treaties, ancient tales and legends, Roman and Greek history, genealogies." Melusine refrained from sounding too eager. "Even a few reports from Julius Cesar on how to construct bridges, roads, and war machines."

Pope John's stare intensified, as if he searched for hidden motives in Melusine's face. "And that would be for your husband's library?"

More educated than Sigefroi, and possibly more knowledgeable than the pope himself, Melusine only smiled. "At the dawn of a new power in Luxembourg, I feel that knowledge is the very basis of prosperity."

Archbishop Henri scoffed his diffidence.

The pope ignored him and kept his gaze upon Melusine. "Very wise, indeed."

Encouraged, Melusine went on. "I was also looking for information on how to manufacture glass and bricks and ceramic, how to make colorful dies for hemp and wool, how to weave thicker carpets and raise silk worms, but I found nothing useful on any craft at all."

The pope shook his head slowly. "You will not find these secrets in libraries, child. They are jealously guarded, only transmitted through training from master to apprentice, never to be revealed outside of their guild."

Melusine had feared that would be the case but hoped she could find a way to bring these secrets home nevertheless. She decided to play the part of the helpless female. "So, what am I to do, Your Holiness?"

The pope offered a paternal smile then steepled his fingers in a reflective pause. "You could hire a few craftsmen who just completed their apprenticeship and make them a generous offer. Perhaps give them a shop in your town, where they can prosper and teach new apprentices under your patronage."

Adalberon gasped. "Your Holiness would allow such valuable craftsmen to leave Rome?"

"For the benefit of this dear child and the greater prosperity of the Roman Empire, certainly." The pope turned to Melusine. "But I will not allow our best masters of the arts to leave our city. They have too much work here decorating our churches, for the greatest glory of God. You will have to recruit newly trained craftsmen."

Delighted, Melusine let her excitement hurry her words. "Thank you, Your Holiness. The people of Luxembourg will praise your clemency. Everything is so beautiful in this Holy City, I will take home new ideas to embellish our halls and our walls... for the greater glory of the Holy Roman Empire, of course."

"Of course." Pope John nodded.

But Melusine wanted to make sure she would get everything she needed. "So, Your Holiness, may I have these books and scrolls copied?"

The pope made the sign of the cross over her head. "You have my blessing. But who will read such an extensive library?"

"That is my next request, Your Holiness."

The pope sighed in mock impatience then smiled indulgently.

"We need scholars to educate our young nobles." Despite her effort to control them, the words just tumbled out of Melusine's mouth. "Our boys only learn battle skills and the girls weaving and embroidery, but their education lacks in true knowledge."

Archbishop Henri stopped fidgeting and seized both armrests as if to rise. "Women do not need such an education."

The pope flashed a brief smile. "I could send a score of Benedictine monks to open a monastery on your lands. Your young noblemen could learn much from them."

The last thing Melusine wanted was a bunch of nosy monks keeping an eye on her. "Your Holiness is too generous. But my lord husband already owns several important abbeys. Besides, I do want to educate the girls as well. If you agree, I would hire lay-scholars from this beautiful city and take them to Luxembourg and Saarburg to educate our people."

The pope frowned. "Lay scholars?"

Sensing his hesitation, Melusine sent him a slight mental nudge. "Aye. They can teach our people to read and write, speak proper Latin, and understand mathematics."

Archbishop Henri slapped the arm of his chair. "Such knowledge without the Church's perspective is most sacrilegious!"

Distracted by the rude interruption, Melusine let go of her mental hold on the pope. She struggled to get it back.

The pope turned a severe face to Melusine. "What about God in all this? What's in it for God?"

Melusine bowed to hide her struggle. "The Almighty will gain the eternal gratitude of Luxembourg, Your Holiness. Within a few years, God will have a wise, civilized and prosperous new nation to draw upon for financial and military support."

"Impressive for a woman." The pontiff chuckled. "I'm not sure I envy Sigefroi such an intelligent wife." The pope turned to Archbishop Henri. "Like you, I favor keeping women ignorant of political matters."

Adalberon nodded.

Melusine did not let it affect her concentration. She kept her voice even. "Do I have your permission, Your Holiness?"

The pope sighed as if beaten. "If Otto sees the good in it, you have my blessing, child."

Melusine genuflected. "Luxembourg thanks you for your selfless generosity, Your Holiness."

* * *

The next morning, in the gardens of the pontifical palace, wearing his white and red finery, Sigefroi set down his silver goblet on the white linen covering the round marble table of the terrace. Unable to escape the pope's invitation to break his fast with the princes of the Church, he would have preferred to visit Melusine on this glorious morning. He knew she stayed at a nearby convent, but he hadn't seen her yet.

Deaf to the meaningless conversation, he let his gaze embraced the ceramic frescoes decorating the outside walls of the palace. White columns with grapevines lined the water front, and reflections from the Tiber River below played on the striations. He breathed in the sweet smell of oleander blossoms.

The pope hooked his hands together and rested them on his round belly. His white robe shimmered in the morning sun and fluttered in the soft breeze blowing from a distant sea. "Ondines?"

The incongruous word pierced Sigefroi's reverie.

Adalberon, in purple silk robes, picked at dark red grapes from a silver bowl. "Aye, Your Holiness. According to my studies, ondines can look like ordinary women, then once every so often they transform into water creatures."

"Ridiculous." Sigefroi sighed. "Isn't that how ancient Babylon fell? While its religious leaders discussed the sex of angels?"

Pope John's beady eyes twinkled. "Fascinating, is it not?"

Archbishop Henri's flabby jowl trembled as he spit the seed of the olive he had been chewing.

Adalberon looked ecstatic at the pope's interest. "An instance of such transformation was witnessed over a hundred years ago along the Moselle River, by one of Charlemagne's archbishops."

Sigefroi perked up at the mention of his illustrious ancestor.

The pope narrowed his gaze on Adalberon. "And what, pray tell, prompted your interest to look into these ancient demons?"

Adalberon flashed a smug smile. "You see, Your Holiness, a number of recent sightings of ondines were reported in Luxembourg and in Saarburg."

Sigefroi stiffened at the mention of his two estates. Luxembourg and Saarburg. The two places where he resided with Melusine, who disappeared one day each month.

Thinking back, didn't all these sightings happen on her pilgrimage days? Why had he never made that connection before? Could it be? Nay. He refused to believe in legends and magic. There were no such creatures as ondines. Yet, the pope himself admitted to their existence.

The fat archbishop cast him an incendiary glare, but Sigefroi shrugged it off. Too much bad blood had flowed between them to mind his veiled accusations.

Archbishop Henri's expression softened as he addressed the pope. "Your Holiness, I read similar stories in my youth in Aachen. If I remember correctly, while mermaids have a fish tail, ondines have more of a sea-serpent tail."

"Truly?" Adalberon seemed fascinated.

Henri glanced at the three other men then straightened, full of self-importance. "They are said to remain eternally young. Some scrolls even claim that they can sprout wings, like a dragon, and fly away if threatened."

"Wings?" Sigefroi laughed to ease the tension building inside. "I thought this was a gathering of erudite minds, but I hear only superstitious talk." He picked up his goblet to hide his inner turmoil.

The pope creased his forehead in disapproval but remained silent. Since Emperor Otto insured the safety of the pontifical throne, Pope John would never speak against Otto's best general and friend. If ever deprived of military protection, the pope might incur the fate of his predecessors, assassinated by the ruling families of Rome.

Sigefroi smiled inwardly at this small advantage on the pope, but the image of Melusine, the first day he glanced at her naked, waist high in the Alzette River, superimposed upon his mind. He did not see her legs that day. And Thierry said he only saw a big flapping fish when she dove under the frigid waters.

Now Thierry was dead. The thought sobered him.

Still, hard as they'd searched that day, they'd found no trace of Melusine onshore. Was it because she swam underwater like a fish? And later that day, he heard a woman sing in a pure enchanting voice like that of the legendary sirens.

Sigefroi shook his head to banish the thought. That could only be coincidence.

"What recourse do we have against such calamitous beings?" Adalberon sounded very serious. Did he truly believe in ondines?

Pope John absentmindedly turned in his hands the gold seal hanging on his chest. "We won't know until we study them."

"But how?" Adalberon did seem to believe.

Archbishop Henri's face flushed. "The best would be to catch such a creature in mermaid form, which might prove difficult if they can fly."

The pope nodded. "But first, we must investigate the recent sightings and see where they lead us." He turned to Sigefroi. "Since these happened on your lands, I place you in charge of interrogating the witnesses and record whatever you can find out. Then send a messenger with your findings to Adalberon, who will in turn report to me."

"Are you serious, Your Holiness?" Sigefroi could not imagine himself questioning people all day about such a ridiculous matter. "A military ruler has more important things to do than ask around about legendary creatures."

Pope John raised his gaze to the pure blue sky above, as if asking God for patience. Then he addressed Sigefroi as he would a child. "Evil is more insidious than most believe, my son. Never underestimate the dark powers Lucifer unleashed on this world. I am giving you a chance to be a soldier of the Almighty and apprehend evil lurking on your lands."

Sigefroi's chest whirled in turmoil. "But my people will make fun of me."

The pope gazed sternly into Sigefroi's eyes. "Or would you prefer I send my own investigators?"

"Nay, Your Holiness." Sigefroi did not want an army of prelates to descend upon his lands and establish their religious rule. Better accept the task and remain the master of his estates. "I'll look into it as soon as I return home."

With an ingratiating smile, the pope relaxed against the back of his padded chair. "I have no doubt you will make a remarkable investigator, my son."

"I must protest, Your Holiness!" Archbishop Henri tapped the table impatiently. "How can you trust the sons of a murderer with an inquiry of that importance?"

Sigefroi's blood curdled at the archbishop's words. The accusations were true, of course, but he could not let the insult go unchecked. "I wish you used civilized language in noble company."

"Noble?" The archbishop leaned heavily over the table. "You lost two hundred knights in a village skirmish. How noble is that?"

The pope waved a hand in entreaty. "There, there, now. We need to forget the past and look to the future."

"Your father killed mine and deprived my family of its lands." Archbishop Henri reached and gripped a handful of Sigefroi's silk tunic. "You owe me reparation."

Surprised by the fat man's strength, Sigefroi rose and twisted the intrusive hand on his chest, forcing it to release his tunic. "The weak does not deserve lands they cannot protect."

The pope waved nervously. "The Holy Roman Empire needs a united front. No petty quarrels will be tolerated. Emperor Otto and I are in total agreement on that point."

Red-faced, the archbishop massaged his bruised wrist but still glowered at Sigefroi. "Do not be surprised if one day soon, you find my personal army at the walls of your precious Luxembourg, claiming your estate to replace what I lost."

Sigefroi half-drew and slammed Caliburn back into its scabbard as a warning. "Attack Luxembourg if you dare, Lord Archbishop. I will be waiting for you."

Scarcely nodding to the pope, his blood roiling with wrath, Sigefroi marched down the terrace steps and out of the pontifical palace gardens.

* * *

214

To the sound of his determined steps ringing on the paved streets of the golden city, common sense returned to Sigefroi. Ondines? Who could believe such laughable tales? His capable wife, the gorgeous woman he loved, the mother of his children, an ondine?

The slapping of Caliburn on his hip reminded him of the vow he had taken in exchange for the miraculous sword. Never try to find out what she did on those strange Wednesdays...

A bell rang up a steeple, close by, calling the faithful to church. He collided with a gawking pilgrim leaning heavily on his walking stick. Sigefroi's hand went to Caliburn's bejeweled hilt. He realized he was in no danger and relaxed his grip on the sword. Was he ready to give up that wonderful weapon?

How could he believe the sword to be invincible while denying the existence of occult forces? But he had seen Caliburn in action, and that... he could not deny. If Melusine really were a demonic creature, however, it would greatly complicate his plans.

Ignoring the good people of Rome going to market or to church, Sigefroi passed the glass-blower's shop and thought about buying a trinket for Melusine but saw nothing precious enough to be worthy of her.

His mind wandered to her impossible parentage.

According to the scroll he had confiscated from the library in Trier, if Melusine were who she claimed, it would make her over a hundred and fifty years old, and she still looked twenty, like the day they first met. She hadn't aged despite giving birth three times in almost four years.

And what could have caused her sudden illness at the baptismal font? Holy water perhaps? Sigefroi must confront Melusine. But could he face the truth if she happened to be a satanic creature?

Aye. Since the pope forced his hand, Sigefroi would clear the mystery of the ondine sighted on his lands. And Melusine would have to give him answers.

* * *

215

The knock at the door startled Melusine. "Do come in."

The nun in gray veils skittered in like a mouse, flushed with excitement. "Mother Superior sent me. There is a visitor for you at the gate."

Melusine felt the blood drain from her face. "Who is it?"

"A man." The nun blushed even more, as if it were possible. "Only confessors and prelates are allowed inside the sanctuary. Other males must wait in the gate building."

Was it Sigefroi? Who else? Despite her profound revulsion for what her husband had done, Melusine could not help but rejoice at his presence. He had come to see her. He missed her.

But her joy quickly faded. He was a loathsome murderer. How could she allow him in her bed or around her children? As much as she understood his motivations, she could not sanction his actions.

Melusine steeled her resolve for the confrontation ahead. She knew her husband well, and Sigefroi would not easily accept her rebukes.

The nun touched her arm. "Are you well, my lady?"

Melusine attempted a smile to cover her brief moment of distraction. "Aye." She smoothed back her hair. "Just show me the way."

As she followed the nun along the corridor, she realized she wore a yellow gown. Sigefroi liked yellow on her. It set off her tan skin and made her clear gray eyes sparkle. But she did not want to seduce him today. Or did she? Although she had struggled to nurture her anger on the long road to Rome, she now felt empty of rage.

She followed the nun through the rose garden, wondering whether their conversation would have witnesses. A nun would never be left alone with a man, but Melusine wasn't a nun, the man was her husband, and their high rank came with privileges.

She saw him before they reached the building. Sigefroi stood outside the open door, a stonethrow away, one foot propped casually upon a wooden bench. At his feet a patch of vermillion narcissus mimicked his leonine mane set ablaze by the morning sun. Melusine had almost forgotten how handsome he looked, straight and wide-shouldered, in white and red silk cinched with leather.

Melusine recognized Caliburn at his hip. Sigefroi, as formidable in his finery as in full battle gear, watched her intently, like the great lion of Luxembourg that pawed the air on his tunic.

Melusine touched the nun's arm. "You may return to your devotions, now."

As if relieved of a great burden, the nun nodded then darted away toward the main buildings.

Melusine managed to walk without faltering. Her insides roiled, partly from the anger she failed to bring to the surface, and from something else. Desire! She suddenly realized how much she had missed him.

She struggled to bring forth the bloody vision of her nightmare, but somehow, the anger had worn itself out. Still, Melusine would confront her husband. She could not and should not accept what he had done.

The closer she moved, the faster she walked. Now she wanted to run into his arms. But as she closed the distance, something in his stance, the fierce knit of his brow, slowed her steps. She halted four paces away. He remained still as the garden statues where doves perched and cooed.

He spoke first. "You look beautiful but why the frowning face? Are you sick from the journey?"

"Nay." Melusine's chest tightened.

Sigefroi lifted his foot from the bench and stepped toward her. "This is not the happy reunion I had imagined after months of separation."

Melusine stepped back. "Why did you do it?"

Surprise arched his brow and he stopped in his track.

"Why did you maim and kill all those women and children?" Her throat clenched and her voice cracked.

His frown fell away and he suddenly looked sad, eyes downcast. "Oh, that?"

"Please look at me and tell me it's not true." Against reason, Melusine wanted to believe his innocence. "Tell me you did not do this."

"But I did." He turned sideways as he stared down at the narcissus. "When I saw Thierry lying in a pool of blood, something clicked in my mind. These villagers had poisoned us, slit the throat of our best knights. We were all dying, or so we believed. Nothing mattered but justice."

For the first time, Melusine realized that Sigefroi could have died as well. As much as she mourned Thierry's death, she rejoiced to see her husband alive.

Her voice trembled as she uttered feebly, "Justice? You call that justice?"

"Aye." Sigefroi scratched his brow then sighed heavily. "What I did in a moment of crazed battle frenzy cannot be undone. I will have to bear the guilt for the rest of my life. I will never forgive myself."

Melusine's resolve melted but she could not give in. "I thought I married a courageous knight, not a vengeful executioner."

"I never claimed to be a saint." He finally raised his amber gaze to her, as in supplication. "Can you ever forgive me?"

He looked so vulnerable, but Melusine could not weaken. "Never."

His gaze hardened. "Who are you to judge me?"

"Any human worth his salt would balk at such cruelty."

His cold stare searched the depths of her soul. "But are you really human, Melusine?"

The slow, deliberate remark stabbed Melusine like a dagger between her ribs. She gasped for air but the pain did not subside. Chilling tendrils of fear made her shiver in her yellow gown. A drop of cold sweat snaked between her breasts. She must not panic. "What are you implying?"

"Perhaps you can tell me why our peasants sighted an ondine on several occasions on our lands, and always on the days you disappeared from the castle. Maybe you can explain how one grows a serpent tail in the river eddy at sunset and reclaims human shape the next evening."

"My lord, I thought you did not believe in magic and legends." Melusine fought not to faint. She stumbled toward the bench and dropped onto it.

He did not move to help her but remained distant. "Legend, is it?"

"Of course, what else?" She clutched the side of the bench to prevent the world from spinning around her.

"Is it legend when many have seen it? When the archives speak of bishops who witnessed it, when the pope himself just charged me of investigating the facts?"

"What facts?" Melusine wanted to heave.

"Why is it that we did not find you the first day I saw you under the bridge? Were you hiding deep underwater?"

Melusine felt trapped. Nowhere to run. Should she keep denying? Should she tell the truth? Nay. The truth would only get her killed.

Sigefroi did not relent. "Why did you need tunnels leading to the river in both our fortresses?"

Melusine struggled to remember all the details of the curse. It had been so long ago... If Sigefroi found her secret but kept it safe, they could still live happy together. She realized with a start that despite his savagery, she still wanted this man.

Torn between her love for him and the refusal to accept his violent nature, she still wanted to remain at his side. Wasn't it her destiny? The condition that would free her from the curse? Melusine couldn't imagine returning to a solitary life, abandoning her husband, her children, her happy life at the castle.

Sigefroi seized both her arms and forced her to gaze into his blazing eyes. She saw in his stare traces of a power she had noticed many times before, faint but there nevertheless... Fae power?

"Tell me the truth. Are you that ondine?"

"And what if I were?" The words escaped before Melusine could stop them. She realized, too late, that he had made her tell.

He let go of her as if of a venomous toad and his hand grasped Caliburn. "I should kill you right now."

Panic threatened to drown Melusine. "My lord, you can't. The curse would take you, too."

His hand stilled on the hilt and his amber eyes narrowed on her. "What curse?"

"The curse that made me an ondine." Melusine caught her breath and gripped the back of the bench for support. "It is my curse. But if you kill me or if you tell anyone, you and your male descendants will be doomed for nine generations."

Sigefroi emitted a long, sarcastic whistle. "Quite a curse for my ambitious plans to start a new kingdom."

Sigefroi slowly averted his eyes then remained quiet for a moment, his back to her. Finally, he faced her, a smirk on his face. "No one is perfect. We all have weak links in our chain mail, do we not?"

Melusine held her breath. Her life hung on her next words. "Please my lord, in the name of what we had, do not tell anyone."

Sigefroi scoffed. "Tell whom? Tell what? That I made a pact with the forces of evil? That I owe my power to a changeling? A demonic creature?"

"If the bishops find out, they will kill me in the most horrible manner."

"Woman, you are lucky that my faith doesn't run deep and I do not fear the fires of hell. I do not care from whence my power comes, as long as it serves me. But the wrath of the Church could cost me my place in the civilized world."

"I am sorry, my lord. You were never meant to find out, only to benefit from my Fae gifts."

His eyes softened. "It would be a shame to throw away such a beautiful and powerful bride." He paced away from her then turned about. "If I overlook your imperfections, will you forgive mine?"

Melusine remained silent. He had offered a truce. But how could she forgive his cruel behavior? Then how could she not, when he just forgave her. He'd looked so regretful about what he'd done.

Melusine thought back to her own mistake, her own moment of madness, when she had condemned her father to a solitary life and death in a crystal cave. Had she deserved to be cursed for it? Aye. But now that she felt remorse, Melusine yearned for forgiveness. And so did Sigefroi.

She exhaled a deep breath. "I am willing to try."

Gently, he took her hand and squeezed her fingers. "Then your secret is safe with me. But from now on, you must trust me. No more lies, no more excuses, and I want you to tell me everything about that curse. I want to know the whole truth about you and your past."

"Aye." Although she had no choice, Melusine felt suddenly light, as if she had carried a heavy burden since her wedding day. "It feels good not having to lie anymore."

When he grinned, Melusine sensed his strength. A dangerous man to be sure, but a man unafraid of her most terrible secret.

He winked. "Should we get you out of this holy place, my little hellcat, and move you to my temporary villa?"

The word hellcat made her flinch, but Melusine knew it was Sigefroi's way of showing affection, and she thanked the Goddess for such an understanding husband. For the first time in years, she felt hope swell inside.

"Aye, I would like that very much."

* * *

Two days later, Melusine walked sedately at Sigefroi's arm toward the imposing entrance of St Peter's Basilica. The circular courtyard looked as busy as when it served as the market place. Today, however the square rumbled with a festive throng in colorful attire. Bells rang, scaring the pigeons from the roofs and calling the most powerful nobles and rich citizens of Rome to the venerable edifice for an unusual ceremony.

From all over the empire, nobles had flocked to answer Otto's summons. They came from faraway kingdoms, duchies, counties and marches to witness the coronation of

221

a nine-year-old heir, whose father was still alive. A curious new trend in the Roman Empire.

As she passed the threshold on Sigefroi's arm, among the high nobility allowed to enter the basilica, Melusine walked as if she floated, disembodied, like in a dream. Since her new understanding with Sigefroi, her fear of churches had lessened.

He dipped his fingers in holy water and pretended to touch fingers with Melusine as if to pass the holy water. She pretended to take it from him and signed herself. Only Sigefroi ever touched the dangerous water, but the traditional gesture made Melusine look like an irreproachable Christian.

Many heads turned as the rulers of Luxembourg crossed the venerable edifice to reach their appointed place in the first row of dignitaries. Soon the vaults shushed as the emperor and his son took their seat at both ends of the altar.

The emperor wore his jeweled crown in evidence atop his blond ringlets. Otto junior, his childish blond head bare, looked frail and vulnerable as he sat on his oversized throne.

Pope John, whom some influential families outside the empire only recognized as Bishop of Rome, made a grandiose entrance to the sound of harp music. An impressive number of bishops in purple robes filed in perfect order behind him and lined the back of the altar. Then Pope John started the ritual mass, and Melusine recognized the polished Latin of a true scholar.

When the time came to crown the young prince, Pope John walked to Otto's chair and reached for the crown on the emperor's head. Otto waved him away. A murmur flew over the assembly as the pope stepped aside. Otto then rose and walked to his son's throne on the opposite side of the altar.

As if they had rehearsed it many times, Otto Junior knelt in front of his father.

The emperor then lifted his own crown and held it aloft for all to see. "I, Otto the First, Emperor of the Western

Roman Empire, crown you, Otto the Second, as my heir and successor, with all the powers of Holy Mother Church, to govern over the kings of Christendom with justice, strength, and wisdom."

In a deliberate, solemn gesture, he set the crown upon his son's head.

The boy's voice came loud and clear. "God willing, I, Otto the Second, when my time comes to reign, will defend Holy Mother Church and rule over Christendom with justice, strength and wisdom."

When the young boy rose, very straight, wearing the big crown, he looked taller. Filled with obvious pride, he gazed at the crowd of nobles with new confidence.

Bells pealed, filling the vaults with their carillon, and other bells answered from churches throughout Rome. Many nobles cheered, others applauded. A few hats flew toward the high arches of the central nave. Melusine wondered how many of the guests felt delight and how many only sought to gain the emperor's good graces. Otto was a hard man to please and many coveted his favors.

The two emperors, father and son, followed by Pope John and the bishops, now walked down the central aisle out of the basilica. Sigefroi offered one arm to Melusine then led the nobles in a long cortege. The procession crossed St Peter's square then snaked through the streets of Rome.

In the city, the populace looked happy. Was it for the crowning? Most did not really care who ruled the empire. But the baked goods and honey sweets the children in the cortege threw at the good citizens probably accounted for some of their happiness.

On the way to the pontifical palace for the traditional agape, Melusine felt like a queen. Against all her expectations, Sigefroi had embraced her cause and become her champion. As long as they showed a united front, nothing could hurt them, and Luxembourg would continue to prosper. The Goddess would be served. Leaning confidently on Sigefroi's strong arm, she smiled at him then waved at the delirious crowd.

Somewhere in her heart, however, Melusine doubted her good fortune would last. What If the Church found out? Her happy family would be doomed, along with all the good people of Luxembourg.

Chapter Fifteen

Luxembourg - Spring of 973

"What?" Melusine still could not believe what she just heard.

Little Kunigonde at her breast, she stared at the imperial messenger, muddy and drawn from a hard ride. The women's quarters of Luxembourg castle were usually closed to men, but the urgency of this morning's message hadn't allowed any delay.

The messenger cleared his throat. "The emperor is dead, my lady. Long live our new emperor, Otto II."

"So suddenly? How did he die?"

"Wounded by the Saracens in southern Italy." The man's gaze darted everywhere to avoid staring at her naked bosom. "Looked like just a scratch when he returned to his palace in Memleben. But then the fever took him. He fell unconscious and died in his sleep a few days later."

Melusine did not know the Emperor had been wounded. How would his son, now seventeen, deal with war and politics?

She covered her breast and gave the child to Alyx. "So young Otto is now emperor..."

The messenger, obviously more comfortable now, gazed straight at her. "Aye, my lady."

With Otto dead, Melusine realized there might be a shift in the complicated weave of allegiances that kept the balance of power. Otto had reigned through force. Many kings and dukes would not be so intimidated by his young son.

"Will there be a public funeral?"

The messenger nodded. "In ten days, my lady. When the emperor was wounded, a message was sent to his heir and to Lord Sigefroi in Italy. They should be back very soon."

"If my lord husband is on his way home, I have much to do." Melusine had missed Sigefroi so much, she couldn't wait to see him again. "Thank you my good man. Go to the kitchen to get some food, and rest as long as you wish."

* * *

A few days later, when the horn sounded joyously from the watchtower, Melusine knew it was Sigefroi's party. She climbed the stairs to the top of the rampart to catch a glance of the riders fast approaching on the Roman road. About a hundred knights rode hard under the white and red banner of Luxembourg.

From her vantage point, Melusine could see the entire valley. As she turned, she gazed with pride upon the plateau across the gorge. The new town had grown and now spread far and wide. She marveled at how much had changed in Luxembourg since the crowning in Rome, seven years ago.

Many acres of forest had become green fields and pastures. The craftsmen Melusine had brought from Rome now held shop in the town. Each month, new families came to settle from Trier, Aachen, Metz, Verdun. The word of Luxembourg's prosperity spread throughout the empire.

The men took employment among Sigefroi's soldiers. The women and children worked the fields, tended the flocks, or apprenticed new trades. Many learned weaving, glass-blowing, or tanning, and most pottery shops took new apprentices.

The river brought traders and visiting merchants. Throughout town, smithies resounded with hammering blows and the breath of bellows, as the smiths mended chain mail and forged new weapons. The silversmith catered to the castle, of course, but also to the prosperous houses of merchants and craftsmen, and to the landless nobles of Sigefroi's entourage.

The castle library had become a study room where Melusine's children, Henri, Frederick, and young Thierry, named after Sigefroi's deceased squire, attended school with other children and adults from the castle who wished to learn. Not that the boys cared for knowledge. They much preferred the fencing yard, or violent fist brawls in the stables, from which they returned bruised and bloody.

With a twinge in her heart, Melusine thought of her nine-year-old daughter, Liutgarde. The girl still hated her mother and resided in a convent in Trier, where the nuns saw to her education.

As the riders closed the distance, Melusine barely recognized Sigefroi on his destrier. Now thirty three, he did not radiate the same strength as ten years ago. He rode stiff and weary in the saddle. While Melusine had not aged one day since they met, Sigefroi showed the wear of endless seasons on the battlefield.

If he must become the most powerful man in the new empire, he would need more youthful strength. Melusine wondered whether her knowledge or her magic could help him overcome old age. Caliburn made his arm invincible, but what if his body weakened so much he couldn't wield the sword... what then?

The riders disappeared into the woods on the road ascending the plateau. Melusine climbed down the rampart and fetched Kunigonde to welcome Sigefroi at the gate. Gone for many months, he had yet to meet his new daughter.

Soon, the clattering of hooves on the drawbridge brought cheers from the assembled castle folk. Stable boys ran for the horses. It seemed to Melusine that it took Sigefroi a little longer than usual to dismount, and when he pushed back his mail hauberk, his flaming hair looked dull and streaked with pale sandy strands.

Never before had Melusine noticed the creases in his stern face, and suddenly she felt sad. The man she loved was growing older.

She walked to Sigefroi, the baby girl in her arms. "Welcome home, my lord. Meet your new daughter, the mild and lovely Kunigonde."

"You named her after my mother?" Sigefroi took the baby from Melusine and held her high for his knights to see.

The men whooped and clanged swords against shields.

Under this ovation, Sigefroi lowered the child and took her in one arm then encircled Melusine with his other arm and kissed her cheek. "I like her already."

Melusine held Sigefroi's waist as they walked toward the keep. "This child needed a queenly name, since she will marry an emperor some day."

Sigefroi laughed. "An emperor?"

"Aye." Melusine winked. "I have my sources."

* * *

That night, in their bedchamber, as she brushed her long hair, Melusine watched Sigefroi unbuckle his baldric and sighed. "I wonder how young Otto feels, with the weight of the empire on his head. He looked so innocent last year, when we attended his Byzantine wedding."

Sigefroi winked then sat heavily on the bed. "I just learned that his lovely bride, Theophano, is with child."

Melusine rejoiced at the thought. "Wonderful. I hope it's a boy. A new emperor needs heirs. Who would have ever thought of a Byzantine princess on the German Imperial throne?"

"Aye." Sigefroi pulled off his soft boots and wriggled his toes. "But now that we made peace with the Byzantines, the Saracens are threatening Rome..." He sighed heavily. "It never ends."

"Well, young Otto inherited a good wife out of that deal. The girl is as smart and bright as she is beautiful, and he will need her support."

"If young Otto can stay alive long enough." Sigefroi scoffed. "When I swore to his father I would protect and advise his son, I did not expect it to be so soon."

"No one did. At least, with you standing in his shadow, no one will dare question the new emperor's authority." Melusine set down the brush. "Maybe you should remind young Otto of the arrangement we made with his father for the marriage of our son Henri to his younger sister."

"Aye." Removing his tunic, Sigefroi revealed a well-muscled chest striated by battle scars. "The heir of Luxembourg must marry an imperial princess to further strengthen the bonds between our two families."

"And some day our newborn Kunigonde can marry Otto's future heir and become an Empress."

Sigefroi shook his head. "Is that what you have in mind for her?"

Melusine smiled mysteriously. "This baby is a very special child. The Goddess showed me her future. She will become not only an empress, but a Saint celebrated in all Christendom."

"The daughter of a Pagan, become a Christian Saint?" He frowned.

"It's all the same, dear husband. Fae folk are descended from angels who mated with humans. Many Christian saints have Fae blood in their veins."

"The fact that I accepted your protection and agreed to keep your secret doesn't mean that I embrace all the implications." Sigefroi fell back heavily on the bed. "I feel too tired for philosophical debates."

"How about another kind of activity, then. We don't have to talk." Melusine crossed the chamber and joined Sigefroi on the furs. She kissed the soft light hair on his chest.

Sigefroi caressed her long tresses then pushed her back gently. "I had a long day and my bones are aching, sweet wife. Take pity on your aging husband."

Feeling the sting of rejection after months of celibacy, Melusine bit her lips and hid her tears. She blew the candle then lay down beside her husband on the furs. Soon, Sigefroi snored loud enough to shake the frame and the draperies of the great bed.

Wide awake, Melusine decided it was time to act.

She rose and went to the stone basin behind the privacy screen and filled it with water from the pitcher. Then she set a row of tallow candles on the circular rim. With a spark of Fae power, she lit them up all at once.

When her reflection in the basin smiled back, a great peace descended upon Melusine. Focusing on the water surface, she conjured in her mind the image of one of her sisters.

"Palatina, are you there?"

A young woman in white, her hair severely tied back, answered the call. She smiled at Melusine with startling gray eyes. "Sister? What a joy to hear from you! How is the world doing without me?"

Melusine, always surprised by her sister's striking resemblance, felt as if she was speaking to her own image. "I see you look well, dear sister, but the world is aging and I need your knowledge."

"I would be glad to help. I feel so useless alone in my cave."

"This could be your chance, then. I need an elixir to keep my husband young and vigorous in the furs."

Palatina's eyes widened in shock and she gasped. "You are talking to a virgin, Melusine. What would I know of such things?"

Melusine shrugged. "You know what I mean. With your knowledge of plants and spices and healing potions, in all the books you read, in all the secrets you learned, isn't there one that can help me?"

"Perhaps." Palatina's forehead creased in concentration. She looked away then moved beyond Melusine's field of view.

Melusine stared for a moment at the water basin reflecting the ceiling of a dark cave. She felt sorry for her sister. Such beauty and knowledge locked away while the centuries went by.

Their father had suffered a similar fate at his daughters' hands, though. Children could be cruel, and Melusine had done her share of hurt in childhood.

When Palatina's reflection reappeared in the basin, she held a large volume of bound parchment and leafed through it, slowly, following the lines with one finger.

"There it is." Her finger stopped. "Thistle milk, licorice root, black currants, hawthorn, apricots... a complicated formula with many elements, but the book says it keeps the skin smooth, the heart strong and the mind alert. You can mix it with wine and honey, and your husband should drink a cup of it each night before bed."

"That's all?"

"Nay. You also need a magic spell to make the potion."

"What magic spell?"

"I'll explain in a minute. Also make sure you feed him mackerel, salmon and sardines to ease the pain in his bones."

Taking mental notes, Melusine rejoiced at the idea of Sigefroi regaining his former strength.

Palatina licked a finger and turned the thick page. "Some elements might be difficult to find. They come from the orient, like the root of a plant called ginseng, and another plant called gingko. They are said to keep a man's body young and strong, and keep his mind sharp and alert very late in life."

Melusine smiled. "I know some astute and devoted merchants who might be able to get me the special plants I need. Little sister, you are a blessing. Now, explain to me how to make the potion..."

* * *

The next morning, Melusine watched Sigefroi leave for Memleben with a small escort to attend the emperor's funeral. There, along with all the kings, dukes, counts, and marques of the Roman Empire, he would publicly swear fealty to the new emperor, Otto's son.

Melusine did not offer to accompany him. Sigefroi could take care of himself. Besides, in order to help him fit into this brand new empire, she had an important potion to make that would require much time and many errands.

Melusine gave Alyx a list of herbs to get from the town healer who gathered and dried his own healing plants. Meanwhile, she visited the spice merchant.

The big man rose from behind a row of earthen jars on a trestle table. His bearded face broke into a smile when he recognized Melusine. "What an honor to have you in my humble shop, my lady. What is your pleasure?"

"I am looking for rare plants from the orient, one called ginseng and another called gingko."

The man's eyes lit up. "What would that be for? I've heard the names but I don't know their uses."

Melusine saw no harm in educating the man. "One keeps your body strong and the other keeps your mind sharp."

The merchant grinned. "So that's how you remain young and beautiful after birthing six children. My wife wondered about that."

"Give her my regards. Maybe she can use these plants herself." The scent of coriander from an open jar filled the air, along with faint traces of other spices Melusine could not identify. "Do you know where to find these plants?"

The portly man removed his cap to scratch his head. "There is a trader in Trier who supplies the imperial court. He carries almost everything one can find in the empire. I will get these plants for you and make sure I have them in my shop, if you'll be kind enough to buy them from me in the future."

"Thank you my good man. But I need it urgently."

The man's eyes lit up. "It would cost extra, my lady, but I could send a fast rider to Trier this afternoon and have the merchandise delivered to the castle late tomorrow."

Melusine smiled as she handed two gold coins to the greedy man. "I will pay the price. As long as I can count on you."

The big man took the coins and bowed profusely. "I promise you will be satisfied, my lady."

It took Melusine an entire week to brew the potion in a cauldron in the hearth of her bedchamber. The sweet smell clung to the stone walls. Then she mixed the decoction with some of the castle's best Italian wine. It took another day to perform the spell to enhance the elixir's potency. Finally, Melusine filled a barrel and set it in a wall niche in the bedchamber, next to Sigefroi's favorite silver goblet.

* * *

Sigefroi returned a few days later, with his brother Bishop Adalberon, and Melusine ordered a private feast. Although it was almost summer, she had fresh salmon and mackerel brought from the seashore at great expense.

That night, she wore the yellow dress Sigefroi liked so much. She intended to seduce her husband and reclaim him as a lover. Melusine noticed his sidelong glances, but he looked weary from his travels.

During the repast, Adalberon turned to Sigefroi. "Brother, did any new sightings of ondines occur on your lands?"

Melusine held her breath. Since Sigefroi found out her secret in Rome, seven years back, she had been extremely careful. She now swam far from the town, far from the ramparts of Luxembourg, in the wild tributaries of the Alzette, deep in the forest, where no living soul would venture alone.

"You still believe these old tales?" Sigefroi scoffed. "I told you years ago they were only legends... we could not find any reliable witness, only drunken sailors who hardly remembered their name when sober."

Adalberon shrugged. "Just asking... I tend to believe there is truth to the old stories. A new sighting would definitely help verify the legend."

Hiding her apprehension behind a smile, Melusine changed the topic. "Did you taste the fish, Adalberon? The cook prepared the salmon in a delicate white sauce, with baby onions and fresh cream."

With dainty fingers, Adalberon ripped a strip of pink salmon from his bread trencher. After dipping it in the sauce, he nibbled on the fish. His eyes smiled approval. "Delicious indeed."

Sigefroi skewered a piece of salmon with his eating dagger and ate with obvious pleasure. "I bet Gunter in Saarburg does not eat this good."

"Aye." Melusine smiled. "But he might be drinking our best wine with a curvaceous wench on his lap."

Laughing, Sigefroi almost choked on his food.

Adalberon made a disgusted face then blotted his mouth with the hem of the white tablecloth. Obviously, he did not approve of Gunter's taste for wine and women. He cleared his throat then turned to Melusine. "Did you know Archbishop Henri of Verdun did not attend the emperor's funeral?"

"Really?" Melusine knew such an insult to the emperor meant serious trouble to come. "Was he indisposed? Did he send a representative?"

Adalberon shook his head. "Not even that."

Sigefroi drank a sip from the silver cup he shared with Melusine. "I wonder what that bastard is fomenting behind the fortified walls of Verdun."

"Nothing good, I'm afraid." Adalberon sighed. "To think he is a man of the cloth!" Adalberon's face relaxed. "Brother, while we are on Christian matters, when are you going to reform your abbeys?"

Adalberon's smile made Melusine shudder with foreboding. He looked like a cat about to pounce.

Sigefroi shrugged and dropped his eating dagger on the table. "I knew you would find a way to spoil this family meal with Church business."

Adalberon arched one eyebrow. "It is past time for monastic cleansing."

Sigefroi wiped his mouth with his sleeve. "Listen, brother, I pay to maintain the abbeys, I reap the profits of their vineyards and decide by whom they are administered. But whether the monks take wives, concubines, or remain celibate does not interest me in the least."

Adalberon turned a shocked face to Melusine then stared down at his bread trencher. "Shame on you, brother. You of all people should be giving the example and pushing the reforms."

Sigefroi's face tensed. "Why? What's wrong with the secular canons? They have been in place at Eternach for over a hundred years. The change may not be welcomed by the congregation."

"The old rules are too tolerant." Adalberon cleared his throat. "Besides, as the leader of the spiritual cleansing, I would expect my own brother to support my reforms. Popular or not, you can impose your will. Unless your will does not favor my new vision for the Church..."

A cold shiver coursed over Melusine's spine. She laid one hand on Sigefroi's thigh under the tablecloth. It wouldn't do to make an enemy of Adalberon.

Sigefroi's fist tightened on the table then relaxed. He nodded to Melusine then turned to Adalberon and offered a strained smile. "I guess you are right, brother. Family must stick together. Would the roles be reversed, I would expect you to support me as well. I'll speak to the abbots."

"Excellent!" Adalberon beamed.

* * *

Later that night, in their bedchamber, Melusine took Sigefroi to the niche and the barrel containing the youth elixir. "A special gift for you, my lord."

Sigefroi inspected the barrel. "What is it? Wine?"

"A very special wine." Melusine filled his silver cup and handed it to him. "Tell me how you like it."

Sigefroi took the cup and tasted the brew then smacked his lips in appreciation. "Unusual... bittersweet but pleasant enough. Is it a cordial?"

"More like an elixir, my lord. One cup each night before bed should keep you healthy and strong for many decades to come."

Sigefroi's amber eyes widened upon her. "A magic potion?"

Melusine chuckled. "Only if you believe in such fables."

"Could it be dangerous?" Sigefroi stared suspiciously inside the half empty goblet. "I'm warning you I'm hard to kill. I have been poisoned before, and it did not take."

Melusine laid her hand on his shoulder, enjoying the warmth of his body through the white silk tunic. "Is my invincible knight afraid of an elixir?"

"Nay." Sigefroi grimaced. "But I wouldn't want to turn into a toad in front of my knights. They might make fun of me and I would have to kill them."

"No danger of that happening, my lord." She smiled with all the love she felt for him, hoping he could read her heart.

"In that case..." Sigefroi drained the cup and smacked it down on the stone surface next to the barrel.

Melusine came closer and faced him. "I'm so glad you like it."

Sigefroi encircled her in his arms. "I knew you were good for more than building fortresses. Woman, you know how to take care of a man."

She rested her head on his hard chest, listening to the strong beat of his heart. How she enjoyed feeling safe against him. "As long as you love me, my lord, I will take great care of you."

Sigefroi laughed, the vibrations shaking his chest. "There must be something to this elixir of yours, my little hellcat. It makes me feel twenty again."

"Then prove it to me." Melusine smiled coyly.

He swept her off her feet. "If proof you require, my lady, proof I shall provide."

She kissed his corded neck as he carried her toward the high bed. Then he dropped her in the middle of the mattress, like a sac of grain, sending the hem of her yellow dress flying in the most immodest fashion.

She laughed and watched his tall, wiry frame as he loosened his sword belt and slipped the baldric off his wide shoulder to hang it on the bedpost. He pulled his tunic over his head, revealing his muscled and scarred chest. Was it an

236

illusion, or did his skin glow with new vitality? It could be a trick of the dancing light, but his scars seemed less conspicuous.

Heat surged at her core as Melusine noticed the prominent bulge in his chausses. She hadn't expected the elixir to work so quickly, but she was delighted that it did.

Sigefroi kicked off his boots then joined her on the bed and covered her with his body. His lips traced a burning trail on her throat. One hand explored the folds of her yellow dress and the other dislodged her breast from her low neckline.

She gasped when he took the hard nub between teasing teeth. How she'd missed his attentions. Her breasts swelled under his touch. Her back arched of its own volition. He pinned her under him and her breath came short as he made full contact with the length of her body. How strong he was, how potent.

Then his roving fingers climbed under the hem of the yellow dress and he stroked the sweet spot where she generated so much heat. She moaned with unspent desire, undulating under his ministrations but unable to escape the sweet torment. She loved the way he imposed himself upon her, held her entirely at his mercy.

She shivered at the contact of his warm skin against hers. She drank the nectar of his mouth like a river of spiced, honeyed wine soothing her parched throat. "It has been so long... I missed you like that."

"It's been too long, my sweet. I won't let it happen again."

Melusine welcomed him inside her as they joined, savagely at first, then lovingly, for a very long time. Indeed, the elixir worked miracles that night, for Sigefroi made her sing in the furs, and better than she had in many years.

For tonight, Melusine forgot about Adalberon and his religious zeal. As long as Sigefroi loved her, they could handle the obstacles together... be it an assault from the jealous Archbishop of Verdun, or an investigation of ondines from the Church.

She hadn't expected the draft to work so well. And since her sister mentioned cumulative effects with regular use... there was much happiness in store for both of them.

She fingered a strand of copper hair at Sigefroi's nape. "I love you, my magnificent lion of Luxembourg."

He kissed her forehead softly. "And I love you, my little hellcat."

She smiled at the pet name. "I'm glad the future looks bright for our beloved Luxembourg."

Sigefroi relaxed on the pillow and closed his wide amber eyes. "Amen to that."

A rooster crowed outside. Almost dawn. Melusine drifted off to sleep against Sigefroi's warm body, reveling in his masculine scent. In her drowsy state, she saw the Great Goddess smiling upon them.

Melusine exhaled a contented sigh then whispered, "Thank you O Great One, for making me the happiest woman in the civilized world."

The end

If you enjoyed this book - please leave a review. Authors need reviews. Please help readers find this author.

Other Books We Love titles by Vijaya Schartz

Curse of the Lost Isle series (medieval fantasy romance):
Princess of Bretagne – Book 1
Pagan Queen – Book 2

Seducing Sigefroi – Book 3
Lady of Luxembourg – Book 4
Chatelaine of Forez - Book 5
Beloved Crusader - Book 6
Damsel of the Hawk - Book 7
Angel of Lusignan - Book 8
Curse of the Lost Isle Boxed set (Books 1-2-3-4)

Ancient Enemy series (sci-fi romance):
Snatched (Sci-fi Romance)
Alien Lockdown (Sci-fi Romance)

Ashes for the Elephant God (reincarnation love story)

Asleep in Scottsdale (contemporary romance)

Archangel books (speculative fiction):
Crusader – Book One
Checkmate – Book Two

Born in France, award-winning author Vijaya Schartz never conformed to anything and could never refuse a challenge. She likes action and exotic settings, in life and on the page. She traveled the world and claims she also travels through time as she writes the past and the future with the same ease. Her books collected many five star reviews and literary awards. She makes you believe you actually lived these extraordinary adventures among her characters. Her stories have been compared to Indiana Jones with sizzling romance. So, go ahead, dare to experience the magic, and she will keep you entranced, turning the pages until the last line. Find more about her and her books on her website at http://www.vijayaschartz.com

Lightning Source UK Ltd.
Milton Keynes UK
UKHW011255200120
357276UK00005B/1823